THE CASTLETON AFFAIR

BENEDICT BROWN

Storm
PUBLISHING

Ebook ISBN: 978-1-80508-192-0
Paperback ISBN: 978-1-80508-194-4

Cover design: Rose Cooper
Cover images: Alamy, Shutterstock

Published by Storm Publishing.
For further information, visit:
www.stormpublishing.co

ALSO BY BENEDICT BROWN

The Marius Quin Mysteries

Murder at Everham Hall

The Hurtwood Village Murders

Lord Edgington Investigates…

The Izzy Palmer Mysteries

AUTHOR'S NOTE

Unlike most of my books, this novel mixes a dash of espionage and intrigue into my usual whodunnit plot. This was the eighth book I wrote in 2023 and I needed to do something a bit different to keep me motivated. It also afforded me the opportunity to cram the plot full of even more twists and turns than normal. Of course, this being a Benedict Brown book, nothing is quite as it seems, and I hope that the story I've written is a really satisfying one.

If you read the About this Book and Research chapters at the end, you'll learn a little about the history and influence of spy and invasion fiction in the early twentieth century. You'll also find a character list and some interesting vocabulary you might not know. I hope you enjoy my attempt to combine genres, as many writers in the 1920s did. And if you don't, I have all sorts of classic mysteries planned for the year ahead and normal service will soon be resumed.

ONE

I was sitting at home in my writing room when the kind of adventure I'd always dreamed about knocked on the front door.

I initially ignored the sharp rap. I was staring at two piles of papers and had no wish to be distracted. To my left were the notes for the new book I hoped to write, though the story kept changing, and I couldn't get a firm grip on it. I knew that I wanted my third novel to be bold and different – not just the same old tired mystery with a tightly defined group of suspects in a country house. The plan was to throw in a dash of intrigue and adventure, but the plot I'd constructed seemed so complex that I was no longer sure it made any sense.

To my right, there was a stack of legal files from around the time my father disappeared, but their contents had led me precisely nowhere, and I was trying not to think about them.

The knocking became more insistent, and it pulled me from my daze. I normally caught sight of people approaching my flat through the front window, but St James's Square had been quiet all morning, and I'd barely seen a soul. Even pressing my face up against the glass didn't help, so I accepted that I'd have to go out to see who was there.

"Are you Marius Quin?" A man in a camel trench coat and tweed Trilby was leaning against the white column beside the door as if he didn't wish to be noticed.

"That's right."

"The Marius Quin of Marius and Co.?" He had a terribly flat voice and gave the impression that the answer was of little interest to him.

"I very much doubt there's another Marius Quin in the whole of England."

He closed his eyes as he replied. "Just answer the question please, sir. Are you the Marius Quin of the Marius and Co. Detective Agency?"

"I am. But if you're a hawker, then I'm not interested in whatever you have to sell."

His nostrils flared a fraction as he emitted a cold laugh. "It's nothing like that, Mr Quin. I'm here to offer you a job."

I was so taken aback by his nonchalant manner that I didn't think to block the way as he pushed the door open and squeezed past. He took one look at my messy writing room and correctly concluded that it wasn't the place to receive guests, so he continued along my sparsely decorated corridor to the main salon. I was glad that my mother wasn't at home. I would not have looked particularly professional with her fussing over me. I suppose I could have pretended that she was my tea lady, but then she would have called me "Marius, darling" and spoilt the pretence.

"Can I offer you something to drink?" I asked as he took a seat without being invited.

"I didn't come here for refreshments." He pointed to the chair in front of him, but I remained on my feet, loitering in my own home.

This odd fellow was quite different from anyone else I had encountered. He reminded me of certain policemen I'd met, but that may have been down to his coat. He was furtive and arrogant, and a sense of superiority bubbled within him.

"Will Lady Isabella Montague be here soon?" he asked in a manner which suggested that he knew she was due to arrive at any moment. "I would like to speak to the pair of you at the same time."

"I think you should start by showing me some form of identification," I demanded, but before he could respond, there was another knock at the door, so I raced back down the hallway to let my fellow sleuth into the house.

"I thought we were going out for lunch," Bella said, when I turned back to the sitting room without speaking. "Marius, is everything all right?"

"I really can't say. You'd better come with me."

Bella and I had been childhood friends then sweethearts, and after a decade without speaking, we'd established a detective agency together – so in other words, the same old story you've heard a thousand times. Dressed in a blue and yellow floral gown and complementary summer hat, she followed close behind me, as I puzzled over the identity of the uninvited guest.

"I didn't know you had company," she muttered when she saw the curious little man. I hadn't noticed how slight he was until now. Something about his presence rather filled the room.

"Not to worry, Lady Isabella." He did not stand up to greet her. "I've come here today to contract your services."

"How wonderful. What sort of job did you have in mind?" My childhood friend was instantly relaxed and went to sit in front of the stranger.

He glanced briefly through the doorway as though afraid someone was listening. "It's not the kind of thing that can be discussed so freely, if you understand my meaning."

Bella nodded enthusiastically just as I found my voice. "No, we do not understand your meaning, Mr...?"

"My name is of no importance. I am merely a *conduit* for

the information you require." He over-pronounced certain words, as though proud of himself for knowing their meaning. *Conduit* was one of them.

I wouldn't let him off the hook. "What are you? Police? Military?"

"Something like that," was the only answer he would give as he looked critically at the unlit fireplace.

I wouldn't let him get away with such evasiveness. "I'm sorry, but we can go no further until you show me your card."

He rolled his eyes and released an impetuous breath as he extracted his wallet and stamped across the room to me. "There we go."

I'd rarely seen such a sparsely worded calling card. It simply read, *Section Manager, GC&CS.*

"What's GC&CS?" I inevitably enquired.

"You'll find out in good time. First you have to accept my conditions."

"Mr..." Bella began, in an attempt to calm the situation before remembering he was unwilling to share his name and starting again. "Perhaps if you tell us the problem that needs solving, we can be of service. We here at Marius and Co. are particularly suited to clandestine work."

We here at Marius and Co. had actually only completed two investigations, but she wasn't about to tell him that.

"I need you to find someone." Our potential client had a long, gaunt face and mud-brown hair. I'd got the impression that he was mildly amused by Bella's approach, but he became quite serious again. "A man by the name of Ernest Castleton left his work on Monday night and was walking through St James's Park when a man with a gun seized him. There were a couple of witnesses, one of whom was shot to death when he got too close to the kidnapper."

Bella stifled a gasp. "That's awful. Do you know who took him?"

The man's nose twitched much like a rabbit's. "We can't be certain. That is why I have come to you."

"What's his job?" I fired back at him. "This Castleton you mentioned. What does he do and why would someone want to take him?"

"He worked for the government."

"Do you work for the government?"

He smiled. "We all do in one way or another, don't we?"

"No, I certainly do not." I presumably sounded hostile, but I didn't like knowing so little about the man who wished to employ us.

Bella was determined to keep things professional, and her calm, sensible approach was bound to elicit more from him than I could. "Are we to understand that Mr Castleton's work was in some way... confidential?"

The man nodded, apparently impressed by her deduction. "That is exactly it. I can't go into too many details, but I am at liberty to tell you that Ernest Castleton is the chief aide to a very important man." He paused, and I thought he would stop there, but he provided one more morsel of information. "He works for the Foreign Secretary."

"Lord Darnley?" I said with just a hint of excitement. "You're telling us that Lord Darnley's aide has been kidnapped. Why hasn't it been in the papers?"

He released a long breath as though to steady himself. "I told you that this was a sensitive matter."

"But how could you keep it from the public?" Bella enquired. "Surely someone will find out. His family must at least have reported it to the police."

He gave a curt shake of the head. "The people I work for made sure that didn't happen."

I finally took the seat beside Bella. The room was comparatively tidy and, regardless of the stranger's disdainful look at the fireplace, it was May, and the air was warm. I wasn't about to pick an argument over such a petty topic, though, and had something more important to ask him.

"Very well, but why come to us? The police would be better placed to solve such a case."

"You have a point." He pinched his nostrils together absent-mindedly before continuing. "In ordinary circumstances, we could rely on the invaluable help of the Metropolitan Police Service to resolve this matter. However, these are far from ordinary circumstances. My bosses believe that Mr Castleton may have been taken by a foreign party. A *very* foreign party... if you get my meaning."

It was hard to know what sort of background the man had. His nasal voice offered little evidence of his class or breeding. In fact, everything about him was decidedly nondescript. He was a man without an identity – a thoroughly ordinary human being – and I concluded that he was just the kind of person to excel as a spy.

"So you're afraid that another country could be involved?" Bella clarified, and he nodded so subtly I wasn't quite sure what I'd seen.

"Then the military should be involved," I told him. "I can't imagine for one moment that Bella and I are the right choice to conduct such an investigation."

He breathed out more loudly this time, and I could see that his patience was, if not wearing thin, then at least fraying at the edges. "I've come to you because, for one thing, the men who give me my orders are impressed by your work. You were ahead of the police on two tricky cases at Everham Hall and Hurtwood Village." He ground to a halt, as though debating with himself whether he should share anything else. "More importantly though, if you get caught, we can deny any knowledge of your actions. No one will believe that the British government would have anything to do with a fly-by-night detective agency."

This sudden revelation amused him, and I now understood why the man had grated on me from the first moment. His whole plan was to throw us to the wolves.

"So the reason you've come here is to avoid a diplomatic scandal."

"Precisely, Mr Quin."

"And what if we get caught?" Bella asked, the apprehension clear in her voice. "What if one of us were to be killed?"

"Then you would be dead, and there would not be a great deal I could do about it. Either way, you or your families would be generously reimbursed for your trouble."

"We're not motivated by money," I was quick to reply.

The stranger chuckled to himself, and I caught another glimpse of the man inside him. "And that's why I know you'll take this case."

I wanted to disagree with him. I would have loved to tell him that he was wrong and that he should get out of my flat and never come back. I truly wished I could wipe that look from his face, but the mystery he'd presented had sparked my interest, and I couldn't back out now.

He stood up and, from within his coat, produced a manila folder which he dropped onto the coffee table between us with a satisfying thud. "I'll leave this here and show myself out. If you accept the proposal, put a mark in red lipstick on the front window of the flat by tomorrow morning. You've got forty-eight hours to find Ernest Castleton and bring him back here. If you need any more information, I'm afraid you're on your own."

"But what happens when we find him?" Bella asked. "How will we let you know?"

"You needn't worry about that. We will be watching." He pulled his hat lower over his face. "Goodbye, Lady Isabella. Goodbye, Mr Quin. For the sake of Great Britain and every last person in the nation, I wish you the best of luck."

And with that, he was gone. Bella and I listened to the

sound of his soft steps as he picked his way along the hall. Not a
creak emerged from the floorboards. Not a squeak came back to
us from the hinges on the front door as he opened it and slipped
outside.

"This is insanity," I said once I was sure we were alone.

"Absolute madness," Bella agreed but, in the very next
moment, we lunged forward to find out all we could about
Ernest Castleton.

TWO

"'Conditions of engagement,'" Bella read from the first sheet. "'By opening this dossier, Marius Quin and Lady Isabella Montague agree to act in a manner befitting agents of His Majesty's Government.'" She paused then and looked at me from her spot beside the mantelpiece. "Are you happy so far, or should I stop?"

"I don't know. I really don't." I was torn between jumping headfirst into the case and burning the file before it could get us into any more trouble. "I can't help thinking that there were reasons that man came to us which he didn't want us to know."

My friend showed no such hesitation and smiled a guilty smile. "It's possible, but you didn't answer the question. Should I stop now or keep reading?"

I sighed and ran my hands through my hair. "Fine. I think we can go a little further."

She did just that. "'By accepting these conditions, you agree not to contact any police or military representative, either British or foreign. You are also forbidden from sharing the information herein and any subsequent discoveries with members of the press and their relevant institutions.'"

"That's enough banana-oil," I told her. "It's just as the man said; we're on our own. Should we trip up in any way, we'll be before a judge if we're lucky and thrown somewhere dark if we're not."

Far from this frightening the sweet-natured aristocrat before me, she was positively ecstatic. "It's wonderful, isn't it?" She cleared her throat and turned the page. "Here we are: Ernest Castleton. His people come from Castleton Square, a village and manor near the city of Derby. His brother is Lieutenant General Henry Castleton of the Green Howards, who is tipped to make general very soon."

"I'm sorry," I interrupted from my comfortable spot on the sofa, "but is that information on the paper you're reading, or are you reciting it from memory?"

"A little of both," she admitted. "My father knows the lieutenant general. The man is something of a brute, so let's hope his brother is a shade nicer." I gestured for her to continue, and she took a moment to find her place once more. "Ernest is thirty-two years old and attended Harrow then Cambridge. He studied law and jurisprudence at St Ignatius' College before going into the Foreign Office. He started working in Whitehall around the time I was there."

I'd forgotten that Bella had worked in the Home Office before her father fell ill. I had to wonder whether this was the reason we'd been chosen for the task.

"So far, so predictable," I said under my breath and leaned forward to examine a photograph that had fallen from the file. "He certainly looks a dependable sort. I have no doubt that Lord Darnley is missing his top aide."

The picture showed a cleanly shaven man dressed in a featureless brown suit. He had a broad, open face and was every bit the anonymous civil servant. I would have struggled to pick him out in a crowd, and yet there was something odd about the composition of the photograph. It was as if it had been taken

unawares. The angle was slightly askew, the focus a little
blurred and, rather than an office behind him, or the background of a photographic studio, he was standing in front of a
brick wall. It made me wonder how the picture had been
obtained, and that returned me to the question of which secretive branch of the government wished to hire us.

"This is interesting." Bella had been reading ahead and
came to sit down next to me. "It talks about the jobs to which
Mr Castleton has been assigned under the Foreign Secretary.
He apparently acts as a liaison between Lord Darnley and the
GC&CS. Parts of the document have been crossed out, but it
sounds as though it's responsible for code breaking."

"That was the name on our new client's practically blank
calling card. It said that he is a section manager there." I moved
closer to look over the paper she was holding. One word in five
had been obscured with heavy black ink and there were no
names visible except Castleton's, though the expression *crypt-
analysis* stood out in several places.

"It's hard to know what to make of it," I said as I read along
with her. "If a foreign government has got hold of Castleton, we
must assume it was connected to his work. Perhaps he discovered something that our enemies would wish to suppress or use
to their advantage."

Bella flicked through the folder to see what else she could
discover. "There are more documents like this one. He appears
to be involved in various different areas within the Foreign
Office." She had a quick mind and swiftly extracted the necessary information from each page. "The promotion of British
interests abroad, international conferences, diplomacy—"

"That's all well and good, but code breaking and counter-
espionage are more likely to get you kidnapped." I managed to
prise one of the papers from her grip so that I could examine the
general information on Castleton for myself.

"Yes, but how are code breaking and counter-whatever-you-just-said going to help us find our man?" She posed the question but, after a few seconds, gave up waiting for an answer. "We know nothing about secret organisations or foreign agents, so we should start with his personal life. That may well bear more fruit."

I didn't entirely agree with her suggestion but decided we had to start somewhere. I scanned the page for information and realised that there really was only one salient detail on anything but the man's work. "It says here he has a fiancée by the name of Hermione Ravenscroft. She works in the same building as him on Broadway on the other side of the park. That's a fifteen-minute walk from here."

Bella swapped the stack of papers for the photograph of Castleton. "I wondered what kind of woman would agree to marry such a man. He looks very..."

"Dry?" I thought it rich that she could ponder such a question when her own boyfriend was as interesting as a week-long lecture on the different varieties of dust.

"I was going to say earnest, but perhaps that's a little too on the nose. He certainly has a nice face."

"Will that help us identify his kidnappers?"

"It might." She nudged me with her elbow. "Now tell me what else it says about his fiancée."

"I've told you everything." I stood up from the sofa to move towards the door. "Are you sure you don't know her?"

"And why would you think that?" She almost sounded offended but was soon on her feet chasing after me.

"Because well-bred young ladies like you know everybody."

"No, we do not." She definitely sounded offended.

I seized my keys from the telephone table in the hall and the faint jingle caught my basset hound's attention. Percy had been asleep beside my desk all morning and not moved an inch. The prospect of a walk was enough to stir him.

"You knew Castleton's brother," I reminded her. "And I'd

put a pound on the fact that your father has crossed paths with Lord Darnley, too." Bella knew a lot of people, but her father, the Duke of Hurtwood, was in another league altogether.

"I'll have you know that Daddy has never 'crossed paths' with Lord Darnley." She spoke in an indignant tone, then confessed the truth in a murmur. "They were at school together and, as it happens, he's my godfather."

We'd reached the door by now, and I had to turn back to look at her. "Your godfather is the Foreign Secretary?"

"What of it?"

"I'm just surprised you never mentioned it."

She pulled the door open before I could and flounced out into the street. "There you go then. You don't know nearly as much about me as you think."

With her canine devotee at her heels, Bella positively marched across the square towards the park.

I had an inkling for why she was being so waspish. "You do know her, don't you!"

Percy gazed adoringly at our beautiful companion. Her silky black hair shone in the sunlight as she returned this fond look, but she wouldn't even glance at me.

"Marius, you're jumping to conclusions again. Just because my father could afford to send me to a good university – and my mother can trace her family back to the Domesday Book – you assume I know every bright young thing and musty old boy in England. However, I'll have you know that I've never met Hermione Ravenscroft in my life."

Silence fell between us so that the only sound I could hear was Percy's panting and the *click-clack-click*ing of Bella's heeled shoes on the pavement.

A little floored by the force of her words, I decided that the only way to make it up to her was to apologise. "I'm terribly sorry, Bella. I certainly didn't mean to cast any aspersions. I just wondered whether—"

She had a kind heart and stopped me before I could say any more. "I've never met Hermione Ravenscroft, but I do know her sister Petunia. We shared a house at Oxford."

It was tempting to point out that I'd been right all along, but discretion is the better part of valour and all that, so I bit my tongue. Which isn't to say that I could stifle a laugh.

"It's not funny," she (incorrectly) insisted, even as she joined in with my increasingly raucous mirth. "I've never even seen Hermione's photograph, let alone met her, so your theory is inaccurate."

We stepped into the park as she said this, and I did my level best to keep a straight face. "Of course, Bella. I was a million miles from the truth, and I hope you can accept my apology."

Percy saw a squirrel at this moment and went hurtling ahead of us. It is one of only two things that is guaranteed to make the lazy pup break into a run – the other being food of any description.

"If her sister is anything to go by," Bella began when the laughter had subsided, "Hermione is a curious sort. I grew fond of Petunia, but it took a year or two to be sure she liked me in return. From what I've heard, though, Hermione is the jollier of the two."

There was a note of reservation in her voice, and I wondered what this meant for the interview we would conduct. Many of Bella's rich acquaintances were superior and stand-offish to her pauper friend from the village (that's me). If she felt the need to warn me in advance about the Ravenscroft girls, it did not bode well for us.

It was a mild day and, as we crossed the suspension bridge over St James's Park Lake, the sun hit the water and the view towards the spires and towers of Westminster was just magnif-icent. I would have liked to settle down on the grass with a picnic and a bottle of wine. I was wearing a cream summer suit that was perfect for such an occasion, but there was no time for jollification. In fact, Bella was so serious that I didn't even suggest it as a joke. It appeared that the thought of meeting Hermione was more upsetting to her than the possibility of prison or disavowal by our government. For my part, I was still trying to imagine why the Marius and Co. Detective Agency had been chosen for the job. Whatever the unnamed spy had told us, I felt there had to be more we were yet to discover.

To avoid further distress, I didn't say another word for the rest of the journey – except to keep Percy from jumping into the water on the other side of the lake. He would have swum all the way to the pelicans on Duck Island if I hadn't seized him just in time.

The three of us soon made it to Broadway Buildings which, confusingly enough, was a single building, though it really was located on Broadway. It was a grand office block built in Portland stone with classical pilasters on the façade and a high mansard roof, which had a great number of windows dotted all over it. Bella was about to approach the building when I stopped on the corner of the street.

"We can't just walk into her office," I told her. "We should wait out here and see if anyone emerges who looks like your friend."

"That doesn't sound like much of a plan." Her tone was even less cheery than before.

"It is almost twelve, and she's bound to take her lunch soon."

"Unless she's working a morning shift and stays in the office until it's finished." Bella was rarely so negative, and it didn't suit her. Pessimism was my pastime, not hers.

Luckily we were standing in front of an old pub that, while it had seen better days, would surely provide us with refreshments, and so I steered us inside.

"We should eat while we can. If we have to skulk about the

city looking for a kidnapped man, we'll be doing a lot of waiting around."

We walked towards the bar, and I would have told her an anecdote about the time our friend Inspector Lovebrook had to follow a famous actor, but she spoke first.

"That's her." Without pointing – because she was far too polite ever to commit such a faux pas – she signalled across the room to a young woman in a long grey skirt and jacket who looked as though she'd spent the morning sucking on a Scotch bonnet pepper. "She's just like her sister."

The woman in question raised one hand in the air as she spotted us. "Lady Isabella Montague?" Hermione called. "Is that really you?"

THREE

Though Bella had never seen a photograph of her, Hermione Ravenscroft evidently recognised my friend.

"My goodness me!" She spoke in a very loud voice, as though she wished for people hundreds of yards away to know what she was saying. "My goodness, goodness me. Just wait until Petunia learns that I saw you. I'll go straight home tonight and say, 'Petunia, guess who I saw in a public house beside my work today?' And she'll say, 'Hermione, I haven't the faintest idea.' And I'll say, 'Petunia, I saw your old housemate.' And she'll say, 'Stephanie or Isabella?' And I'll say, 'Why, Lady Isabella, of course. I've never seen so much as a sketch of Stephanie Moorland, but I'd recognise Bella Montague anywhere.'"

"How nice," Bella replied, as though she was uncertain it was the right response to make.

"Lady Isabella. My goodness me." Hermione was still shaking her head in disbelief. "Petunia never stops talking about you. I don't think she's ever liked another person as much as she likes you, including myself and our parents. You would not believe the number of times she's taken out her scrapbook from her university days and told me tales of your time together."

"I'm sure I wouldn't."

"And this must be your young man." Hermione Ravenscroft was a surprising young woman. She was not the cold, reserved type I'd had in my head, but a steam train of chatter without any brakes. "Gilbert, isn't that your name? Gilbert Baines the banker?" Before I could correct this terrible assertion, she continued her nattering. "Such a pleasure to meet you, Mr Baines. And what a handsome fellow you are." Though only a year or two older than I, she assumed the pose of an elderly lady inspecting her grandson. The only surprise was that she didn't pinch my cheeks. "You know, you rather remind me of my handsome young man. Did Petunia tell you that I'm engaged?"

Bella looked as though she'd recently suffered an aerial attack from a German gunner.

She could only nod, and so I answered for her. "We did hear something along those lines. Castleton, isn't that his name?"

"Yes. Ernest and I just adore one another. We're hoping for a spring wedding. Though he's convinced me that we should wait a year or three until his job is more secure. You know, I'm not supposed to say anything about it, but he works for someone very high up in the government. He prefers me to be discreet, but I'm sure he won't mind me telling you that it's the Foreign Secretary himself. That's how we met, actually. I work in the building just around the corner, and we started talking in the foyer one day. He said that, from the first moment he heard me speak, he knew I was the woman he would marry."

"Such a lovely story! And what exactly does Ernest do for the Foreign Secretary?" Sometimes, being a detective is much easier than one might expect.

She didn't even look around to check whether anyone was listening. "Oh, I don't know half of what he gets up to but, as a receptionist there, I do hear some interesting things." She leaned in closer to reveal yet more secrets. "Though the sign on the door of number 54 Broadway says that our company produces lawn mowers, I've never seen any proof." She had at least dampened her foghorn of a voice to reveal this.

"How interesting," Bella murmured. "And would you say that your fiancé—"

Hermione appeared to live her life at twice the speed of anyone else, and it was at this moment that she burst into tears. "Oh, Lady Isabella, I haven't told the whole story. You see, I wanted to impress you, but the truth is that I haven't seen Ernest for days. I think he's left me." She'd switched from supreme confidence to sheer despair in the space of a few seconds. It was quite fascinating to watch.

We were still on our feet beside her table and Bella looked at me as though I was the one who was supposed to be good at talking to people. She eventually gave up on that idea and sat down beside Hermione.

"Come along now. There's nothing to worry about. I'm sure he hasn't left you. Perhaps he's..." This was as far as she got.

"Perhaps he's been kidnapped," I suggested when nothing else came to mind. Honesty is supposed to be the best policy after all, though I can't imagine spies hold to that particular maxim. "Perhaps the clandestine work assigned to him by Lord Darnley has endangered him in some respect and he's being held by a group of nefarious criminals or what have you."

To my amazement, this made her feel better about life.

"Do you really think so?" She wiped her eyes on the sleeve of her long cream jacket. "Do you think that some terrible ruffians have stolen him away?"

"Of course." Bella rubbed her shoulder sympathetically. "Why would he ever leave you?" How she managed to ask this with a serious expression on her face was truly astonishing.

Hermione had passed through ecstasy and agony and now

became quite sober. "That *would* make sense, actually. You see, he told me that something like this might happen one day. It was months ago, and I thought he was just joking, but when we first fell in love, he explained that his job was a dangerous one. I should have realised that he really meant it, but I'm a fool and thought he was pulling my leg."

If there were two ways to say one thing, Hermione could be relied upon to use both. She had a mania for repeating the same information, but neither I nor Bella had the courage to interrupt her.

"I see now that everything in his behaviour over the last year was down to the situation in which he found himself. Even his wish to delay the wedding! I thought he wanted to put it off because he had cold feet, but I think the real reason is that he was worried about his safety... and mine. Oh my goodness! He was thinking of me all along."

I couldn't extract much of value from any of this, but I did my best. "Do you mean that he was prepared for this very scenario?"

She looked straight at me. "Yes, that's just it. He said that if there was ever any sort of trouble and I couldn't contact him, I was to go to the reading room of the British Museum and find a pamphlet by the noted mycologist Christian Gottfried Ehrenberg."

"And you haven't been there yet?" Bella asked, as Percy pawed her foot and whimpered. We really were the most monstrous people to ignore him so.

"No, I didn't even think of it until now. I believed he'd had enough of me." She looked down at her hands and a wave of unexpected self-awareness passed over her. "I talk so much that the poor man must be half deaf. You don't think that he made it look like a kidnapping to get away from—"

"No, I do not," I jumped in to reassure her, as, despite her eccentricities, I was fairly certain she had a kind heart underneath all that fluster and her thoroughly modern attire. "I don't suppose you've heard, but Bella and I have some experience of investigations. We could go to the British Museum on your behalf to see what this pamphlet might reveal about Ernest's whereabouts."

She looked up at me as though I was a saint who required veneration. "Would you do that for me, Gilbert? Would you really?"

I had no wish to respond to that name, but it was too late in the conversation to explain that I was not Bella's terribly dull boyfriend. "Of course we will... on one small condition."

She reached her hand out across the table to take mine. "I'll do anything! Just say the word."

Bella knew what I was thinking and looked down at Percy. "You don't happen to like dogs, do you?"

It turned out that Hermione had left work early that day as she was so upset by Castleton's disappearance. Perhaps unsurprisingly, her superior had insisted she take all the time she needed. It was lucky we'd caught her in the pub at all, and even luckier that the sight of my basset hound seemed to revive her flagging spirits.

"I'll take the very best care of him I can," Hermione promised as she pushed aside her plate of salad, having consumed approximately one stick of celery and a piece of lettuce. "We'll go to the park together, won't we, Percy?"

"Jolly good," I replied. "You won't lose him, will you?"

It was at this moment that Hermione started crying again, and Bella kicked me in the shin. She was a violent sort of person to spend any length of time with; I still had the bruises from our last case. Of course, I eventually realised that what I'd said might be construed as insensitive to a woman who had recently misplaced her fiancé.

"Come along, Percy!" She took him by his lead and, much

like Bella a few minutes earlier, was no longer willing to look at me.

"It wasn't my fault," I tried to convince my oldest friend as soon as we were alone. "I was trying to make sure that she would look after my dog properly."

Bella walked off ahead, and so I gave up arguing. She walked with some speed, too, and it took me a moment to catch up with her.

"I haven't been to the British Museum since I was a child." There was excitement in her voice as she said this. "It's a shame we won't have time to see the mummies in the Egyptian galleries. I always found them thrilling."

"At the moment, I'm more worried about my feet and my stomach."

"I beg your pardon?"

I couldn't entirely blame her for not understanding me.

"We're already late for our lunch appointment, and it must be a forty-minute walk from here to the museum. Perhaps we should take the tube."

She didn't respond but walked to the roadside and waved one hand in the air. There were no cabs in sight, and I couldn't understand what she was thinking until a camel-brown 1914 Sunbeam drove up to us. Her sullen chauffeur immediately exited the vehicle to usher his mistress into the back seat. I didn't know the etiquette of such things, so I waited for him to open my door, but Caxton paid me no heed and climbed into the front of the car.

"You had your chauffeur follow us?" I asked with some disapproval once we were all inside.

"You prefer it that way, don't you, Caxton?"

The loose skin at the back of his thick head ruffled in response. "That is correct, madam. I'm only too happy to serve."

Caxton had never liked me and, under the pretence of

checking for approaching cars, sent a glare over his shoulder as he turned onto Victoria Street beside Westminster Abbey.

"How the other half live!" I lamented, before adding a caveat. "If ninety-nine per cent of the other half had a staff of thirty, that is."

Bella was a charitable person who, from what my mother had reported over the years, had given a great deal of her time and money to various well-meaning organisations that were devoted to ridding the world of the blight of poverty. That being said, she saw nothing strange about the fact there was a man whose sole job it was to drive her around on the odd occasion she required such a service. However, this was not the moment to point out the discrepancy in her thinking or the injustices built into our society, as I was frankly appreciative of the lift.

FOUR

We shuttled through Westminster, Whitehall and on towards Trafalgar Square.

Although I had been living in the centre of London for several years, I rarely had the time to enjoy the sights as I did that morning. I was normally too busy complaining about the traffic or the sheer number of people who drive like maniacs to notice such attractions. But there was Admiral Nelson standing proudly atop his granite column, and sitting around him were the famous Barbary lions, poised as though they expected the command to attack at any moment. As we swung towards Shaftesbury Avenue, I felt really rather spoilt. Bella was clearly thrilled by the prospect of the case before us and, despite the fact we were being driven by the most taciturn human being I'd had the misfortune to meet, her positivity lifted me up.

In just a few minutes, we'd crossed Piccadilly Circus and woven a path through Soho, all the way to that most stately of museums in the centre of the city. *Le British*, as the French presumably call it, was high on the list of places that I'd always planned to visit, and it was certainly no hardship to have a peek inside.

Caxton dropped us off on Great Russell Street, and I appreciated the authority with which Bella marched towards the grand entrance, much like a tour guide leading a group of unruly school children. The heels of her shoes *clip-clip-clopp*ed on the flagstones, and I trailed after her, wondering whether there were as many columns in the whole of ancient Rome as on the façade of that singularly wide and impressive edifice.

We passed through the entrance hall (and yet more columns) before following a sign that promised to lead us to our destination via a wood-panelled corridor.

"Have you been inside before?" Bella slowed down to ask me.

"No, I tend to research my books in the London Library beside my house. I doubt that the British Museum dedicates too much space to sordid murder cases from the Victorian era or old penny dreadfuls that I spend my time reading." I was worried for a moment that this sounded terribly gloomy, so I tried to be more positive. "I've always wanted to visit, of course."

"Then your wish is about to come true."

We'd reached the end of the corridor and, breaking with the usual way of things, my lady friend pushed the door open for me. To say that I was amazed by the sights within would be an understatement. We emerged in an immense domed rotunda, and the curving walls above our heads led up to a glass oculus at its pinnacle. The ceiling was like an upturned flower, with its open petals marked out in gold and blue. Yet, somehow, the architecture was not the most remarkable thing before me.

The huge, circular space was lined with books on three levels, and I got the immediate sense that the corridor we had just taken passed under a great deal more. Directly in front of us were thirty or so extremely long desks, which were arranged around the circle like the numbers on a clock, though they stretched right to the centre of the room. There were a few dusty scholars with their heads in books, but for the most part, the place was quiet, which I suppose I should have expected from a library.

"How can I help you, madam?" the most lethargic librarian I'd ever come across enquired when we reached the enquiry desk in the centre of this very simple maze.

"My name..." Bella hesitated. "My name is Cecilia Long-horn. I'm a research assistant to Dr Eggingwhite, the noted mycologist from Oxford University." I assumed she was refer-ring to me and so I nodded and tried to look worthy. "We'd like to consult a pamphlet by the..." She paused again, and I believe she was about to repeat herself, but she found a better option. "...legendary mycologist Christian Gottfried Ehrenberg."

It was a good thing she'd remembered the name of the writer whose book we needed, as I certainly hadn't. I might just about have managed a vague description of it, but I doubt that would have helped.

The man behind the counter pushed his glasses further up his nose and looked unimpressed. "Fill out your details on this form." He shifted a piece of card a half-inch in our direction. "And then consult the folio catalogues behind you to find the location of whatever it is you require. Certain items which are deemed too fragile or valuable will have to be brought to you by one of my colleagues."

This was all the unmistakably bored man had time to explain before he turned to an open notebook on the half-moon desk and made it perfectly clear that we were no longer of any interest to him.

I smiled in his direction all the same before Bella and I turned to look at the shelves immediately behind us. They were crammed full of tall, leather-bound volumes.

"Where on earth should we begin?" she asked, and now that the talking was over, it was my turn to be helpful.

"M for mycology, presumably. Except for the name of the

author, that's the only information that Castleton gave his fiancée, so I hope it's enough."

She really only needed the first uttered sound of my response to send her off in search of the right catalogue. The folders marked A–C were of little use to us, so we travelled four shelves along until we reached M–O, which was halfway around the room. So that was the right section. Now we just needed to locate mycology, and one specific book in the largest library in Britain, and we'd be hot on the trail of Ernest Castleton once more.

"Why did you give false names to the librarian at the desk?" I asked as we both seized volumes which referenced subjects beginning MY-.

Bella's nose wrinkled the tiniest bit when she was vexed, and it happened right then. "It's obvious, isn't it? Whoever kidnapped Castleton could be following us. The police clearly think this case is too dangerous for them, so just imagine the peril through which we are currently wading."

"You could have at least chosen more believable names. Dr Eggingwhite and Cecilia Longhorn sound like characters from a romantic novel."

"I could have." Her eyebrows flicked upwards for a moment. "But I decided otherwise."

"You're enjoying this, aren't you? Here I am worrying about the consequences of our actions and whether we should even take the case, and you're having a whale of a time."

She looked down at the weighty tome which she had laid on top of the dark wooden shelf. "Of course I am. This is the best treasure trail I've followed in years. Don't you find it just electrifying?"

"If you are happy, my dear Bella, then that is all I could wish."

"Mycology!" she exclaimed. "Christian Gottfried Ehrenberg's sole text is on floor number two, stack L, shelf forty-seven.

This whole detective lark is child's play." She clapped the book shut with a satisfying snap and then tried not to run as we crossed the immense chamber in the direction of the nearest staircase. "It reminds me of a treasure hunt I was on a few years ago with Lord Elles' daughter, Pandora. We wiped our boots on the opposition. You should have seen us."

Beyond the rotunda was a vast grid of book-stacks which surely occupied more room than the famous central space. Iron staircases led us to iron walkways, and the shelves themselves were supported by great iron girders. Natural light came in through the floor above us, and I must say the whole thing reminded me of a child's Meccano set – which I didn't mind one bit!

"Mycology!" Bella exclaimed yet again, but her jaunty tone soon faded when we discovered that shelf number forty-seven was gigantic and divided up into various subsections. "Perhaps we missed one part of the reference."

"Perhaps we did." I couldn't help laughing as the amaranthine confidence she had possessed now faded a fraction.

We looked at the headings over each section of the seemingly endless shelf and I read a few aloud. "Lichenology, Zymology, Mycorrhizae—"

Bella put one hand on my shoulder and had a confession to make. "To tell the truth, I haven't the first idea what mycology means."

I failed to hide my shock. "You went to university, didn't you? You must have studied Latin and Greek."

"I certainly dabbled in those languages but—"

"Then what's the root of the word? What does myco- mean?" I asked this question as though the answer were painfully obvious.

"That's the thing. I've clean forgotten."

"Tut-tut, Lady Isabella. I'm surprised at you. Mycology is

the study of..." I pulled a book from the shelf, but nothing on the cover gave me a clue as to the subject matter.

It was my turn to acknowledge my ignorance. "Oh, fine. I don't remember what it means, either."

"Fungi." She pointed at a sign behind me that said *Medicinal Fungi*. "That's it. Mycology is the study of mushrooms."

Her squeal of delight was met with two very loud shushes from unseen men at either end of the row.

"You're a genius," I exaggerated. "Now, if we only knew in which branch of mycology Christian Gottfried Ehrenberg specialised, we'd be on the right track."

We stared at the shelves once more, but it was impossible to know where to begin.

"Perhaps if we..." Bella suggested without actually suggesting anything.

I ran my fingers along the books in the hope that some pertinent detail might jump out from their spines. It didn't and none of the long, hard-to-pronounce words I read helped me understand what we were doing there. For all they meant to me, terms like anastomosis, foxfire and oomycetes might just as well have been written in Russian or ancient Aramaic.

I was about to suggest that we go back downstairs to have another look at the catalogue when a man in ill-fitting trousers and an unseasonably thick overcoat pushed past us. In a particularly knowing manner, he selected a series of books from the shelves on either side of the passageway. He was an unkempt sort, with wild hair and the makings of a patchy beard, but he evidently knew something of the topic.

"I'm sorry to bother you," Bella said before I could, "but we're looking for a book by the mycologist Christian Gottfried Ehrenberg. I don't suppose you could point us in the right direction."

If anyone had ever refused my uniquely charming friend a request, I had yet to see it. The scruffy fellow stopped what he was doing and looked at Bella as though he was in the middle of a heavenly visitation. Her porcelain skin and green eyes had that effect on people, which is a fact I know better than anyone.

"Christian Gottfried Ehrenberg was primarily a zoologist and naturalist," he replied in a nervous squeak. "Of course, he is commonly thought of as the father of micropalaeontology."

"Oh, I see. So perhaps the information we had was incorrect."

"No, madam. It's not that." He could no longer look at the Aphrodite before him but glanced down at the ground as though the luminosity of her beauty was too great to bear. "Ehrenberg wrote his doctoral thesis on the biodeterioration of paper when he was just twenty-three years old. You know he was the very first person to describe *stachybotrys chartarum*."

He seemed to think that this was rather impressive, but as we stared back, our mouths hanging open, he came to understand we were no great thinkers.

"I beg your pardon." He tapped the side of his head as if to knock the thoughts into their correct places. "*Stachybotrys chartarum* is black mould to most people." He turned away to scan the titles of the furthest bookshelf in the row. "The work itself is fairly rudimentary compared to more recent publications, but if you're completists, it may be worth your while."

Supporting his own substantial pile against his chin with one hand, he neatly extracted the pamphlet we required and held it out to us.

"Thank you so much," I said as I accepted it. "Are you a scientist yourself?"

"Me?" He laughed and blew his frizzy fringe from his eyes. "Oh, no. I just come here to escape the elements. I started with classic literature several years ago, then spent some time reading up on history before moving on to the sciences. It's incredible what you can learn in a library."

He nodded to us and, with a great smile on his face, plodded on down the metal walkway back towards the reading room. Bella and I regarded the pamphlet in my hands like archaeologists who had found the Holy Grail. I don't know why we were so excited. This was the easiest part of our quest and we'd achieved virtually nothing, but progress is (almost) always a good thing. We were about to discover the information that Ernest Castleton had considered crucial enough to hide it in such an elaborate fashion.

"Well, open it then," Bella demanded as I continued to stare at the thing.

I did as instructed and, to my disappointment, the contents of the booklet appeared to be just as the unkempt autodidact had implied. The text of the slim volume was in Latin. There were no notes or marginalia that I could see, and it wasn't until I got to the final page that the letter we were looking for dropped out of it.

Bella was quick to seize it from the floor and ripped open the eggshell-white envelope with a fervent desire to know what the paper inside would say. We huddled together as she read it aloud.

Dear Hermione,
If you are reading this, then clearly something terrible has happened.
Love you as I do, I do not wish to upset you any more than is necessary. As a result, it is not likely that you can do anything to help me.
Over the last year, I have been so immeasurably happy with you, my sweet little Nightingale. Time passes differently when you are with me, as if the world can spin a fraction more quickly than normal.
Of course, if this really is the end, I pray that you may go on to find the happiness you deserve.
So much of that which we have lived together, I will treasure to my dying day.
To me, you are everything.
Always, your Ernest

"No!" Bella growled in frustration which led to another "Shhh!" and also a "Hush!" and, this time, one of the scholarly gentlemen from the neighbouring aisle stuck his head around the bookshelf to glare at her.

"It tells us nothing!" she declared in the quietest yet angriest tone I'd heard in at least an hour. "It's little but a romantic farewell. Because of the work in which he was involved, Castleton must have put this here for Hermione on the off-chance that something happened to him. Sadly, it's quite unrelated to his current situation."

"I wouldn't be so sure." I was already scanning the text to make sense of what we had discovered, but no great secrets leapt from the page. "Unless he is a hopeless romantic and was afraid that our country's enemies would snuff him out before he could say goodbye, I believe he left this here for a reason."

Bella reacted to the sheer vagueness of my statement with an unimpressed frown. "And what might that be?"

"I haven't a clue, but hopefully the man's fiancée will be able to tell us."

FIVE

I pocketed the letter, and Bella returned the book to its place alongside all the other fascinating texts on household moulds. Castleton had presumably chosen it as the chances of anyone wishing to consult the first ever text on black mould were somewhere between nil and none.

I made sure to give the unhelpful librarian a cheerful wave as we delivered the requested piece of paper, and he looked suitably perplexed by my display of bonhomie. When we got back to the street, Caxton was still waiting for us where we'd left him. It wasn't until I'd climbed into the Sunbeam that Bella remembered she had a telephone call to make and nipped over to a phone box. This left me alone with her chauffeur for the first time since he'd caught me playing in Lady Montague's rose garden when I was ten. I can honestly say that I now found him more frightening than when I was a child. I could see his beady eyes glaring back at me in the newly fitted mirror, and his breathing was noticeably noticeable.

"Caxton, old man," I began in the warmest and, yes, poshest tone I could muster, "would you mind awfully if I were to ask what it is you have against me?"

He didn't need long to consider his answer. "Yes, I would."

"Well that rather kills the conversation." I could have forced the issue, but Bella returned, and I decided to put off the discussion until another day... or possibly never.

"Back to St James's Park, please, Caxton," the mistress told her devoted employee. "I hope that Hermione hasn't taken Percy for too long a walk, or we'll struggle to find them."

"But when we do, we'll have an even more important task to complete," I told her.

"Which is?"

"Eating lunch. I had nothing but a few crumbs of toast this morning. If we don't eat soon, I shall stop the car and go to the first Lyon's Tea House I can find."

As we retraced our route through the city, London still looked spectacular in the spring sunshine. The glittering theatres on Shaftesbury Avenue were each more majestic than the one before. The trees on the Mall had turned vibrant green in preparation for the summer, and I'm beginning to sound as if I've been paid to advertise my adopted city, so I'll stop there.

Luckily for us, Hermione Ravenscroft was easy to find. It was not because of the loud fuchsia blouse she wore beneath her trim black working clothes or her even louder voice; we were only a few yards into the park when we saw her sitting on a bench. My dog was rolling about on the ground, and she was making the fuss of him he duly expected.

"Did you find it?" she asked when Bella sat down next to her.

I stood beside Percy in the hope he might be pleased to see me. He stopped his rolling and looked judgementally in my direction, so at least he'd noticed that I'd been away.

"We did, and there was a letter in the book you mentioned, but it doesn't seem to provide any answers." Bella shot her hand out, and I duly provided the object she desired.

I'd put the letter in my inside pocket for safe keeping and

now handed it to Bella, who gave it to Hermione, who sat before us reading it. Well, she started to do so, but had burst out crying again by the time she'd managed a few lines.

Bella always softened her tone appropriately in such situations. "I'm sure it's difficult to read, but you must tell us if there's anything that stands out as being strange."

Hermione had a handkerchief at the ready and dabbed her eyes before composing herself and reading the rest of the note.

"He is such a sweet, kind man. It breaks my heart to think that he knew of the danger he was in and still managed to write this."

"That's fabulous," I told her in entirely the wrong tone of voice. I sounded both sarcastic and impatient, but I promise that was not my intention. "Is there anything in the letter that could suggest a hidden meaning?"

She glanced back at the missive and read it again with this in mind. I'd read it myself three times in the car and had yet to identify anything out of the ordinary.

"There is one thing," Hermione revealed, her manner more tentative than before.

"Oh, yes?" Bella is so good at saying this sort of thing without sounding as if she is barking out a demand for more information. I really must find out how she does it.

"He calls me his 'Nightingale'."

"Yes, that's very affectionate, but it won't lead us to whoever has taken him." You see! There I go, needling our sobbing witness when I should have been helping her along. And worse than that, I'd distracted her from what she wanted to tell us.

"So you still believe he was kidnapped?"

Luckily, Bella took Hermione's hand at this moment and wrenched the discussion away from me. "It certainly seems that way. We can't know until you tell us your impression of the letter he wrote."

Hermione took comfort from this, and her eyes focused on

the neatly folded paper as if to will the information from her mouth. "It's this term of affection. He's never called me that once in all our time together. He calls me Flittermouse, Sweetikin or Cariad, but never Nightingale. That's quite odd, don't you think?"

I sat down on the other side of her to look at the letter, but nothing new came to mind.

"Perhaps he chose that word to suggest that all was not as it seems," Bella posited. "Perhaps he wanted you to know that there was something more in the letter than a first reading would reveal."

The Hermione there in the park was an entirely different person from the brash, outspoken character we'd met in the pub beside her office. She no longer had the courage to respond, and I wondered what, beyond her fiancé's sudden disappearance, could have scared her so.

"If there's a hidden message, I'm afraid I'm not the person to find it. You should take it to the police."

Now it was my turn to be cagey. "We will, of course, but not yet."

She apparently didn't question why this wouldn't be our first course of action and continued looking glum. "Please contact me again if you find out what's happened. I can't tell you how much I miss my dear Ernest. If I'd known how dangerous his work was, I would have told him to resign."

She was on the point of tears once more, and so I squeezed her hand. I must say I felt truly sorry for the woman. It's easy to treat the people on our cases as nothing more than bit-part players in the grand adventure of Marius and Co. But whatever sort of person she was, and whatever we thought of her, Hermione Ravenscroft was clearly suffering, and I was glad that my friend was emotionally astute enough to comfort her – even if my overriding instinct was to seek out some lunch.

"You'll see," my companion told her. "Everything will work out for the best."

"You know, you're just as nice as my sister has always told me," Hermione said through the sobs. "You can't imagine how happy I was that you were the ones to come and help."

"We'll do all we can to find Ernest. I promise."

She looked so downbeat that I considered lending her my dog, but Percy was already up on his feet, ready for whatever excitement lay ahead.

"If you think of anything else that could help, you can find me in the ground-floor flat at 15 St James's Square," I told her gently. "If I'm not home, my mother should be." This was not the most professional farewell, and so I formed a resolution to print some calling cards for our detective agency (and, in future, not mention my mother so often).

We left her to her thoughts and finally set off towards the Cavendish for lunch. The Cavendish Hotel was not the grandest, the best kept, or the most luxurious establishment in the neighbourhood, but the food was unrivalled. As a bonus, it was a lot more affordable than most places in which Bella would usually set foot, and I preferred its relaxed atmosphere to Hotel Russell, Claridge's or the Ritz.

It helped that the place was run by a real character of a woman who, when we arrived, was dashing in and out of the kitchen, laughing and shouting to her staff as she went. Rosa Lewis was known as the duchess of the establishment, and she was certainly confident and commanding enough to be given a royal appointment, though perhaps her manners needed some polishing.

"Don't just leave the lady and gentleman standing there, Benjamin!" she bellowed, and a smartly dressed employee rushed over to us.

The maître d'hôtel showed us to our table in the outside courtyard, and I was pleasantly surprised to find an oasis of calm in the bustling city. I hadn't been there in warm weather before, and the internal patio was filled with potted trees and small plants, along with ivy creeping up three of the walls. The only disappointment was that our table was already occupied by a man with a dour expression and no charm.

"Bella, my dear, I was expecting you hours ago." Gilbert Baines crossed his arms over his chest, and I bit my tongue to stop myself from saying anything rude to my companion's boorish boyfriend.

"I'm terribly sorry, Gilly," I replied so that Bella didn't have to apologise. "It's all my fault. I got the pair of us muddled up in a simply thrilling case of intrigue and espionage." I knew the only way to get under Gilbert's skin was to remind him of all the fun we were having without him, and so I did just that. "We've already raided the British Museum for clues and enjoyed some sunshine in the park. What did you get up to this morning?"

Percy is a terrible judge of character and went to sit on Gilbert's feet.

My brawny opponent, meanwhile, just bristled. "I'll have you know that I've been incredibly busy this week working for my new client." Baines was a banker of... some description. I'm sure that he had told me what he did on numerous occasions, but I evidently hadn't paid attention. "After my previous client died within an hour of meeting you, I had to find another."

"Now, now, boys. There's no need to bicker," Bella intervened, then pushed me into my seat. "Marius, we all know that you weren't responsible for dear Cecil Sinclair's death. And Gilbert, I am sorry we're late, but I called to tell you as soon as I noticed the time."

His voice became shrill. "Yes, but that was twenty minutes ago. I'd given up waiting and eaten my lunch by then."

It was at this moment that the waiter arrived. He was a smart young Londoner with a white shirt and a black apron tied around his waist. "Sir, would you care to finish your meal with a hot drink or perhaps a digestif?" He looked a little puzzled by our presence and added another suggestion. "Or maybe your friends would like to see the menu."

Within a minute or three, we'd ordered our lunch and, just to be sociable, Gilbert opted for more food. Pig's trotters have never been to my taste. Eating pig's trotters twice within a matter of hours would positively turn my stomach, but Gilbert tucked into them.

"Perhaps you can help us," Bella proposed between courses.

"Do you really think we're at liberty to reveal our secrets?" I asked, partly because we were dealing with a highly confidential matter, but mainly to annoy our dining companion.

"Of course we are." Bella refrained from tutting... this time. "Gilbert is the third member of our team. And our employer only said we couldn't talk about it with foreign agents, the police and the press. He didn't say anything about our close confidants." She squeezed his hand, and I wished I hadn't said anything.

A few minutes later, Belly had told Gilly the whole story, and the note we'd found was laid out before us on the table.

"We believe that this letter, which Castleton hid in a terribly dry text in the British library, must contain a hidden message," she summarised, "but we don't know what it is."

I was tempted to make a joke about mould not being dry, but I couldn't find the right wording and it probably wouldn't have been very funny anyway.

She pushed it across the table for Gilbert to read, and I moved around to see it. My white metal chair screeched across the paving stones, which caused the people at the table beside ours to cover their ears. I was torn between wanting that dullard to discover the information that had eluded us and crossing my fingers that he would draw a blank.

I gave it one last try myself in the hope that the competition would drive me to success. I read the message backwards in case I should find a run of words that, when reversed, would reveal something significant. That didn't work, and so I tried reading the lines in the wrong order. The language was vague and sentimental, so this technique was never going to uncover a significant address or some explanation of the project that had placed Castleton in danger. And therein lay our problem. It would not be easy to hide a phrase such as "experimental weapon" or "top-secret investigation" in a love letter.

He must have known that I was trying to do the very same thing as he was, as he kept darting glances in my direction. I doubled or possibly redoubled my efforts and looked for new patterns in diagonals, as in a jumble letters in the paper.

"I've got it!"

Gilbert and I looked at Bella in awe. Our esteem for that fine young lady was surely the only thing we had in common.

"'Nightingale' is the key after all. Look at the beginning and end of each line."

Neither of us responded. We turned back to the letter, both desperate to be the first to complete her instructions. Yes, we are very juvenile and competitive. I may enjoy being friends with the first woman I ever loved, but that doesn't mean I have to like her odious boyfriend.

My eyes searched the page, desperately trying to see what she'd spotted and, just as she said, it was the ends of the lines that stood out.

"Of course!"

"What? What is it?" Gilbert was immediately flurried. "All I can see is a perfectly maudlin note to the poor fellow's sweetheart. There's certainly nothing that might relate to the inner workings of the Foreign Office."

"The lines break off unexpectedly," I explained without the hint of a patronising tone. "Some are fairly short, others fill the width of the page, and we already knew that he never called Hermione 'Nightingale'. It's so obvious."

"What is? What's obvious?" He was awfully vexed by now.

Bella liked the man more than I did and put him out of his misery. "The lines break off in odd places because the first letter of each spells out a name." She was proud of her achievement and rightly so. "He chose the word *nightingale* – and not sweet pea or honey pie – because they didn't start with the letter N. Otherwise, it wouldn't have communicated the hidden message."

I ran my finger down the letters at the start of each line. They spelt "Dillon Costa", and the truth is I felt a fool for not noticing the words earlier.

"Who or what is Dillon Costa?" Gilbert asked, and the pair of them turned to me for an answer.

"It's obvious." For once, I was quite confident. "Dillon Costa is the next mystery we will have to solve."

SIX

I don't know if you're aware of the fact that London is a rather large place. Finding a person among the millions who live here is as big a challenge as identifying one specific conker in Hyde Park in the autumn. And yet something about the name Dillon Costa sounded familiar. While I couldn't remember meeting any half-Welsh, half-Spanish people – or should that be half-Irish, half-Italian? – whatever his nationality, the name kept playing in my head like a song that I'd known for years.

It was no great shock that Gilbert had nothing useful to say on the matter. He would not be the man to solve this or any other conundrum and, when the meal was over, I took my fickle pup and retreated to my cave in St James's. Bella had to see her invalid father in her village and would be occupied for the rest of the day, so I was left alone, tormented by the thought that the answer to the next part of the puzzle was just under my nose. It really was most unnerving.

Fortunately (or perhaps otherwise), Bella allowed me to keep the letter, and I spent an hour or two in my writing room, searching for different ways to read it. Dillon Costa certainly seemed like the obvious message that Castleton wished his fiancée to uncover, so perhaps she would know who that was. Sadly, until Bella arrived at her house a ninety-minute drive away, I didn't have any way of contacting her.

Egad! What did people do before telephones were invented? Criminal cases must have taken months to investigate, with detectives spending most of that time waiting for a response to their letters. Thank goodness for modern technology.

The situation was so desperate, I gave up entirely and decided to look through the papers concerning my father's disappearance. This now seemed a less intimidating prospect than the hunt for Ernest Castleton, even if I'd spent two whole months looking into the circumstances and knew little more than when I'd begun.

Good old Dad had disappeared from Hurtwood Village when I was just eighteen, and after a brief search by the police, no one had tried to look for the beloved local solicitor in the ten years since. However, my mother had recently revealed that, shortly before he went missing in 1918, Father had represented a man named Lucien Pike in a murder trial. All I'd found out about Pike, though, was that he was a thug who'd been accused of killing his best friend. My father had made sure he didn't go to prison for his crime. And that terrible knowledge – the antithesis of everything Terence Quin had stood for throughout his career – was the reason I was so happy to run off on any new adventure, instead of sifting through the stark details of his final brief.

I read the papers for the fiftieth time, which resolved precisely nothing. The man I had known – the kind-hearted, charitable sort who had defended every underdog he'd ever heard whimpering and fought the corner of those in need – was not represented in the cold language of the legal files on my desk. There was nothing of Dad there. His very existence was eclipsed by Lucien Pike's, and I had to wonder whether that savage criminal had done away with my father when he was no longer of use to him.

I was so caught up in the list of problems in my head that I didn't notice the sun dropping low behind the buildings opposite, or my mother coming into the room to chastise me.

"Really, Marius. You could at least turn on a light. You shouldn't be working away like this in such a dim room."

I was caught in a fog, and it took me a moment to come back to the world. "You're right, Mother. I'm sorry. I have a lot on my mind."

"You certainly will have if you go blind." She pulled the curtains a little wider in an attempt to eke out the daylight.

I stood up and stretched my legs. "I'm not certain that the medical foundation of that sentence is particularly solid, but in future I will certainly turn on a light."

She glanced at the papers and swallowed hard. "I don't suppose you've found anything yet? About your father, I mean."

I took her lined hand in mine and traced the veins on the back as if they were roads on a map. "Nothing, but I plan to talk to my friend at Scotland Yard about Father's case again. He may have had more success than I have."

The only positive development that afternoon was related to the Castleton affair rather than my own problems. You see, there was one person in my social orbit who knew more of the great and good of London than Lady Isabella herself. Luckily for me, he was about to ring the doorbell.

"I'll get it," Mother was quick to say, but I was faster on my feet and dashed ahead much as I had as a child whenever anyone called to see us.

"Bertie!" I positively cooed when I opened the door to my publisher. He was standing on my doorstep with a bottle in hand and his wife on his arm. "And Margery too, what a lovely surprise."

"Marius, my boy!" Mrs Price-Lewis was a jolly woman with ruddy cheeks and reddish hair. She had always liked me and rushed forward to smother me in a hug. "It's been too long. It's been *too* long!"

I was just as fond of her myself and returned the warm embrace. "Thank you so much for coming. I've had a trouble-some day, and it's wonderful to see a cheery face or two."

Bertie came to bat me about the shoulder with his spare hand. "Then you're in luck, my boy. We just made the acquain-tance of your aunt and uncle. They're on their way in now."

Why did it not surprise me that my uncle had befriended two passing strangers in the street?

As Mother welcomed our visitors, I stuck my head out of the door to see my grinning uncle, who was pushing Auntie Eleanor along the pavement. I should probably mention that she was in a wheelchair. He wasn't rolling his wife up the road.

A similarly jolly scene now played out as my relatives arrived with much noise and excitement.

"Oh, Marius, it's a pleasure to see you," my uncle exclaimed in his usual over-eager manner. "It's been far too long."

I bent down to welcome my aunt, who was far less effusive than her husband but just as kind.

"I read your mother's copy of your new book, Marius," she told me as I followed the others into the lounge. "It was as good as the first. Although I think they would be even better if the detective had a dog."

"Everyone's a critic," I replied as I pushed her chair along the hall.

"That may be true, but it is also the case that the vast majority of people like dogs. What about a dachshund? Your detective would be far more human if he had a dachshund."

I didn't have the heart to tell her that I couldn't imagine the stern, relentless Inspector Rupert L'Estrange carting around a sausage dog on a murder investigation. That being said, I'd taken Percy with me on all of my cases so far, and he was not the obvious choice for a detective's assistant. He was, however, extremely happy to have company. He couldn't decide who deserved to lavish him with attention first so, once we'd all settled down in the lounge, he walked from chair to chair, allowing each person a brief stroke before he moved on again.

I told my visitors the details of the case, without going into the specifics of the file which Inspector Ordinary, as I'd come to think of him, had entrusted into our care.

"The fellow sat right where you are, Bertie," I said after I'd told the unlikely tale. "It was the oddest experience in my life..." I considered the truth of this statement. "Or this year, at least... Or perhaps just this month, as I've had a rather extraordinary time recently."

"A secret policeman?" The usually cheery Welshman looked a little alarmed. "It sounds very cloak and dagger. Soviet Russia uses such people to suppress dissidents, but I wouldn't expect that sort of thing in Britain."

"You're concentrating on the wrong matter entirely, Bertie," his wife intervened. "Whatever the reason the police came to Marius, it shows how highly they must think of him."

"I'm most worried about this Dillon Costa," I continued. "British spies and code breakers must know what they're doing, but I'm not sure that I do. If Bella and I can't find the next clue that will lead us to Castleton... Well, I don't like to imagine what will happen. We only have until Saturday to solve the case, and time is ticking."

"I knew a Dillon Lewis once," my mother contributed. "But on saying it out loud, I've realised how entirely irrelevant that statement is." She carried a tray of wine glasses from the walnut cabinet in the corner and placed it on the table for me to pour snifters of Madeira for each of us.

Though my lounge is not as bright as the rooms at the front of the flat, it is a perfectly comfortable space and just right for entertaining friends – not that I tend to throw wild parties. In fact, since moving to London, I'd spent a portion of my time writing and the rest staring at a blank page whenever the muse failed to strike.

"Dillon Costa," Margery repeated. "It definitely rings a bell, but why?"

"I was hoping you might know who he is, Bertie."

My publisher was normally both the spark and conductor of every conversation, and so the few seconds for which he had been silent were truly remarkable.

"I'm thinking," he eventually explained. "It's not an everyday sort of name."

"Much like Marius Quin," Auntie Elle pointed out when I was too slow.

"It sounds rather like a sailor to me," her husband suggested. "Not an English name."

"Much like Marius!" My aunt beat me again.

"Dillon's a Welsh name, isn't it?" I asked Bertie, whose own family came from a South-Walian mining valley.

"Only if it's spelt with a Y. Was it spelt with a Y?"

I tried to imagine where the letter Y would fit into the name Dillon and soon had to give up. "No."

"Either way, did you expect me to know every Welshman in London?" he asked to chastise me.

I took him his drink in the hope that it would lubricate his thoughts. "Of course not, but you do know most politicians, a good few judges, several lords and half the England cricket team. Surely if Dillon Costa is someone worth knowing, you or one of your acquaintances will know him."

Bertie had fallen quiet again, and I believe that everyone in the room leaned forward in anticipation of what he might say. Percy was the exception, of course. He was getting comfortable on Margery's lap and appeared to have no interest in the conversation, which is hardly surprising as Percy is a dog.

"I can certainly put a few pertinent questions to some well-connected individuals," Bertie said to break the tension. "But it is possible that Dillon Costa isn't a person at all. It could be the names of two streets that cross somewhere in the city."

"I've never come across a Costa Street around here." Uncle Stan scratched his rough sideburns as he spoke.

"Or perhaps it's a reference to another book in the British Museum," my clever aunt suggested.

I was reflecting on the openness of the question, and the sheer number of potential solutions to it, when my mother put forward a thought of her own.

"It could be two separate people." She did not possess the unfailing confidence of the Price-Lewises, and she was no gabster like her brother-in-law, but she'd made a good point.

"You mean like a double act in the theatre?" Auntie Elle mused. "That's a thought."

"I once saw a man-and-dog act called Dillon and Crackers at the Kilburn Empire." Uncle Stan's light tone made it clear that Dillon and Crackers were not the man and dog that we were looking for.

"We're dealing with spies and secrets, so it's unlikely to be anything so glamorous," Margery replied. "Could it not be the name of a firm of solicitors? Messrs Dillon and Costa of Clerkenwell."

Like a speck of soap circling a drain, the fact that had been on the periphery of my brain all day finally dropped into place. "Dillon and Costa!"

"What have you realised?" Bertie asked. He was an enthusiastic fellow at the worst of times, and right at that moment, he was set to explode.

"Dillon and Costa!" my mother echoed, and we looked at

one another across the room with such glee that the others smiled without knowing why.

"Mother, please tell everyone where I'm going." I put my glass down on the table and ran to the door. "It's not quite six o'clock. I might yet catch them."

SEVEN

Not to be left out, Percy scampered along behind me, his crescent moon tail whipping back and forth with every step he took. I left my building and exited the square onto King Street, before turning right onto Duke Street, then crossing the perpendicular road (which held no lofty title but was named after a famous Earl). Piccadilly Arcade was the brightest attraction in that part of town, and I'd always loved strolling along that illuminated walkway. The elegant tailors, cobblers and milliners displayed their wares behind bulging glass windows, which lent a magical effect to the place, as though one were viewing their offerings through glistening bubbles.

But there was one shop in particular that seemed even more unreal and wondrous. Just under the glass dome in the centre of the arcade, squeezed in beside a shop selling antique militaria, was the prettiest jewellers in London. Through the window, I could see velvet trays of bejewelled rings, bracelets and necklaces of every colour. There were rubies, sapphires and diamonds twinkling back at me in the bright evening light that cut through the glass overhead.

It was one of those shops that I'd always wanted to enter but never had a reason to do so. Dillon and Costa had been on the tip of my tongue since Bella had unlocked the code in Castleton's letter, and now I was standing right before it. I must have walked past that shop a hundred times, but it wasn't until Margery Price-Lewis put a conjunction between the two names that I made the connection.

As I placed my hand against the door to enter, it was as if I were travelling to another world that no one had explored before. Which is an overblown comparison to make, though I did now hope to find some answers to the long list of questions that I had accumulated since Inspector Ordinary had knocked on my door that morning.

Percy waddled in after me. He was evidently aware that this was not the sort of place in which to go charging about, and he sat patiently beside me the whole time we were in there.

"Good evening, sir. May I help you in some way?" the wan gentleman asked. He had a rather Victorian aspect and wore a corded velveteen coat, a black silk cravat and a pair of extremely thick glasses, which he presumably used for examining the stones he bought and sold.

"I very much hope you can," I replied in a cheerful voice before realising that the topic I had to broach would not be an easy one. "You see, I'm a friend of Ernest Castleton's, and I'm here to—"

Before I could say another word, he stood back from the counter and, much like an undertaker (which I now realised he resembled), he walked slowly towards a black metal door in the corner of the shop. From the chain around his neck, he produced a key, which he held up to me in dramatic fashion.

Once the door was unlocked, I could see that it concealed a number of small black drawers in a tall cabinet that was built into the alcove in the wall. The jeweller ran his fingers over them and muttered to himself, as if attempting to recall where he had stored something. His hand swayed left and right then up and down before he made a brief, triumphal sound and pulled out the bottommost drawer to bring back to the counter.

"Mr Castleton left me with strict instructions that, should someone come looking for him, I was to pass on something very important."

As he spoke, he removed a burgundy wooden box. Then, from within that, he revealed a smaller one. This process continued, much like the dismantling of a Russian matryoshka doll, until he reached the final item that was no bigger than a matchbox. "Here we are, sir."

He placed it on the counter before him and I was about to reach out towards the glossy red case, when I had the definite sensation that my reward had come too easily and there had to be a catch.

"What's inside it?" I asked, half dreading the answer.

"Now, that's the interesting part."

This was exactly what I feared. "You mean to say that you know, but you won't tell me?"

The jeweller rolled his shoulders. "Not exactly. I know, but I can't tell you until you answer a few key questions."

"Very well." I wore a stern expression as I braced myself for what came next. "Ask away."

I could see that he was sizing me up, but I still wished he would get on with it.

"Question number one: What is the name of Mr Castleton's fiancée?"

This was easy enough. I was not likely to forget the woman in a hurry. "Her name is Hermione Ravenscroft. It's thanks to her that I'm standing before you."

"Very good, sir. And could you describe her to me?"

This was no trickier, and I reeled off a description. "In terms of her appearance, she is a very striking young lady with a pronounced pout and unusually dark eyes."

"And her personality?"

My brows knitted together. "Is that one of the questions, or are you just curious?"

"Does it matter either way?" Despite his pallid complexion, he had a warm manner. I knew that he was playing with me, but I couldn't tell whether it was part of the test I had to complete, or he was just having fun.

"I suppose not." I cast my mind back to the pub that morning. "Well, she's rather loud and outspoken. I think it would be accurate to call her passionate... and plummy, of course. She's certainly that."

"Excellent. Now, my next question is, what does Mr Castleton do for a living?"

"He works for the Foreign Office."

He made a clicking sound in his cheek, as this clearly wasn't what he wanted to hear. "I'm afraid I'll need more information than that."

I tried to extract the specific detail from the file I'd read. "He's an aide to Lord Darnley, the Foreign Secretary."

He shook his head apologetically. "That's all true, of course, but there was a certain fact which Mr Castleton insisted that the person who came here would know."

I could tell that the questions until now had been little more than the build up to this one. "He... he's involved in many different projects. I remember talk of his work on diplomacy and..." The longer I went without summoning the right answer, the harder it was to think. "...and international conferences, he's involved with those, too."

He seized the box from the counter and looked as though he would lock it back up inside the safe. "I'm terribly sorry, sir, but I cannot give you the contents of this box unless you provide the exact answer Mr Castleton requires."

I looked away from him to the floor, but Percy was no help. My eyes roamed over the glass case filled with jewels and jewellery, and I hoped that the sparkling treasures on display might fire the synapses in my brain into action. To my surprise, that's exactly what occurred.

"Code breaking!" I declared far too loudly. "Castleton works as a liaison between Darnley and a government agency called..." This was surely the hardest part of the challenge, but I closed my eyes to picture the card Inspector Ordinary had shown me and read off the letters. "...GC&CS!"

The man I took to be Mr Dillon stopped what he was doing and rubbed his hands together. "That is correct. GC&CS."

This raised the question of how the man in front of me knew what he knew. He gave the distinct impression that he was more than just a jeweller, but there was something ever so theatrical about him, and I had to conclude that he was simply enjoying the role he'd been given.

"And so, my final question..." He paused to build up the tension. "Where in Fitzrovia is Mr Castleton's pied-à-terre?"

The energy drained out of me in a second. I couldn't believe I'd got this far only to fail the final test. "I'm afraid I don't know."

The gentleman bit his lip and sighed. "Ahh, that's going to be a problem." He released a soft tut. "You see, sir, it would be easy enough for thieves to rob my shop and take the item with which Mr Castleton entrusted me, but it is far more difficult to extract knowledge from those unwilling to share it. That is why Mr Castleton came to me. My partner, Mr Costa, and I have established a certain reputation for discretion. You don't get far in this business without people being able to trust you." He spread his hands out and ran them along the glass case in front of him to highlight the value of the goods on display. "Oh, yes. We here at Dillon and Costa are known for our ability to keep more than just jewellery safe."

He tapped his nose and laughed, and I couldn't tell whether he meant a single word he said.

"That's impressive, no doubt, but it doesn't change the fact that I still can't tell you the address."

With a wink, he ducked under the counter to seek out a metal prong which he fitted into a small hole in the shiny red box. He kept his eyes on me as he performed the action, and the hinge sprang open to reveal... nothing.

"It's empty!" I blurted in dismay.

"That's right, sir. I wasn't about to disclose the whereabouts of the very thing you've come here to obtain without first assuring that you were the person who should have it." He tidied away the boxes and the prong and pulled a bronze key from a hook behind him. "You'll need this to get into Mr Castleton's property."

I was even more nonplussed than when I'd entered the shop. "I just told you; I don't know where that is."

"Precisely, sir. You can't get into the door that this key opens if you don't have the address. It is another of the many secrets I store up here." He pointed to the top of his head, and I had nothing left to say to him. It would do me no good to beg or argue, and so I stood there looking like the cat who has been shown the cream only for it to be ripped away just as his eager tongue was reaching out for it.

The jeweller's face suddenly brightened. "Not to worry. I'll write it down for you."

He looked beneath the counter for a pencil and paper and had soon scribbled the details I needed. I took the scrap from him but found it difficult to know what to say.

"Don't look so surprised," he told me. "The address isn't one of the questions; it's the reward for getting them right. From what I understood when he came in here, the property is linked to Mr Castleton's work, and even his girlfriend doesn't know about it. He told me that he'd entrusted the key and the address to us so as not to endanger Miss Ravenscroft."

"Thank you most kindly," I found myself saying in something of a daze, and I clucked my tongue for Percy to follow me. When I got to the door, my curiosity got the better of me and I turned to ask the man another question. "I'm sorry, but I must ask; how much did he actually tell you? Do you have any idea what I will find at this address?"

"I might, or I might not..." He shrugged with the same air of mystery he'd maintained since I arrived, then chuckled under his breath. "Although a more accurate answer would be, no. I do not. Mr Castleton seemed a very discreet sort of person and offered the barest of facts, though I do wish you well with your task. Whatever it may be."

"Then what was all that business with the boxes?"

He pulled at one cuff and took his time to formulate an answer. "That was just a bit of fun on my part, sir. I've always fancied trying my hand at amateur dramatics, but this is the next best thing." He bowed his head sombrely before that mischievous smile broke out on his lips again. "Perhaps you'd allow me a question of my own, though, sir?"

My resultant shrug successfully conveyed my total confusion.

"We've never had such a mysterious case as this one before. It's normally secret notes sent to lovers that people leave here, or heirlooms they want to hide from their families. When Mr Castleton came, I didn't know what to think. I pledged to follow his instructions to the letter, of course, but I ended up wondering whether it was part of some sort of treasure hunt?"

I smiled and allowed him to think he was right. "That's just it. It's a little game that Ernest and I are playing for laughs."

"I knew it!" He clapped his hands together. "I knew it all along."

EIGHT

I was tempted to go straight to the address the jeweller had given me and see what I could find there. Luckily for Bella, I didn't have my own private chauffeur to drive me across the city to 8 Colville Place. I also lacked the energy to walk there, and it was far too hot that evening to descend into the bowels of the Earth to take the tube.

The final straw was my realisation that most shops in London would soon be closing for the night, and I still didn't possess any red lipstick. Inspector Ordinary had told me to leave a mark on my window to confirm that we were taking the case. Whatever doubts I might have had about the reason he'd hired us, I wasn't about to give up after we'd come so far. I went to Fortnum and Mason, where an assistant not so politely informed me that I was in the wrong shop, and then I hurried along Piccadilly, desperately searching for somewhere that sold make-up before finding the very place.

"You're in luck, sir," the female shop assistant informed me. "We happen to have a new range in stock. What shade would you like?"

I thought I'd been clear on this point, but apparently not. "Red. I'd like red lipstick."

She laughed a little too hysterically. "There's a world of reds, sir. How would you describe your wife's complexion?"

"My wife...?" I looked over my shoulder at Percy, who was sitting outside the shop. For all I complain about him, he really is a very well-behaved dog, but he couldn't help me now. "Do you know the shade of red of the new Bentley that came out a few months ago?" I tried. "What about that one?"

She looked a little concerned about me but hauled a heavy box onto the counter. "I have cherry, beetroot, geranium and cockscomb."

I genuinely think that I was more nervous at this moment than I had been when I thought I'd failed the jeweller's test. "I want the reddest one."

"Natural it is, then." She tutted at me as if I was being quite unreasonable and went scrambling under the counter for another box.

"Natural red. Yes, that sounds right. Were the others somehow unnatural then?" I emitted a soft laugh.

She did not think me funny. "No, sir, but they were kissproof. Are you sure that you wouldn't prefer the cockscomb? There might even be a scarlet in the box somewhere if I dig deeper."

"No, no. Natural red is just the ticket. My wife and I barely kiss these days anyway."

She didn't seem to know how to take this comment, and I certainly couldn't imagine why I had made it, so I handed over my (exorbitant) two and six and hurried from the shop. I got a few suspicious looks from the remaining customers, not to mention the guard at the door. I could tell that they were thinking, *What a queer fish! Sneaking into the shop just as it was closing in the hope that no one would notice. Some people are loons.*

I would have liked to tell them that the lipstick I had purchased was not for me but my imaginary wife, though I doubt they would have believed me. I went back to my house on St James's Square and took my purchase from the paper bag. I painted a large X on the front window, wondering the whole time what the postman would think when he came past the next morning.

With that done, I rang Bella to tell her the news about the key and Castleton's secret flat in the city. She promised to come first thing and, as we were both unable to disguise our excitement, our goodbyes lasted almost as long as the call itself.

I was pleased to see that my friends and family were not only still at home but getting on like a forest fire. Mother had inevitably pulled out her accordion. Uncle Stan was at the piano, and good old Bertie was leading everyone in a particularly rousing rendition of a raucous Welsh song.

"Sosban fach yn berwi ar y tân,
Sosban fawr yn berwi ar y llawr,
A'r gath wedi sgramo Joni bach."

If I had to guess, I would say it was about a saucepan, but that surely couldn't be right.

"Marius, you're back!" Margery said once the song was over, and they'd finished clapping.

"Yes, and I have the next clue on our endless trail. I would tell you all about it, but I simply must go to bed."

A great hubbub struck up as the elderly – or at least aged – masses clamoured for me to stay.

"It's not even seven o'clock yet. Don't be such a killjoy," Stan complained, and even his reasonable wife objected.

"You wouldn't want to be the skeleton at the feast, Marius." She rolled her chair forward a half rotation to reason with me. "Come in for one drink and some of your uncle's cheese scones.

I promise you can go to your room to ponder the case just as soon as you've told us what happened."

They were right of course. I was being a spoilsport, and so I went in to talk to them. Still, I stuck to my guns and was in bed by midnight. I would have probably stayed up even longer, but Margery declared that the night was still young, and they set off to Leicester Square in search of a late dinner. Percy and I waved them off from the doorway, and then I was finally free to go to bed with Bertie's irritatingly catchy song stuck in my brain. I didn't know the original words, so I made up my own.

"Saucepans are fun. I use them all the time.
Saucepans are great. Has anyone seen mine?
If not then Johnny better give it back."

Percy looked at me like I was the weird one, and I fell asleep as soon as I collapsed onto the bed. I may have had a few too many glasses of the Welsh whisky that Bertie had brought us. He claimed it was very old, and it certainly tasted it.

Approximately seventeen seconds later, I was woken by the sound of someone coming into my room.

"Come along, Marius. Why aren't you awake?"

"Because I haven't been to sleep yet," I murmured, before realising that the warm body next to mine was Percy's. You'll be pleased to hear that I soon pushed his slobbery face away from me.

"Marius, I'm serious. We have to leave now. Just imagine what the savages who took Ernest Castleton are doing to him. They've already killed an innocent bystander."

I opened one eye only to discover that the morning had sneaked up stealthily when I was least expecting it. Dressed all in black for some reason, Bella was standing at the end of the bed, silhouetted by daylight.

I put my hand over my face to stave off blindness. "My goodness! How did you make the night pass so quickly?"

"It took just as long as always, you giddy fool."

I tried to push myself up to sitting, but it was too much effort, so I stared at the clock on the mantelpiece instead. It was eight o'clock. "When you said that you'd meet me here first thing, I assumed you meant at ten or eleven like any reasonable person. In future, I would prefer you to come at third or fourth thing if it can be helped."

"What have you done to yourself?"

The pressure of my hand weighing on my head told me that I would not be feeling top notch for some time. I swung my legs off the bed and was pleasantly surprised to discover that I was far readier for the day than I had imagined. "Oh, how wonderful. I'm already dressed."

"Nonsense, you can't go out like that. I'll wait for you to wash and change." Bella was gazing through the curtains, as if to check whether anyone was watching us. As we were at the back of my flat and the windows gave onto a small, shared garden, I very much doubted this would be the case.

"Bella, my dear old friend, why is it that, whenever you're around, I feel as though I've done something terribly naughty?"

She did not answer but pointed to my bathroom. The look on her face told me I should not challenge her again. I was dressed and clean in mere tens of minutes and, standing in front of the bathroom mirror in my summer whites, no one could have guessed what I'd been up to the night before.

Percy was still asleep, so we crept from the flat to speed back to Fitzrovia. It now made more sense that Castleton had hidden the first clue on our treasure trail in a book in the British Museum. His pied-à-terre was minutes' walk from the grand old institution. It's just a shame he hadn't revealed the address in the letter. It would have saved us the best part of a day and another journey with Bella's grumpy chauffeur.

"Did you have a peaceful night, Caxton?" I asked, mainly to vex him.

"Perfectly, thank you, sir." He had to be polite when his mistress was there, and I was determined to make the most of it.

"Jolly good. I don't like the thought of you skimping on your beauty sleep."

"That's very kind of you, Mr Quin."

Bella smiled at us for talking to one another like adults. She was normally too smart not to see through such a façade, but she had a definite blind spot when it came to Caxton.

We soon arrived at Colville Place, which was a quiet walkway between two rows of modest brick houses. It looked like a calm place to live in the centre of the city. The residents had placed potted plants in front of their homes, and there was a group of children playing with a ball below a sign which read, "No Ball Games".

It was easy enough to find number eight. There were only twenty or so houses in the whole narrow lane and it stuck out for being the one house without plants in front of it – or any sign of life, for that matter. It was smaller and shabbier than most in the row and looked to all intents and purposes like an office rather than a dwelling in one of the smartest parts of London.

To tell you the truth, there was a moment of panic when I put my hand into my inside jacket pocket and wondered whether I'd remembered to bring the key with me. Thankfully, I soon felt the touch of metal on the tip of one finger and took the key out to open the front door. This brief shock helped sober me up somewhat.

"Ready?" Bella asked, as she must have seen my relieved reaction.

"'As ready as a borrower's cap,'" I replied and turned the key in the lock.

The sense that this was not a place where anyone lived was

only reinforced when we went inside. There was little of the personal within the small parlour we entered. There was a telephone on a low table, a crate for dirty shoes, and an umbrella stand. The next room was no different. It was a lounge with two sofas and a fireplace, but it had no photographs on the walls nor knick-knacks on the mantelpiece. I can't say exactly why, but Bella and I moved through the house as quietly as spiders. It was not out of fear that someone might be in there with us – the thought hadn't entered my mind. No, I believe it was down to our sense of decorum. We were intruders and, even if this was not someone's home, there was no need to make it any worse.

It wasn't until we reached what should have been a dining room at the back of the house that we found anything worth finding. While the previous rooms had looked much as they would have when the house was first built, this new one was something of a mess. It was not merely the newspaper clippings, scribbled notes and photographs that were pinned haphazardly all over the walls. The floor was equally covered with torn papers. I had the sense that whoever had assembled this strange tableau had done so in an immense hurry.

"What do you think Castleton was doing that made him a target for the kidnappers?" I asked myself as much as Bella.

She approached the main wall that had been, for want of a better word, redecorated in the aforementioned style. "I suppose we're about to find out."

I noticed photographs of burly men in long beige raincoats looking quite out of place in the seaside cottage they were inhabiting. A little higher on the wall, there was a clipping about the forthcoming visit of the French Foreign Minister, Aristide Briand, but the majority of the papers bore long chains of mathematical symbols, and what I took to be indecipherable codes.

"These two men look dangerous," Bella concluded as she

stood ever so close to one of the photographs. "Why would Castleton have assembled all this information?"

It was a far from simple question to answer, but there was one thing I felt confident to say. "He clearly believed that they posed some sort of threat. What's harder to determine is, assuming these are the people who've taken him, and he knew their location in advance, why wouldn't he have told his superiors so they could send someone to arrest them?"

"Perhaps that was the very reason they scrobbled him. He found out too much about some terrible criminal organisation or a nest of foreign spies and was dealt with accordingly."

Bella fell quiet as we studied the house in the photograph. It was a small white cottage with a curious front garden dotted with fanciful wooden decorations. There were miniature windmills and woodpeckers that, I could only imagine, rocked back and forth in the wind. They were the kind of novelties you found in souvenir shops at the seaside, and just the sort of thing that eccentric people who retired to such quaint towns favoured.

"Do you have any idea where the photos were taken?" I asked when we'd studied the evidence for a few minutes without passing further comment.

"I can't say it looks familiar." As she replied, she moved aside an overlapping sheet of paper to reveal a wide-angle photograph. It had been taken from a pebbly beach and showed a row of houses in the background, with the white cottage noticeable in the middle. "It could be the south coast. Perhaps Brighton?"

I shook my head, as I knew Brighton a little from my visits to see a soldier pal. "I don't think so. The seafront there has a lot of grand buildings. This looks like a smaller town. I might be wrong, of course..."

My sentence trailed off as I noticed a close-up of one of the ruffians. He had a broad face, and I'd rarely seen a steelier jaw outside of the boxing ring. He had the look of a man who had been bred to stand in front of buildings, terrifying passers-by. His eyes were cold and oddly intimidating, even in that colourless photograph, and I hoped I would never have to cross his path. There were pictures of the two men coming in and out of the house. In some, they were carrying what I took to be groceries – though there might well have been something more sinister hidden in their paper bags. In others, they were empty-handed.

I needed to make sense of all that we'd found, but before I could translate my thoughts into words, Bella spoke for me. "Castleton left a trail to this place, and it's clear that he didn't live here. So let's assume that these materials were too sensitive to keep in his own home. That would explain why Hermione didn't know anything about this property."

"Yes, Castleton suggested as much when he left the key with the jewellers. It's interesting that he would even trust such information to Messrs Dillon and Costa, though. I assume he paid them a good sum to keep his secrets."

"That's not our most pressing concern," she was quick to remind me. "We followed Castleton's clues to this address, which means something here must tell us where to go next."

I looked at the quirky house again. It was the perfect place to hide something you didn't want anyone to discover. If I'd been an international criminal, I wouldn't have stashed my treasures in a high-walled fortress or underground safe as everyone would expect, I'd have found the quaintest, most tranquil location in the British Isles, with plenty of friendly little-old-lady-and-gentlemen neighbours.

"This could be it," Bella said to break through my daydreaming. "It's the only note without a single Greek letter or mathematical symbol." She tapped the wall with her hand, and I went to read it.

Sure enough, there was a line of text on a scrap the size of a cigarette paper.

"'A rocky road where Harold fell,'" I read aloud.

"It doesn't give us a great deal to go on," she replied and, just for once, she was wrong.

"How silly of me." I hit my forehead with the ball of my hand. "I knew there was something familiar about those photographs. I went there when I was a child."

She looked a little put out that I'd solved the clue so quickly. "Oh, really. You know the answer from six mysterious words?"

"Yes, and so do you." I put my finger beneath the key part. "Where did Harold fall?"

"Who's—" she began, before realising how simple it really was. "King Harold?"

"That's right."

"He died at the Battle of Hastings! Which is a town on the sea."

"Actually he died in a place about seven miles—" I cut this sentence short when her glazed-over expression informed me that this was not the moment for a history lesson. "Hastings is by the sea, though, so that must be where we have to go."

"Do you actually believe that Castleton is being held there?"

"Unless they've already cleared out, yes, I do. These photos must have been taken before he disappeared, but he didn't trust his colleagues with what he'd found and, when the criminals got hold of him, they took him to this..." I searched for and failed to find a word that wasn't too childish. "...hideout."

She stepped back then, as if it wasn't just my plan that frightened her. "Shouldn't we tell the people who employed us? What good are we going to do against those monsters on the wall?"

I dropped my voice so as not to alarm her. "We're on our own, Bella. That man yesterday made it perfectly clear that it

THE CASTLETON AFFAIR 67

was down to us to save Castleton, and it's obvious now why that had to be the case."

She might have forgotten a few of the facts we had learnt in history class together, but she had as sharp a mind as any other person I knew. Her eyes travelled from photograph to photograph until she found the cutting about the French Foreign Minister.

"You mean to say that the police commissioned us to take charge of Castleton's rescue because they couldn't risk a diplomatic set-to with the French?"

"It certainly seems that way."

"And so our allies across the Channel kidnapped a high-ranking British civil servant?"

I hesitated then. "I know it sounds improbable, but what about this case isn't? Every clue we've followed has led to an unexpected turn of events."

She needed some time to contemplate the path ahead of us. To me at least, it looked as though there would be nothing but twists, turns and bends for some miles.

"Very well." She took a deep breath. "We have to go to Hastings. But we haven't worked out what the note means when it talks of rocky roads."

I pulled out the pin which held the piece of paper to the wall. "We don't need to know that. The house is on the seafront. All we have to do is get to Hastings and drive along the prom until we find the scene in the photograph."

A cold thrill passed over me then, and I believe that Bella felt it too. We fell silent for a moment, and when she spoke again, there was an unexpected glimmer in her eyes.

"I think we've done it. I think we've found Ernest Castleton."

NINE

Bella suggested that Caxton drive us to Charing Cross Station so that we could nip down to the coast on the Southern Railway. There was only one problem with this. Well, there were probably more, but an important one sprang to mind.

"How would we take our rescued hero back with us?"

"The same way we got there, obviously."

Bella was apparently unable to see any issue with her plan, and so I offered a brief critique. "Let's say that we find the place where Castleton is being held. We distract his guards, manage to free him from the house and escape."

"That all sounds good so far," she replied in a less than accepting tone.

"Yes, it's just what we want, but how exactly will we get away if those two giants we saw in the photographs are running after us? Even if we make it through the town, we'll get back to the station and have to wait for the two-fifteen train. I very much doubt the outwitted criminals will give up and go home. They'll do all they can to recover their prisoner."

"Ah, I see. So it does make sense to have a car with us." She leaned forward to talk to the chauffeur. "Caxton, I'm afraid we'll have to drive to—"

"No, you misunderstood me," I interrupted before she could rope him into the plan. "We won't need Caxton. I have a better solution."

If there is one good thing that has come of our attempt to be somewhat professional sleuths, it's the extra value I have been able to extract from my ridiculously fast car. I already loved that exquisite feat of British engineering, but now that I regularly get the chance to speed about the place chasing ne'er-do-wells, I appreciate my glossy red Invicta all the more. I can't imagine I would have been nearly so confident heading to Hastings to face the twin ogres who were guarding our man if I hadn't had such a wonderful machine to whisk us back home again.

When we got to my flat, Percy was sitting on my desk, peering out of the window. With his long jowls and soulful eyes, he was never the most ebullient canine, but when he saw me step from Bella's Sunbeam, he almost looked as though he were smiling.

This made the fact that I couldn't take him with us all the more painful.

"I'm sorry, old boy," I called, though I doubted he could hear through the glass or, for that matter, understand complex sentences. "If we took you with us, there'd be no room in the car for the man we're supposed to rescue. And that's without mentioning the fact that where we're going isn't safe. You're better off staying here with Mother."

I'm not normally the type who wallows in unnecessary pools of guilt, but the sight of those big brown eyes staring out at me struck some previously unknown pressure point that made my throat sore, my heart ache and my gut sting. He's a manipulative little rascal.

Bella cordially said goodbye to her chauffeur – I did not – and then we got into the Invicta. Not so long ago, the journey to

Hastings was a treacherous affair along little more than country lanes. I remember arduous voyages to get there in the back of my father's old Humberette when I was a child, but with the clear tarmac of the A21 now before us, we practically sailed to our destination in a little under two hours.

The air was warm and rushed over our bodies as it whistled past, and there was a sweetness in the air that I found quintessentially British. Was it the flowers in the fields alongside us? I'd never smelt that same scent in France during the war, but then perhaps that was because the land had been blown to pieces by German fighter planes or crushed beneath the tracks of tanks.

The smoothness of the journey that morning was at odds with the rolling tides inside us.

I have no doubt that we were both thinking the same thing, not least because, after fifteen minutes of silence, Bella confirmed it.

"I'm beginning to worry this is a bad idea."

"I don't know what you mean," I lied. "I'm certainly not frightened that we're in over our heads, having bitten off more than we can chew as we row past our own reach." Unsurprisingly, this did not set her mind at ease.

"Yesterday morning, we knew nothing of secret codebreaking agencies or kidnappings. I'm merely concerned that this is a case too far for us."

"So I should turn back?" I asked, to stop either one of us from relying on another cliché to explain our feelings. "Perhaps we're fools to try, but I must admit that I haven't felt this involved in anything since before the war. It's all very well my sitting at home making stories for a living, but this is different."

She had looked terribly cautious until now, but her face suddenly blossomed with the prettiest smile I'd ever known. "I know just what you mean. After all, this was what we wanted when we decided to go into business together. It may be dangerous, but we can't turn our backs on a true adventure."

"That's the spirit!" I said with a cheer. "Where would the world be without reliable fools who jump in headfirst while the angels hang about in the background, terrified of where to set their feet?"

"Righto!" She laughed and joined in with the joke. "This country was built on the back of dunderheads like us throwing caution to the wind."

"Precisely. We have nothing to fear."

"Nothing whatsoever."

This brave act wouldn't have fooled Percy, and our smiles soon faded. It was all very well following clues around London, but the men we'd seen in the photographs on the wall of Castleton's secret flat were frightening. Whether they were criminals or foreign spies, they would surely be carrying guns. All we had were our wits, charm and, in Bella's case at least, beauty.

When we arrived in Hastings, it instantly brought back memories of the perfect summer I'd spent there with my parents when I was about ten years old. Elderly holidaymakers in prematurely short trousers peered through shop windows as their ice creams slowly melted. The funicular railway descended the hill as we drove past and, on several of the streets, gleaming new trolleybuses were picking up locals to ferry them about the town.

But as much as I would have liked to visit the pier and buy a stick or two of sugary rock – or, even better, taken off my shoes and socks to run along the pebbly beach kicking at the surf – we were not there for the tourist attractions, and so I drove east to a quieter part of the town. The tall houses and hotels that characterised the seafront soon gave way to older, less glamorous constructions. A brief glance at the huts and sheds that dotted the beach told me that the furthest point of the bay was mainly populated by fishermen and their families. There were countless coloured rowing boats left upturned where they'd been dragged from the sea that morning, and lines of men were selling their catch on the narrow promenade or loading fish onto carts to take to neighbouring towns. The smell had changed somewhat since the beginning of the journey, but I still enjoyed that distinctive aroma of sea air.

"There it is!" Bella whispered to interrupt my nostalgic musing.

I realised what she meant and slowed the car to a walking pace. She was looking at the façade of a funny little house with a front garden that was full of whimsical wooden sculptures that were waving and wiggling in the breeze. I had a quick enough mind to realise that, if we didn't want to be spotted by our adversaries, it was a good idea to keep driving. I barely glanced at the building but found a space to park a hundred yards along the road.

"That was the easy part," I said once the car had come to a stop. "Now we have to work out how we can get the men away from the house and Castleton out of it."

"Oh," was all Bella could say in reply, and we both knew that the odds were against us.

We sat there without moving for some reason. I don't know if it was a lack of energy to confront the problem before us or our trepidation coming to the fore, but this inertia gave me an idea.

"How long do you think you can make a packet of chips last?"

Five minutes later, we were sitting on a bench on the promenade, twenty yards down the road from the little white cottage. We had two piping hot parcels on our laps that were wrapped in clean newspaper. Bella had chosen plaice to go with her chips, while I'd gone for sole in crispy batter. This was another element of youthful holidays to the seaside that I still appreciated. You simply cannot go wrong with such a meal, especially if it provides the opportunity to observe a ruthless pair of kidnappers.

Despite the precarious situation in which we found ourselves, the food was delicious, and we were having a rather nice time until Bella said something that shook me to the very foundations of my being.

"I've never eaten fish and chips before."

I was speechless, truly speechless.

"Why are you looking at me like you've just swallowed a bone?" she asked, before coming to worry that she had answered her own question. "Wait, have you actually swallowed a bone?"

"No, of course I haven't. I'm trying to make sense of the person sitting before me. I thought I knew you, Bella. I mean... we grew up together. We were best friends through most of our childhood, and now this."

This was her cue to punch me. It was one of her favourite pastimes. "It's not my fault that my parents failed to expose me to a wider range of experiences."

I tried to look sad for her sake. "Yes, it must have been tough. All those trips to Italy on holiday and countless excursions to the opera, but they never once thought of the joys of greasy chips and fried fish. My poor friend. In some ways, the Duke and Duchess neglected you."

"Very funny, Marius." Though she delivered this sentence in a sarcastic tone, her subsequent laughter undermined the message. "But if you must know, I would have preferred fewer trips to Covent Garden and more to the sorts of places that children really enjoy. I'd take these salty and delicious potatoes over Wagner's *Ring* cycle."

For once, I didn't respond with a quip. Something in her words made me question what I'd really thought of the rich little girl who lived on the hill. My parents had always scrimped and saved to pay their way, and perhaps one of the reasons I'd come to love her as an adolescent was because I wanted to be just like her. I wanted the life that she had.

"What? No witty rejoinder?" she asked when I still hadn't replied.

I hated to disappoint her but, not only did nothing particularly amusing come to mind, I was distracted by the sight of a giant. He was walking along the road straight towards us, and so I leaned closer to Bella to put my arm around her shoulder and my forehead against hers.

"Don't be alarmed but..."

She spoke over me. "Marius, I..."

"...one of the men we saw in the photographs is walking on the same side of the pavement as us." I paused to glance innocently along the road, and I felt her muscles tighten. "No, don't look now. Just pretend that we're in love and you have eyes for me alone."

She followed my instructions surprisingly well, which was a novelty in our relationship. "Is he still there?"

"Yes, he's coming now."

I put my hand up against her cheek but kept my eyes on the great hulking chap in the gabardine mackintosh, which was entirely unsuited to the warmth of the day.

"He's walking up the steps into the house," I told her. "He's knocked at the door, and the other man, who looks rather like his identical twin, has opened it. They're both peering about suspiciously. They must be afraid that someone is coming for Castleton."

Bella pulled back and could finally gaze at the house without fear of discovery. "What do you think the first man was doing out here?"

"Stretching his legs, I suppose. It must get terribly boring guarding a prisoner. Perhaps thugs get mandated breaks, like men who work in factories."

She looked withdrawn but did not explain herself and nodded at what I'd thought was a perfectly silly idea.

"We'll have to wait until the other one takes his turn," she said in a whisper, as though our enemies would overhear. Perhaps *enemies* was too strong a word for them. After all, they were just earning a living like us. I did hope that we were better at our jobs than they were at theirs, though.

Bella's fear had not abated. "Isn't this the moment at which you amaze me with an incredible plan to get Castleton out of the fisherman's cottage without anyone shooting at us?"

"No," I said, before popping a chip in my mouth. "This is the moment we finish our lunch."

TEN

The downside to eating fish and chips on a bench is, of course, the fish. Chips are easy. They were surely designed to be eaten by hand, but there is no practical way to eat a whole battered fish without looking uncouth or ridiculous. Well, that was what I thought until I saw Bella attempt it. After this, I came to believe that she could make gargling the national anthem look graceful.

When not a scrap of food remained, I said, "And this is the moment we walk around the cottage to see what hope we have of actually rescuing Ernest Castleton."

She had recovered her good spirits somewhat and, with a quick dab of a paper serviette, was up on her feet to carry out the next part of the plan.

"There's a waste bin just in front of the house,' I said, apropos of nothing as we walked past.

"And whoever owns the place has dubious taste in garden decorations." Bella took in the strange collection as a weather-vane depicting two men cutting the trunk of a tree seesawed back and forth in the breeze.

"A bin plus seaside curiosities... I'm not sure that's enough for us to free him, but we'll see what else we can find."

The most important factor we had to examine on this brief reconnaissance mission was always going to be the rear of the building. There was an alley that separated the row of houses from the ones on the street behind. This was lucky as, if we'd had to scramble through other people's gardens to get to Castleton, it would have made for a slow getaway. Best of all, though, we could see into the rooms at the back of the house.

"Look up there." I pointed to a first-floor window. "The curtains are drawn, I bet that's where they're keeping him."

"Or perhaps one of them has gone for a nap," Bella unhelpfully suggested, and I chose to ignore her.

"What we have to do is really very simple." I didn't necessarily believe this, but I was trying to sound positive. "You create a diversion at the front of the house, whilst I climb over the wall here. I'll go through the garden, scramble up onto the roof of the conservatory and then in through the window to free our man."

"Simple." She clearly couldn't decide whether to laugh at my unexpected optimism or cry at the danger we faced.

I kept blathering in the hope that I could distract her. "And with that done, I will take our friend Ernest out to the road at the end of the alley where you will pick us up."

"I'm allowed to drive your car?"

"Just this once." I wasn't nearly so possessive over my Invicta – or Vickie, as I had taken to calling her – as everyone thought.

We returned to the seafront and, on the way, I noticed that the name of the street was Rock-A-Nore Road, which fitted with the "rocky road" part of the clue that Castleton had left in his flat. I still had to decide how we could tempt one of the guards outside, of course, and we didn't know for certain that the kidnapped man was in the house, but I wasn't about to tell Bella that.

As we waited for a plan to come to us, we gazed over the wide expanse of beach. There were larger fishing vessels down by the distant shoreline and, closer to the land, a group of bald but bearded fishermen – yes, each of them had a beard and each was bald – were stretching out an immense net between themselves to look for holes.

"The bin," Bella eventually muttered to break this ponderous silence.

"Fire!" I responded, as I thought that was what she wished to imply.

"I beg your pardon?"

"I said, fire. We can set a fire in the bin outside the cottage and the guard will have to come out to see what's happening."

"Oh..." She pouted disapprovingly. "I was merely going to suggest that we upturn it loudly and run off, but I suppose that a fire would be more likely to draw him out."

I was barely listening to her as the previously undetected pyromaniac inside me suddenly emerged. "Yes, that's it. I'll pour some sort of accelerant into the bin. Then you'll walk past and drop a cigarette which will ignite whatever's in there and create a real spectacle. If that doesn't get the swine out of the house, then nothing will."

"Or you could simply set fire to the cottage itself." Bella maintained her serious expression. "That way, the thug will have to bring Ernest out with him."

I rubbed the side of my cheek with my thumb as I considered the possibility. "Well, it might work."

"Yes, and it couldn't possibly have any negative side effects."

I did realise that she was being sarcastic. "Or perhaps my first plan was the better option."

"I think it might be." She finally allowed herself a smile. "Now, do you have a cigarette for me?"

"No, I don't smoke. It's a filthy habit, no matter what health benefits the doctors claim it possesses." It suddenly occurred to me that I might have offended her. "Sorry, do you?"

"No, no. I'd rather stick my head in a fireplace. Gilbert takes a pipe from time to time but—"

I wasn't particularly interested in her boyfriend's habits, or her boyfriend for that matter. In fact, I had turned to walk along the beach to a small news kiosk next to the spot where we'd parked Vickie.

"Afternoon folks, lovely day." The newsagent was a short man in a flat cap that was pulled down so tightly on his head it must have been difficult to see us.

"Good afternoon," Bella replied in her poshest voice. I was surprised she didn't call him "my good man".

"What can I get for you this fine day?" he continued. "Bucket and spade? Bathing cap? Shelter from the wind?" He pointed at the various items that were strung up around the kiosk.

Bella looked bemused by the selection and so I answered on her behalf. "Thank you, but all we need is a packet of Senior Service, and a copy of the *Daily Mail*."

"Very good, sir."

"And I don't suppose you happen to sell any kind of fuel?"

"Fuel, sir?"

"Yes, you know the sort of thing. Petrol, naphtha, or kerosene should do it."

"Ah-ha." He wagged his finger knowingly and ducked to open a box at his feet. "I normally sell gas for lighting lamps, but it appears that I've sold out." He looked us up and down for a moment, as though deciding whether he could trust us. "Course, if you don't tell no one, I don't mind selling you a bottle of home-made grog."

I stared at the tin container he had produced. "Grog?"

"It's good stuff. Don't worry on that score. It should certainly do the trick if you're looking to light a campfire."

"Yes, of course... a campfire," Bella murmured unconvincingly, and so I took charge once more.

"We'll take it. How much do we owe you?"

He placed my items on top of a stack of newspapers and totted them up in his head. "That'll be two and thruppence, and I'll throw in a packet of matches for free." He tipped his head back to wink at me and I realised that he was far younger than I had imagined. I suppose that's what a tweed flat cap can do to a fellow.

"How incredibly generous of you," Bella replied quite sincerely. I often forgot what a sheltered existence she'd led. Not only had she been born into near-royalty, we came from a village that was hidden away within a dense forest. It was quite possible that, having enjoyed our exotic lunch, buying something from a newsagent was another first for her.

With our purchases wrapped in paper, we said goodbye to the shopkeeper and returned to our bench.

"You know, if the police decide to investigate the case of the burning bin, that nice gentleman who just sold us 'any kind of fuel' will instantly be able to identify the culprit."

"Don't worry about that. The police will think it's an accident caused by your cigarette, and besides—" Before I could say any more, the second guard left the house to go for a walk... or pop along to the pub... or whatever it was he had to do.

This time, it was Bella who grabbed me. She pulled me into her and squeezed incredibly hard so that I had to wheeze a little as the man walked past. I believe that he had a brief chuckle at the sight of us cuddling beside a closed whelk stall and a rotten old boat with a hole in the hull. I crossed my fingers that the last laugh would be on him.

"We must move quickly," I said when he'd gone. "I'll go

first, then you follow along a minute later, drop the lit cigarette, and go to the car. The remaining guard should run outside when he smells smoke, and you can collect Castleton and me from the end of the rear alley. Is that clear?"

She nodded but looked nervous, nonetheless. I'm sure that if we'd stopped to think more carefully, we would both have realised what fools we were being, but there was no time for that.

"What if he doesn't come out?" she called across the road to me as I sped off.

"Then we wasted two and thruppence and scorched His Majesty's bin for no reason." I tried to reassure her with a smile and then nipped across the road.

I kept my eyes on the house as I ran along the pavement. I didn't want the remaining kidnapper to come out and spot me, especially at the moment I was dumping the strong-smelling alcohol into the bin in front of the property. I've never liked the *Daily Mail*. As far as I'm concerned, it's a rag and, sure enough, it soaked up the fluid just perfectly. I gave the tin a good squeeze and considered throwing it into the bin along with the newspaper, but I didn't want it exploding in anyone's face.

I looked back across the road to make sure that Bella was ready for the next step of the plan, then ran around the block to take up my place in the back alley. A tense minute or two later, I heard the first shouts from the road beyond the cottage. I don't know who was out there, but they kicked up just the right amount of fuss to alert the inhabitants of number fifteen. The lower rear windows were open, and I could hear the sound of someone thundering down the stairs.

I strained to listen for the front door opening and then propelled myself at the garden wall to gain access to the house. It was higher than it looked, and I only just managed to clamber over the edge. I hadn't given a thought to what I would find there, but I could never have predicted the army of gnomes that stood in lines on either side of me. The lawn and flowerbeds were covered with them. Their beady eyes locked onto mine, but they were only made of plaster of Paris and would not tell anyone of my intrusion, so I navigated the path up to the house.

Perhaps the first climb had readied me for the second, as I mounted the flat roof of the sun lounge in seconds. From there, it couldn't have been easier. All I had to do was slide open the sash window and— Well, the window was locked, but I wasn't to know that. I tapped on it in the hope I could catch Castleton's attention, before cupping my hands against the glass to look inside.

It was empty.

My heart was beating faster now. My nerves were taut. The shouts and yells that came from the front of the house had grown louder, but I was too busy wondering how to get inside to worry about that. I tried to reach across to the next window, but it was too far, and I almost lost my footing and fell to the ground below.

Although there was only one solution, my body was being obstinate and refused to do what I required. I urged myself onwards, but caution had gripped hold of me, and I couldn't move. I whispered half-formed words to get me going again, and still I just stood there on the roof. It was at this point that I spotted an old lady in the garden next door. She was watching my every move – or lack thereof.

I looked at her. She looked disapprovingly back, and I tried to think of a reason for why I might be up there. "They called me about the guttering, but it seems fine to me." I tapped on the nearest pipe and shook my head. "People these days do nothing but complain."

I jumped back down into the garden before she could question how likely it was for a comparatively well-spoken man in a neat white outfit to know anything about home repairs. This embarrassment turned out to be just what I needed to snap me out of my daze, and I formed a new plan.

Taking a deep breath to steady myself, I pushed the down-stairs window a little wider and climbed into a small lounge. It suddenly occurred to me that there could be a third guard in there somewhere that we hadn't spied before, but I rushed on all the same and had made it halfway up the stairs when the front door banged open and the thug who had gone to attend to the fire rushed back inside. There was nothing I could do. I was certain that he would see me and draw his gun. I froze where I stood and, to my amazement, he didn't look up but carried on towards the back of the house.

My fear was forgotten, and a shock of energy coursed through me. I ran to the landing and was relieved to hear the guard leave again as I began to look in the bedrooms. The first was too small, the second was too big, and the third had a kidnapped civil servant inside it. I can't describe the feeling of relief that ran through me as I saw him, and I must admit it made my manner rather brusque.

"Move it, Castleton. We must leave immediately or there'll be trouble."

Lying atop the paisley sheets on the narrow bed, he had a copy of *The Man in the Brown Suit* on his chest and appeared torn between opening it and going back to sleep. My brusque instructions had apparently stunned him, and when he didn't react, I took him by the arm to pull him from the room.

As we reached the landing, I heard the roughneck walking into the house again. From the sound of things, he was fetching buckets of water to put out the blaze. It was too much of a risk to go back the way I'd come, and so I pushed Castleton to the locked window and swiftly unfastened it before steering him out onto the flat roof. At least I didn't have to push him off to get him into the garden. He jumped of his own accord, but there was still something dazed or dozy about his movement. I had to wonder whether he'd been kept drugged by his captors, so I put my hand on him again as we rushed to the back wall. There was a heap of soil and a water butt on that side, which made scaling it a great deal easier.

"This way," I bellowed when he turned in the wrong direction on the other side. The least I could say for him was that he followed my instructions. He spun on his heel just as Bella pulled to a stop at the end of the alley.

"Hurry! I didn't exactly make a clean getaway," she yelled from the driver's seat, and I helped Castleton towards her.

As we'd realised on a previous case, my fast, fun and ever so attractive vehicle was not built for three people. Castleton looked at the Invicta as if he didn't quite know how to climb aboard. To keep things simple, I pushed him into the passenger seat and flipped up the makeshift dickey for me.

"Hey, what are you...?" a voice began, and I realised that the second guard had spotted us on his walk home. "You sneaky little..."

Bella stepped on the accelerator and sent the car screaming past him just as he pulled his gun from its holster. Unluckily for me, I was the closest to him when he pulled the trigger. Luckily for me, we were already twenty yards away and he missed. He did, however, startle a large seagull who was standing on the pavement, eating what looked like a saveloy sausage.

As the bird took to the air, the ruffian with the pistol realised that he was defeated and put his hands to his head. I believe he would have thrown the gun to the ground had it not been liable to let off another round in his direction. The last thing I saw as we turned off the road was him shouting what I could only imagine was an obscenity.

Evildoers had been vanquished, the goodies had won, and our adventure was at an end, I incorrectly assumed.

ELEVEN

"That was incredible!" I said, leaning over the rear seat as Bella piloted the car ever so carefully out of town. "It's like you said. This is why we got into the detective game in the first place."

"Well, I'm glad you're enjoying yourself," she replied. "I almost burnt my hand off, but as long as you've had a thrilling time, nothing else matters."

"What do you mean? What happened?"

"The alcohol, Marius." She kept her eyes dead ahead, much like Castleton. "You put in far too much and there was a great intense burst of flames. A woman who was walking her dog came running over to blame me. I told her I only dropped my cigarette, but she wasn't having it. Thankfully, the fire caught one of the garden ornaments that was just above the bin. The poor wooden men were incinerated, and then the spinning cockerel next to them caught too and, before I knew it, half the garden was aflame. The people who came to watch didn't know whether to shout at me or do something about the fire. When the big chap from inside came out, I shot off to the car."

"Then we both played our part to a nicety," I perhaps generously surmised before punching Castleton on the shoulder to check that he was still with us. "Eh, fellow! What did you think of that?"

I know that I should have been more sensitive, but I was all nerves and emotion after the rescue. He made a nervous sort of groan in reply, and I wondered once again what had got into him.

Bella still wasn't happy. "They saw us, Marius."

"And we're almost out of Hastings and on our way back to London. They haven't a chance of catching us." Even as I said this, I spotted the flaw in my argument.

"They saw your car."

"Yes, but one bright red car is much the same as any other."

I looked at the vehicles parked along the side of the road and realised that almost every last one of them was black or dark blue. I decided it would be wise not to tell Bella that only a few hundred examples of my car had been produced in any colour since the company was founded. I just had to hope that the quick-trigger minion back in Hastings hadn't noticed the marque.

Now that I had the chance to study him, Ernest Castleton looked quite different from his photo. For one thing, he was no longer cleanly shaven and had thick stubble on his chin and cheeks. His eyes were dark, as if he hadn't slept for days, and there was a sallowness to his skin that made him look a touch ill. I didn't blame him for not speaking after what he'd been through.

"You don't need to worry about anything anymore," I tried to reassure him. "You're in capable hands now."

This did nothing to cheer him up, and so I sat back in my cramped compartment that was originally designed for luggage rather than a grown man. Bella eyed me in the mirror, and while I was fairly certain she was still annoyed at me for nearly setting the cottage alight as we'd planned not to, she looked a little relieved.

And that was how we spent the journey back to the city: in a gloomy hush. The wind over the front windscreen was too noisy to allow for conversation, which gave me time to consider the events of the last thirty-six hours. They seemed miraculous and brilliant, but something didn't sit quite right. We were driving past Sevenoaks by the time I knew what it was, and I still struggled to put it into words. You see, there was something unusual about the way the thug on the pavement had watched us as we'd driven away.

He looked... well, he looked miffed. Yes, that's just the word for it. He carefully shot at the car, with one hand beneath the other to steady his aim, and then when he fired and saw that he'd missed, he didn't appear worried about what would happen to him for letting his prisoner escape. He didn't scream to the heavens in fury. No, he just looked a mite bothered. Not irate or furious, just miffed.

I wanted to ask our new friend about it, but he had closed his eyes and wrapped his arms around himself as though in shock. I had to wonder what had happened to him up in that house and what his kidnappers had planned to do to him. It's the kind of thing that makes men lose their sense of themselves. I'd seen it often enough in the war. I'd spent time with soldiers who'd been taken by the Germans and, for some of them, it was as if they'd had their brains removed and put back in upside down. There was something not quite present about them – not quite able to view the world as everyone else does – and I saw it again in that car.

My initial good cheer swiftly returned when we reached St James's and I got to see Percy again. That might sound senti-mental, but the contrast between the drama in Hastings and the normality of my red-tempered dog pretending he was indifferent to my return was just wonderful. My mother went out to see friends on Fridays, so there was no one else there, but he immediately walked off to the lounge when I came through the door, as if he was in the middle of an important task.

I couldn't help but laugh at the silly creature, whereas Castleton remained just as distant. I took him to my spare bedroom to rest, then went to discuss the situation with Bella.

"How do you feel?" she said out of the blue, although I should probably have been the one to ask this.

"I feel very pleased with myself. Or rather, with ourselves, if that makes sense."

"It makes sense to me." She smiled and everything felt as it should.

All the worries I had accumulated in the forced silence of the car slid away, and I couldn't help grinning along with her. "You were wonderful, my dear."

"We didn't do too badly, did we?" Her shoulders shrugged a little as she laughed. "Who'd have thought? Lady Isabella Montague: the brave adventurer."

"Setter of fires," I teased. "Rescuer of men!"

She stood beaming before the window in my writing room, just as lovely as when she was seventeen. It made me content to see her so happy, and I could have watched her for hours if someone hadn't knocked at the door to interrupt.

"Good afternoon, Mr Quin." Our mystery man was just as stern as he'd looked the previous day, but then he pulled his hand from behind his back and handed me a bottle of Dom Perignon champagne. "I believe that congratulations are in order."

"Yes! Yes, they certainly are. Please come inside." I waved him in but had a quick look at the square beyond. I could only imagine that he'd paid someone to keep an eye out for our return. A group of messenger boys was sitting in front of the East India Club, and their young companion, Jamie, was over in the park. She was the smartest of the lot, and I wondered whether she'd been put in charge of our surveillance.

"Ah, Lady Isabella," Inspector Ordinary said and offered a brief bow. "I don't know how you did it. I don't honestly care how you did it, but if you can confirm that Ernest Castleton is here, I will put you both forward for a knighthood."

Bella came over to welcome him. "I think I have enough titles as it is, but I'm sure that Sir Marius Quin would sell more books than plain old Mr Quin here."

"Come through to the lounge," I told them, and I was already peeling the foil off the top of the bottle. There were glasses beside the drinks cabinet, just waiting to be filled. I really should come up with some hobbies that don't involve drinking, but there was no turning down victory champagne.

"Not for me, thank you!" The spy, or whatever he was, held up both hands as if trying to shoo away a goat. "I never drink on the job. More's the pity." He had a brief titter at the idea.

"I'll get you some water then," Bella told him. "It would be a shame not to join us in a toast."

"Or some kind of cordial, if you have it," he said rather hopefully. "I admit that I do have something of a sweet tooth."

"It's in the cupboard next to the sink," I called after her, as I continued with my task.

"You must tell me everything," he murmured in that oddly confidential way of his. To give him his due, he was more relaxed than the day before. He was clearly just as relieved as we were that the mission had gone to plan.

Bella was quick to rejoin us and, before I answered his question, she handed him a tumbler of lemon squash. "To our success!"

"To your much-deserved success!" he corrected her and tipped the drink down his throat.

We took an armchair each in front of the unlit fire. Percy went to sit on Bella's feet, and I began our extremely unusual story. "It was rather like a treasure trail, really, but we were only able to complete it thanks to Castleton's fiancée, Miss

Ravenscroft. Without her, we wouldn't have known where to start."

He gave a brief nod. "Yes, I did wonder whether she knew something. I talked to her at the beginning of the week, of course, but for whatever reason, she wouldn't reveal anything significant." He cleared his throat then and apologised for interrupting. "Please, do go on."

I looked at Bella as I sipped my champagne, and she was only too happy to reveal the next part of the story. "It's hard to understand why Hermione didn't think of it earlier, but there was a note that Ernest had... Well, there was a note that her fiancé..."

I thought it was rather amusing that Miss Elocution herself was having trouble getting her words out. "Bella, dear. Has the frog got your throat?"

"Frog?" She grinned, but something wasn't quite right. "Cat, you mean, Marius. Cat and tongue, you..."

"Oh, how silly. I..." I tried to speak again, but the words refused to come. "I don't know... I..."

Our guest got up from his chair to walk to the middle of the room. I thought he was coming to see what was wrong, but he just stood there, watching us. I couldn't speak or even think, and the last thing I saw, as my head became indescribably heavy, was Bella lying slumped in her seat.

TWELVE

Even before I opened my eyes again, I knew that I was in a hospital bed. I'd spent a good week in one after a bomb nearly took my legs off in Amiens, and I knew just how they felt. It's not merely the crispness of the sheets; it's the sound of their rustling. I found it familiar and yet far from reassuring.

A list of questions had imprinted itself in the darkness behind my eyelids. My brain had been hard at work as I slept, trying to figure out exactly what I needed to know. Of utmost importance was, *Is Bella all right?* Though I should probably have started with *Where am I?* Thoughts of Castleton and Inspector Ordinary danced in and out of my consciousness, but it was mainly Bella, my mother and even Percy who most concerned me. *Did Mother find us passed out in the lounge? Did that man hurt my dog? Were we supposed to die?*

"He's awake," I heard a voice declare as someone rushed across the room.

I cracked my eyes open to see that, although the bed belonged in a hospital and there was a nurse standing at the door, the room looked more like a salon in a well-appointed flat.

What I could see of the view through the window told me I was on one of the upper floors of a tall building and it was already night-time.

"Marius Quin," a man pronounced as he walked through the door, and I pushed myself up to receive some sympathy for my predicament. "You're a blasted fool, and you've made everything ten times worse."

He came to a stop at the end of the bed and, in my hazy state, I thought he was the same man who had given me the champagne back at my flat. They couldn't have looked more similar. They had the same nondescript clothes and unremarkable features – the same conceited look on their faces. It was really only their voices that struck me as different.

"Did you hear what I said?" this new fellow demanded.

Rather than give in to the pressure and answer, I glanced at the two men who had followed him into the room and was surprised to discover that I recognised them. It was the thugs from the cottage in Hastings and, up close, they were even more intimidating than they'd looked in the photos. I promise I'm not exaggerating when I say that their necks were thicker than my legs.

"He's entirely witless." The featureless character in the beige overcoat looked at his brawny companions, and I got the definite impression that wherever we were and whoever they were, he was the one who called the tune. "And yet he still got past the pair of you."

Rather than admit their error, the twin lumps looked away. I was beginning to wonder whether I'd been taken to a secret facility responsible for producing very bland-looking men.

"Bella..." I managed to murmur. "What have you people done to her?"

The manager-type sneered at me then. "The young lady is fine. No thanks to you." He shook his head and looked as though he was struggling to control his emotions.

"That's not good enough." I tried my best to direct my voice at him, but I didn't have the energy. "Tell me where she is this moment, or you'll get nothing more from me."

"Lady Isabella is in the room beside this one." He made his contempt for me perfectly clear. "My people have looked after her just as they looked after you." Inspector Ordinary's double was not a big man, but he spoke with the confidence of one. "What were you thinking? How could anyone have been so entirely stupid?" He cast his gaze to the floor almost mournfully. "I assume it was stupidity rather than malice that led you to kidnap the Foreign Secretary's chief aide. You certainly didn't do a very good job of it."

"We didn't kidnap—" I began, but my head was still woozy, and I had to blink a few times to know what I wanted to say. "Your bullies there took Castleton. We did what was necessary to get him back."

He had to walk away then. I could tell that he wanted to strangle me. He wasn't the first person to feel such an instinct, and I knew the signs. When he came back, his fingers were squashed together in compact balls, but he managed to control his voice. "So that's what they told you, was it? That we'd kidnapped Ernest, and you had to save him? You fool, they were appealing to your ridiculous sense of adventure. You've been duped, sonny. Duped!"

I was still reeling from whatever had been in the champagne. Accepting this version of events was just too much for me, so I attempted to deny it. "If that's true, why were your attack dogs keeping Castleton prisoner?"

He rolled his eyes, as if I needed any more proof that he disagreed with everything I said. "We were protecting him, you mug." Though he spoke at a moderate volume, every word he said rang in my ear. "He walked out of his office on Monday night and a member of the gang you've been working for almost killed him. It was only because Lieutenant Snipe here happened to be passing that he escaped with his life."

"No. That can't be..." I looked from one to the next of them and wished that the nurse had stayed. I would much rather such news had come from her than this ugly bunch. "Why should I believe you any more than the man who came to my flat and poisoned us?"

"Because we saved you. We brought you here."

"You could be lying."

He ran his hand over his thin, black hair that was parted to one side. "I could be, and I don't blame you for being suspicious, but perhaps you should have exercised such caution when you were sent off to kidnap someone in the first place."

"I told you. We didn't kidnap anyone. We thought—"

"Just forget it." He was a nervous character and, with one finger outstretched, rushed up to the bed to jab at the sheets. "You don't have to trust me. I've called someone here who you're more likely to believe."

He tipped his head back and stood there looking triumphant. After a few moments of silence, I wondered what was supposed to happen next. No one moved. The three of them stood in their triangle formation looking both bored and intimidating and, in time, I caught the soft ding of a lift out in the corridor, and then the fast march of whoever had just arrived.

"Quin." A man of around sixty with a neat white moustache and an upright manner appeared in the room, and the two lackeys parted to let him through. "Do you remember me from the investigation into the murders in Daly's Theatre last year?"

"Chief Inspector Darrington," I replied a little hoarsely. "You're involved in all of this?"

Darrington was an officer of the Metropolitan Police Service and a friend of the great Lord Edgington. I'd only met him briefly when the production of a play I'd written turned into a murder investigation, but he'd struck me as a terribly honest sort of person.

"Not at all. My work for the police does not extend to espionage. However, I knew Mr Rider here long before he became head of the Government Code and Cypher School, and he has told me of his predicament."

With these few sentences, he'd confirmed my worst fears. We'd been working for the wrong side. We hadn't saved the man we'd been hired to help; we'd handed him over to our enemies. On the bright side though, at least I finally knew what GC&CS stood for.

"What happened to Castleton?" I asked, as no one had mentioned him yet.

The chief inspector turned to his acquaintance, who signalled for him to continue. "The staff here were hoping you knew. By the time they located your car, and found you and Lady Isabella unconscious, there was no sign of him."

I almost considered asking whether they'd checked in the spare bedroom, but I had to hope that Rider's men were thorough enough to think of such things.

"He was there when the phoney spy came to congratulate us. We'd just arrived back from Hastings, and he must have had someone watching the flat as he was there within minutes. He brought champagne but didn't have any himself. Almost as soon as Bella and I started drinking, our thoughts became confused, and we passed out. Do you think he intended to kill us?"

Darrington looked at Rider, who answered for him. "We don't know. The doctors have given you medicine to counteract your symptoms, and they've taken blood samples, but until we get the results, we won't know what he put in the champagne or the quantity he used."

I had to wonder how the nasty character had managed to get this dubious chemical into a sealed bottle. In the spy novels

I'd read, such things were achieved with a syringe and a long needle, but I couldn't say whether that would work in real life.

Darrington pulled his shoulders back as if to say, *We must get down to brass tacks.* "Is there anything you can reveal that might help us locate Mr Castleton? I can't tell you how important it is that we find him."

For someone who denied having a part to play in a clandestine organisation, he certainly seemed to know a lot about their activities. I had to think he was at least a liaison between the GC&CS and the wider police force.

"I wish I could help," I replied, rubbing my head in the hope I could soothe the pain. "I didn't notice any unusual cars in front of my house. Your best bet is to talk to the messenger children who hang about in the square. If Castleton was bundled out of there, they'll have seen it."

"Boyle, step to it," Rider said to one of the men we'd crossed in Hastings and the underling immediately hurried away. "Now, what did this fellow who came to your house look like? Can you describe him to me?"

"No, I really can't."

He let out a weary breath. "Come along, Mr Quin. There's no time for games. A man's life is in danger, and it's your fault for meddling in our business."

"I don't mean that I won't. I mean there was nothing distinctive about him. He was as bland and beige as your trench coat." I decided it wasn't a good idea to draw any closer comparison, but Rider clearly understood.

"I wonder where they got the idea to have a perfectly nondescript agent." He wrapped his fist in his other hand, and Darrington took over again.

"There must have been something that made him stand out. He may have been of average height and weight with brown hair and brown eyes—"

"Oh, so you've met him, have you?"

"I know the type. But however normal a man may look, there are no two the same. I'm certain that, if you think carefully, you'll remember something that marks him as different." As the chief inspector spoke, I caught the sound of a door opening and heard footsteps approaching.

"He had an incredibly gaunt, skinny face and a muscle in his neck that was constantly tense," a voice from the doorway revealed, and there was my wonderful Bella with her arm around the nurse for support.

It was almost worth being poisoned and smuggled away to a secret location just for the relief of knowing that she was all right.

"Yes, that's true," I replied as she took a seat in a comfortable chair beside my bed. "But I doubt that will help the police find him. There are millions of people in London. A twitching neck muscle isn't going to stand out if he gets on a train at Victoria Station or boards a plane in Croydon."

It was hard to say whether Mr Rider lived his life in a state of nervous tension, or I brought such feelings out in him, but he had to pace across the room again to avoid exploding. "So we've lost them both – Castleton and his captor."

"Come along now, Rider," Darrington said to calm him down. "It's not over yet, not by a long way."

The little man turned his wrath on his friend. "You don't know the whole story, James. You don't know what's at stake. You can't begin to imagine what will happen if Ernest Castleton doesn't—"

"Boss!" The lackey returned to shout through the door. "He's turned up not far from here. Sounds like he jumped out of a car that was speeding along the Mall."

I can't say that Rider smiled at the news so much as stopped being quite so incensed.

"Well, that's something." He also stopped pacing and

allowed himself a deep breath. "I might not have to throw you in a dark cell after all, Mr Quin."

He stormed from the room with his hounds at his side, and only the chief inspector stayed a few moments longer. "From what I hear, you thought you were helping when you took Castleton from that house. It's unfortunate that your heroics were in vain." He nodded to the pair of us and then followed the others out to the corridor.

Bella put her head back against the chair and laughed in apparent disbelief. "How are you feeling, Marius?"

"I'm feeling annoyed, and a little bit stupid. We were duped, Bella. Tricked from the very word go."

"That's true, of course." She did not look surprised, and it was clear that she'd already sat through the conversation I'd just endured. "But we truly believed that we were helping poor Ernest. We wouldn't have done it otherwise."

"Perhaps, but Rider just told me that I went along with Ordinary's plan because it appealed to my sense of adventure, and he was right. I asked to see our fake spy's identification, of course, but he did such a convincing impression of one that I ignored my every instinct."

"Don't be so hard on yourself. I was there too, and I thought he was genuine. It's not as if he asked us to murder someone. We believed we were doing good and had no reason to doubt him."

It was hard to extract much positivity from any of this. "He played us for fools, Bella."

"Very well. We were naïve." She wouldn't let my negativity dishearten her. "But it sounds as though everything has worked out well in the end. If Castleton is safe, that's all that matters."

"You're right. Except for the fact we're in a secret hospital ward under the watchful eye of a secretive branch of the security services – and the man in charge just threatened to throw me somewhere dark – everything is wonderful."

She really laughed at me now. Perhaps it was the poise that comes with never having to worry about money or where you will live, but Bella had the capacity to exude confidence even at the bleakest times. "You should get some more sleep."

"What a good idea." My head was still foggy, and I couldn't understand how hers wasn't, so I turned on my side and, in no time at all, I was dead to the world once more.

THIRTEEN

I woke up in darkness without any sense of the time or exactly where I was. The windows in my blank-walled room were covered, and the only light came from a lamp in the hallway. Yet I had the feeling that it was morning and, sure enough, when I pushed aside the heavy curtains and peeped through the blinds, the sun came slicing into the room.

Although I could feel the after-effects of the poison in my system, it was more like the impact of a fifth glass of red wine now, rather than the prelude to my head exploding.

I got out of bed to listen to the sound of the building waking up. I was wearing checked blue pyjamas, but my white clothes from the day before were laid out on a chair. I thought it a good idea to change in case I needed to leave in a hurry.

A nurse walked past without looking into my room, and I had to wonder again what sort of place it was. I could tell from the view that I was in central London. I was really not so very far from my own house, in fact. But this didn't explain why the government's code-breaking school had a hospital ward attached to it. It was even harder to comprehend than the story that had sent us to Hastings.

Every time I remembered that we'd fallen for a ruse, the questions piled up higher. Were the clues we'd followed that led us to Castleton real? Or had the criminals led us on that merry dance in order to make us believe their story? Hermione and the British Museum, the letter and the jewellery shop: was any of it genuine?

I had been turning these thoughts over in my head for some time when Rider appeared. With a smile on his face, it was hard to believe he was the same man who had left in a foul mood the night before.

"Good morning, Marius, you gallant knight. Did you sleep well?"

"Quite well, thank you. Can I go home now?"

To my surprise, he'd brought me a cup of tea, which he set down on my bedside table with something of a flourish.

"You can leave whenever you like." The rictus smile on his face was actually more intimidating than the fangs he'd previously bared. "You're not a prisoner here. Although I was wondering whether you'd like to see a little of our operation."

"You're inviting me to poke around in your clandestine organisation before you see me to the door?"

"Something like that, yes. But first the nurses will bring you breakfast, while we allow your sleepyhead friend next door some time to wake up."

He retreated from the room with that same awkward grimace on his face. He had the air of a clown who couldn't abide the little brats he was paid to entertain. He kept his word, though, and the young nurse from the night before soon brought me the most wonderful fried breakfast. I couldn't have asked for better, and I was just finishing it when Bella came to look disapprovingly at me.

"You really should follow a healthier diet, Marius. My father had a cousin who was skinny like you at thirty, enormous by forty, and dead at fifty."

"I'll have you know that my breakfast was prescribed to me by a medical professional. I'm only following nurse's orders."

She shook her head and tried not to smile. I could only imagine that my dainty friend had consumed nothing but a glass of lemon water, a leaf of lettuce and a small box of oxygen for her breakfast. She was dressed in the same black blouse and skirt that she'd had on the day before. I believe she'd chosen such inconspicuous attire for our secret mission, though the fire she'd ignited in that bin had drawn attention to her, nonetheless.

"It's all rather strange, don't you think?" she asked when I'd finished my plate and wiped my face clean.

"Oh, undoubtedly. But what, in particular, did you have in mind?"

She looked for her words. "All this. One minute we were in your flat with that horrible man, and the next – or so it seemed – we'd been smuggled into this nest of spies. I've no idea how we got here or where exactly we are."

"Yes, you have. We're in the building on Broadway where Hermione and Ernest work. I figured it out from the view over the park." I pointed to the window, and she went to see.

"Well, that's one mystery solved. But how did they find us so quickly? Do you think they knew about our previous cases?"

"So many questions, Lady Isabella," Rider said from the doorway. He was apparently rather good at sneaking up on people. "We knew about the cases you'd solved. Such things are soon discussed in the circles in which I move." There was something he wasn't telling us, though I couldn't imagine what it was. "Now, if you'd like to join me, I'll take you for a tour of our facilities."

With that, he sallied off down the corridor, leaving us to scamper after him. A few moments later, he stopped in front of a heavy door that gave onto a set of terrazzo stone stairs, then ushered us through ahead of him. I had a brief panic at the thought that he planned to push us to our deaths (or a short painful fall, at least). Happily, that would not be our fate, and we walked down one floor together before coming out in an equally plain corridor to the one we'd just left.

"This way," Rider told us, tapping a metal plaque on the wall which read "Sinclair Mowers". He approached a double door and held onto them for a moment as he looked back at us. I could only wonder what would be inside. I pictured immense machines, with numerous cogs and levers all over them, recording developments in cities all over the world. I saw sharply dressed gentlemen practising hand-to-hand engagements on one side, and scientists testing brightly coloured solutions on the other. Of course, the reality of what we were about to see was beyond my imagination.

Beyond those dark wooden doors was a very normal-looking office.

There were perhaps fifteen desks inside, separated by low partitions. They were staffed by ten or so listless men in suits who, to a man, all wore glasses. A tea lady was lethargically pushing a trolley around and the only decoration in the whole place was a painting of the King beside a loudly ticking clock on the wall opposite the entrance. All my juvenile dreams of what it must be like to spy for one's country had been destroyed with the opening of a door.

"This is the brain centre of the Government Code and Cypher School. Other floors in the building have other responsibilities, but right here we focus on intercepting and decoding messages from criminals and foreign adversaries who could endanger our way of life here in Britain."

"It doesn't look much like a school," I told him.

"It isn't." Rider spoke in his usual curt manner. "Even that name is a cover. The men before you are some of the smartest, most capable code-breakers in the country. Isn't that right, Adam?" he called to the man at the nearest desk, who was smoking a skinny cigarette that was in desperate need of a good flick.

Adam raised the blue paper file that was in front of him in vague acknowledgement of whatever his boss had just said.

"Make no mistake about it," Rider continued, "these gents are the first line of defence between this nation and the rest of the world."

He was evidently proud of his work, and I didn't blame him. What I couldn't understand was what any of this had to do with us. I believe that Bella was about to ask him this very thing when Rider led us on through a corridor of desks towards a door in the far corner of the office.

The writing upon the glass said, "H. Rider – Head of Sales", and I had to wonder whether he was a Henry or a Harry... or perhaps a Herbert. He let Bella and me go first, and it turned out that the room beyond was already occupied.

An incredibly tall man with a bald head and a tiny moustache was standing between two great windows that looked over the city towards Battersea. On either side of him were the burly agents, Snipe and Boyle, who looked just as unhappy to see us as they had the night before. But the biggest surprise came when I realised who was lounging in a low armchair not far from Rider's desk. Ernest Castleton looked even paler than when we'd last seen him, but he rose unsteadily to shake our hands.

"Thank you for trying to save me, even if..." he said before his words faded.

"We're so sorry for what happened." Bella spoke quite sincerely. "We never imagined that—"

"Madam, you need say no more on the matter." He had a rather pleasant face when he smiled and seemed amused by her apology. "Although I must tell you, Marius, I was terrified when you popped up in my bedroom like that. I felt sure you had a gun in your pocket and had come there to kill me."

"You poor chap." I had to curse our bumbling once again. "I can't imagine how frightening that must have been. It's no wonder you sat in silence the whole way back to London."

"I'll admit I was a little shaken, but it all worked out in the end."

"How did you get away from Inspector Ordinary?"

"Inspector Ordinary?" he asked, looking at his colleagues for clarification before I explained.

"Sorry, that's the name I've been using to describe the man who hired us." I realised at this point that I hadn't said it out loud to any of them before and added a brief caveat. "In my head, at least."

"I see." He smiled a little wider. "Well, I tricked him. I had a brief nap in your flat and, when I woke up, he gave me a glass of something fizzy. I guessed his game and only pretended to drink it. I soon understood that he expected me to pass out, and so I made it look as though I had. He half carried me to his car and, when we were going at a fast enough clip that it would be difficult for him to come back for me, I jumped from the back seat. I probably fractured my shoulder, but I ran like the blazes to get away from him."

The more I heard of this young man, the more I liked him. He was evidently the heroic type that I'd been emulating – though I'm glad I didn't have to jump from a car at any point. Judging by his stiff right arm, he'd done himself a serious injury, but he didn't make a fuss about it.

"If I may ask a question," Bella said, as we settled down in chairs around a coffee table in the middle of the room. "How did Ordinary achieve his goal? We followed a trail of clues that seemed to come from you, Ernest. And yet I can only assume that he wrote the letter we found in the British Museum and sent us on the path around London."

Every time Castleton wished to reveal something, he first looked at Rider, who gave him permission with a silent nod.

"You're quite right, and he must have worked incredibly quickly. From what I understand, he went to see Hermione the day before you did. He told her that my life was in danger and that it was of the utmost importance that she should steer anyone who came looking for me to some obscure volume on mould in the library there. He told her that my life would be in danger if she gave the game away, and the blighter must have spun a different story altogether to the jeweller in the Piccadilly Arcade."

"And the flat we went to in Fitzrovia?" I directed my question to Rider, as I could only assume that he had investigated all this while Castleton recovered from his ordeal.

"It has nothing to do with any of us. The person renting it paid the landlord in cash on Tuesday this week. The photographs on the walls must have been taken in the last few days. Whereas, as far as my team here in the office can tell, the long lines of symbols we found there were Jabberwock."

"Inspector Ordinary may be a criminal," I remarked. "But he's certainly an industrious one. Do you have any idea what he hoped to gain from all this?"

"That's what I've called everyone here to discuss." Rider had a less polished tone of voice than the obviously well-educated Castleton, who was an Oakton boy if ever I'd met one. "We're dealing with a dangerous organisation who we must assume is working for a foreign government. They targeted Castleton and wished to kidnap or kill him. What we can't say exactly is why. Though I hope that Don Carlos here can explain."

All eyes turned to the giant in the corner, who made Snipe and Boyle look like little children.

"Don Carlos is not my actual name, of course." His voice was suitably deep for such an immense creature. "I prefer not to reveal my identity, but I do have permission to tell you all you need to know about Mentmore Towers."

I now wonder whether anyone in that room was using a real name except for Bella and me. H. Rider seemed like it must be a pseudonym. H. Rider Haggard had been one of my favourite writers when I was a child, and I suppose it could have been a coincidence, but I very much doubt it.

It came as no great surprise that Bella had understood more of what the man said than I did.

"Mentmore Towers is Lord Darnley's home," she said in a tentative voice. "He's my godfather. I've been there many times."

The men seemed less sure of themselves all of a sudden, but rather than address her comment, Don Carlos – which, by the way, is a ridiculous alias for a rather pasty Brit– continued with what he was saying.

"The French Foreign Minister is meeting the Foreign Secretary at Mentmore Towers today. We believe there may be an unidentified threat to the proceedings." He stopped talking for a few moments and his moustache twitched. "It is possible that someone there is connected to the gang that wished to kidnap Ernest. What we can't say is whether the traitor will be sitting on the British or French side of the meeting table."

I didn't know who this man was. I never found out his real name or exactly what his job was, but I have no doubt that he was a significant figure in the secretive world we had entered. And yet even he seemed nervous to discuss the matter, which didn't bode well for whatever lay ahead.

The thing that most concerned me, however, was our continued well-being, and so I asked a selfish question. "What has this got to do with us? We're the ones who caused so many of your problems, and we certainly don't have the credentials to investigate a traitor in your ranks."

There was another exchange of glances, but it took longer to resolve this time. Carlos looked at Rider who turned to Castleton, who looked back at the top man, whereas Snipe and Boyle just peered blankly out of the windows.

"They need me," Bella whispered, and this sent a ripple of discomfort through the room.

It was our friend Castleton who tried his best to smooth things over. "Lord Darnley thinks very highly of you, Lady Isabella. He has often talked of his capable goddaughter, and it is nice to meet you in person at last."

This clearly wasn't the official line, and so Rider intervened to help things along. "Ernest will be with you at Mentmore, but as he has to attend to his duties, he won't have the same freedom of movement that you and your boyfriend will be afforded."

"Marius is not my boyfriend," Bella replied, just a little too quickly for my liking.

"We know that," Don Carlos began in his slow, stentorian voice. "But the diplomats and politicians at Mentmore Towers won't."

"Oh, for goodness' sake!" I believe I was more upset by the idea of having to pretend to be Gilbert Baines again than by the dangerous mission they had in mind for us. "Can't I just be her friend?"

"That wouldn't make any sense at all," Boyle muttered before Rider took up the argument again.

"It will be difficult enough to get you an invitation at this late stage. Lady Isabella will have to telephone the Foreign Secretary himself if the plan is to work. I doubt she'd feel comfortable asking whether an old school friend could have a place at an important diplomatic soirée with the French Foreign Minister and his entourage in attendance."

Bella apparently accepted the situation, but I still didn't want anyone calling me Gilbert!

"Very well then. We'll do it, but we need to know more. You can't just throw us in there without telling us exactly what's happening. Why are the French coming here? Is it connected to your work?"

"Yes, very much so." The Don – which, now that I think of it, suits him far better than Carlos – straightened his back and peered down at me. "The British intelligence services barely existed before the last war. We want to make sure that, whatever happens in the future, we're better prepared for it."

"So you're working with France to protect our people?" I put to him.

"That's right. The meeting this weekend between Lord Darnley and Aristide Briand is essential for our continued co-operation. Our work with our colleagues across the Channel is an important defence against any number of potential enemies."

I got the impression that he was thinking of one enemy in particular and, knowing the little I did about the current political situation in Europe, the whole thing put me in mind of the Red Menace from the east.

Bella shifted in her seat before posing a question of her own. "But what does Castleton know that made him a target in the first place?"

The Don hesitated, and Rider suddenly looked nervous again. I imagine he was half-astonished that we were able to follow the conversation let alone challenge them on such matters.

"Lady Isabella, you are clearly an intelligent young lady, and so I'm going to tell you the honest truth." He kept his eyes fixed ahead, as if trying to hypnotise her. "It would be better for everyone if you could complete the task we have set you without my needing to answer that question."

"I understand." Her voice suggested that this was a total, though polite, lie.

"Let me guess," I said, as I'm far ruder than she could ever be. "France and Britain have been working together on some sort of message-decoding system, and the two ministers are meeting at Mentmore Towers this weekend to report on its progress?"

Before I reveal what happened next, I'd like to state that I do not consider myself any sort of genius. Nor am I a clairvoyant or even particularly knowledgeable when it comes to world politics. I'm just a good guesser, but my suggestion led to several dropped jaws, and a stunned silence filled the room.

"How did you know that?" Snipe asked, thus confirming my idea. In return, he received a pained look from his superiors.

The Don leaned forward in his chair. "What have they been telling you?"

"No one has told me anything."

"Don't trust him, gov," oversized Boyle snapped. "He's working with the gang. It's the only thing that makes sense."

"Calm down," I responded with a hint of tetchiness showing. "I'm not a criminal, and I'm not a spy. I'm a novelist and, if I was creating a plot with you people as the protagonists and a meeting between two important diplomats, that's the story I would write."

It fell to the Don to respond. "In which case, it seems that we're sending the right man to the do the job."

"Man and woman," I corrected him. "Not only is Bella Lord Darnley's goddaughter, she is an excellent detective in her own right." My face was expressionless, though I would have liked to wink across the room at her.

"Oh, of course." Rider suddenly sounded rather well-spoken, and I could imagine he often had to put on such an act in his line of work. "And we're immensely grateful to Lady Isabella for her assistance." Only yesterday, he'd been threatening to lock us up and throw away the key, and now he was on the point of grovelling.

The Don was apparently too senior to have to apologise and maintained his steely demeanour. "Do you have any more questions?"

"Yes, I have." I made them wait. I felt it was a small price to pay for our help. "I'd like to know why you think Inspector Ordinary or his bosses chose us to go after Castleton. They already knew where he was and must have had the resources to take him from Hastings themselves."

Rider ceded the floor to the man we'd put in danger. "I've been thinking about their methods a lot since I escaped from that car, and I believe they were trying to keep their hands clean. They already lost one man when they tried to take me the first time. They didn't want anything else to lead back to them."

I found it interesting to contrast the facts I was learning with the story Ordinary had told me. He'd said that an uncon- nected witness had been shot dead in the park on the night of the first kidnapping attempt, but it turned out it was the kidnapper himself.

"Who was it?" I asked. "Who was the man that was killed?"

Everyone looked at Rider then, and I assumed he was the only one who knew the answer. "A very normal person. He worked as a plumber, had no previous criminal record, and we don't understand how he got involved in any of it."

"The whole scheme is hard to fathom." Bella leaned forward to respond this time. "There must be something about us that caught their attention."

"Well, for one thing," Castleton replied, "they knew you wouldn't go in with your guns blazing, so if they wanted to capture me alive, that would have been an incentive."

"And don't forget your record of solving crimes," the Don added, and I thought there was a hint of flattery at play. "We certainly wouldn't be sending you on this mission if we didn't believe you were up to the job. These criminals must know what you achieved at Everham Hall, just as we do."

Even if it was flattery, it worked. Bella gave me a shy smile as Rider hurried things along. "Are you clear on what you have to do?"

I can't say I was incredibly confident, but my friend answered for the both of us.

"I believe we are, though I have another question first." She took a deep breath, and I wondered what new perils she was about to uncover. "A few minutes ago, I described the gang who took Ernest as unidentified, but your reaction told me this isn't the case."

Rider looked as though he wished to say something, but the Don's moustache wiggled to tell him that this was a question he would have to answer. "We don't know exactly what they want or who hired them to go about their business, but we have recently been made aware of certain stirrings."

"Stirrings?" I repeated, as he wasn't the sort to provide information without prompting.

"Yes, we've received word of an organisation known as the Syndicate. If they are the people who have twice tried to take Castleton hostage, we are incredibly fortunate he's still with us. They may sound like something from one of your books, Mr Quin, but there have been any number of rumours about them. Some sources say that they are anarchists hellbent on upsetting the natural order. Others claim that they are a group of home-grown communists who are looking to overthrow the British government.

"However, I believe the most likely scenario is that the Syndicate is an organisation that has taken charge of several large London gangs. Any assassinations, kidnappings and major crimes that occur go through them. Such co-ordination sounded implausible to me, but some people I greatly trust insist that the Syndicate is real and that they've set their sights on bigger things."

"Well, that all sounds terrifying." I released a huff of nervous laughter as the Don turned to me once more.

"It truly is, Mr Quin. We don't know what they intend to do if they achieve their goals – blackmail is one possibility. Or as Mr Rider has already suggested, they may wish to sell any secrets they obtain to our enemies. One thing is certain; people's lives are at risk. Hundreds of thousands of them, in fact."

"We understand," Bella replied for both of us. "And if you need me to call Lord Darnley, then perhaps you should show me to a telephone."

FOURTEEN

With our invitation to Mentmore Towers secured, I assumed that Rider and his men would do what they could to prepare us for our mission. I was wrong.

Boyle escorted me to my house and, as hers was too far to drive back and forth in time, Bella was taken to Kensington by Snipe so that she could buy provisions and suitable clothing for our trip. I had to wonder whether the big brute gave her advice on the colour of shoes that best suited her and whether to wear a hat with the outfits she had chosen.

I had come to the belief that, though they evidently needed our assistance, no one at Rider's office particularly trusted us. We were kept under surveillance until it was time to leave, so perhaps they were just afraid we would back out of their plan.

The conversation I had with my mother when we arrived back home was interesting, to say the least.

"Marius, where have you been? I've been sick with worry," she told me as I stepped over the threshold. The sound of my key in the lock had stirred her. She was even faster than my dog, which shows how worried she was.

"I've been to..." It hadn't occurred to me until this moment that I would have to make up a story. I know that, as a writer, I'm supposed to be good at flights of fancy, but my words failed me.

"...my house," the square-jawed beast beside me exclaimed in a gravelly tone.

"And you are?" My mother was naturally suspicious.

"This is Boyle," I replied. "He's a friend of mine."

"Boyle?"

"That's right. Billy Boyle. Surely I've mentioned him before?"

With each new answer she heard, my clever old mum was less convinced. "Really? And how do you know each other?"

"Boyle is my..." I looked at the big spy and he looked at me. Neither of us was eager to speak, but I eventually came up with an answer. "...tailor."

My mother pulled her neck in as if to say, *When was the last time he made you anything?*

"I'm only just starting out," he explained, before I ushered him into my bedroom so that Percy could go to sleep on his feet.

My dog was still unhappy with me after I'd abandoned him twice in the same week. Once more and he might never have forgiven me, so it was lucky that I'd decided to take him to Mentmore with us. If there was one thing I'd learnt in my infinitesimally short career as a sleuth, it's that a dog is a useful companion to have if you wish to walk about the place without attracting anyone's attention.

I packed a bag with the essentials for the weekend, including my best suit which, now that I thought about it, I'd bought a few months earlier from a tailor on Savile Row. My mother had been there when I went to collect it, but before she could point out this or any other inconsistencies in my story, Boyle, Percy and I had climbed into the Invicta for the journey to Buckinghamshire.

While he may not have been much of a conversationalist,

Boyle was a fine navigator, which was good as I didn't know where we were going.

"Just think," I told the big lug after an hour of near silence, "it was only yesterday that you were trying to shoot me."

"I was aiming for the car," he grimly replied.

I can only imagine he was tired of being used as a seat, but Percy looked perfectly happy on top of him.

"It's lucky you missed then. I would hate to see anything happen to her."

He sank a little lower in his seat but was still much taller than me. "It's not a 'her'. It's a car." He really was a charming fellow.

"I'm afraid I'll have to disagree with you. This car has a name, and that name is Vickie. Why would I call her Vickie if she was not a she?"

"You're talking nonsense." He was growing angrier by the moment. "Cars aren't people. She definitely isn't—"

I was going to drop the conversation, but he seemed to care about it so much that it would have been rude. "You just proved my point."

He sat there stewing for a moment as the wind rushed in around our ears. "I didn't prove your point. I was about to say that she—"

"You did it again. That's twice you've referred to this car as a she. Now I really don't mind what you think, but she's clearly female or you wouldn't have said so."

He folded his arms across his chest, and I thought for a moment that he might explode. For the first time that day, Percy looked rather amused.

"I'm sorry, Boyle," I said to calm him down. "I was only pulling your leg. You see I've recently learnt the importance of not taking life too seriously." He frowned then but said nothing, so I continued speaking. "I spent years after the war feeling sorry for myself. Years thinking that the only way people would take me seriously was if I moped about the place looking tortured, and what good did it do me?"

The answer, of course, was none at all.

"My father hasn't been seen in ten years. The woman to whom I was once very nearly engaged is on a path to marriage with a truly dull man and, for a while at least, there was a real possibility I would be thrown out of my house for not paying the bills. Being glum about all that just made me feel worse, and that is why I am trying to take a lighter view of the world."

He didn't respond for a moment, and I really hoped that my message had been well received, but then he huffed out a breath and, in a mumble, said, "That doesn't mean your car is a girl."

There's no winning with some people, and so I returned us to more serious matters. "You know, I've been thinking about it, and the fact that Bella and I were able to find you so easily shows that your organisation really isn't very secure. Do you have any idea who could have told this gang where you were hiding Castleton?"

He finally came to life. "That might be the first interesting thing you've said since I shot at you."

"It wouldn't surprise me. I'm known for my banality."

Animated by this new thread of conversation, he stroked Percy absent-mindedly. "I'm serious. I've been trying to work it out for the last day. Whoever gave away the location of the house in Hastings is a traitor through and through. But we'll worm him out. You needn't worry on that score."

He spoke just like the spies in the novels I'd read when I was younger. He sounded terribly brave and terribly dim.

"Have you considered the fact that the number of people who would have known was quite limited?"

He held one finger up to disagree with me. "That's where you're wrong. First of all, our organisation is a fair size. We have fifteen code breakers in the office who all know different parts of what's going on, and then there are five or so officers like

Snipe and me. Then you have the bosses, and that's where I think the loose link must be."

"Oh, yes?"

"Yes. It may not have been intentional, but just imagine that Don Carlos or one of his ilk had a conversation with his wife over dinner and the butler heard and decided to make a few bob. Or perhaps the butler himself is the one we're after. Perhaps the Syndicate placed one of their agents close to an important member of our organisation."

"So you're saying we should arrest the butler?"

He swithered for a moment before finding his resolve. "The butler or someone else in the employ of one of my bosses."

"You may have a point."

"I know. These toffs blabber as if no one can hear them, even when they're surrounded by servants."

I found it rather amusing that he was complaining about the loose lips of his superiors whilst gibbering on to me. In fact, now that the tap had been turned, he chatted away for the rest of the journey. He told me that he was the youngest of three brothers, and I learnt more about his cruel siblings than any person outside his family could ever need to know.

It was getting dark by the time we arrived at Mentmore, but just the silhouette of that house on the horizon was enough to impress me. It was like a cigar box sitting on the gently rolling landscape. Sorry, that's a terrible description, as rising up above the central cube were the four ornate towers that gave the Jacobean Revival house its name. I'd say that I'd never seen such a magnificent building, but the truth is that Bella's country pile was similarly magnificent.

The main difference between Lord Darnley's residence and that of the Duke of Hurtwood was that Bella's family's home managed to be both luxurious and ramshackle at the same time. Mentmore Towers looked as though it had specifically been designed for the Foreign Secretary to host retreats with political allies. There was something incredibly businesslike about it. The towers were tall and proud, and the front façade, which was accessed via a tree-lined avenue, seemed to say, *Hurry up! What's taking you so long?* I already felt out of place, and I hadn't yet stepped from my vehicle.

"What will you do while I'm in there?" I asked as I brought the car to a stop in front of a spiky metal gate with a policeman on either side of it.

Before answering, Boyle gave our names – one false, one... possibly false – to the men on duty, and they noted them down and nodded him through.

"While you're living it up with the elite," he eventually replied, "I'll be at the nearest inn with Snipe and Rider."

"I'm sure you'll have a lovely time together."

"I doubt it. We'll be waiting by the phone for relevant information." Whatever bond we might have formed on the journey was now forgotten, and he rolled his shoulders impatiently. "I'll take good care of your car."

"Like you did when you shot at it?"

"Precisely." He gave me a reluctant smile, and I patted him on the back for being a good egg after all.

At the end of the incredibly neat shingle driveway, a lavish collection of cars was parked in rows. There were German Mercedes, British Wolseleys and any number of incredible French vehicles. I spotted a sporty Delage, several stately Peugeots, and a natty little sky-blue Amilcar. There was even a red Invicta, just like mine. So dear Vickie was not unique after all.

I parked on the edge of the cour d'honneur, and Percy jumped from Boyle's lap without a look back or a bark goodbye. I didn't blame him, but it would have been rude if I had followed his example.

"Thank you for your companionship, Mr Boyle. I hope to be contacting you with good news very soon."

"It's Lieutenant Boyle, actually."

"My apologies, Lieutenant."

I was about to turn away, but he looked a little bilious and spoke again. "Quin, try not to make a mess of everything."

I smiled so that he didn't have to. "I'll do my best."

A royal blue carpet had been laid out to link the courtyard to the front entrance of the house so that the visiting dignitaries (and I) wouldn't sully our shoes on the perfectly clean path. There were long wings of the house on either side of me and, now that I could see the building more closely, it rather reminded me of a sculpture of an Egyptian sphinx I had seen in Crystal Palace Park. In fact, that's a much better comparison than a cigar box. The whole building was like a mythical half-man, half-lion, waiting for its moment to pounce.

Percy marched up to a line of servants dressed in long black coats with golden buttons, but I didn't feel ready to talk to anyone just yet and searched for Bella's car in case she'd driven up with her chauffeur. It wasn't there, and I accepted that my hound and I would have to enter the party alone.

We Quins weren't bred to set foot in such places. It wasn't merely the spectacle of all those fancy cars and the sight of the servants awaiting me. The whole place spoke of stuffiness and formality. I cursed myself for always getting into these complicated situations and whistled for Percy to come to heel. He ignored me entirely and walked towards the grand entrance to Mentmore Towers like a standard bearer before his ever so shabby king.

FIFTEEN

"Good evening, Mr Baines," the butler said with a bow. I'd almost forgotten that I was there incognito, so it was a good thing that the men at the gate had presumably let him know my fake name. It's quite possible he would have worked it out anyway. I was undoubtedly the scruffiest member of the party, and the only one likely to be a lowly banker. "I have instructions to show you to your bedroom and then on to the White Drawing Room."

"The White Drawing Room?" I responded, as he clicked his fingers for one of the footmen to fetch my bags from the car. "Does it come in any other colours?"

He closed his eyes in that slightly superior manner that most butlers have. "Yes, sir. There is also a Green Drawing Room here at Mentmore. And I believe that the Blarenberghe Room was previously painted red and known as—"

"The Red Drawing Room, by any chance?"

He pretended to smile. "Sir is most perceptive." With this, he turned on his heel and led me up a glossy wooden staircase that led off the vestibule up to the first floor.

He didn't talk to me as we walked and maintained a three-pace distance between us at all times. I've never liked such formality. Not only do I feel like a fraud whenever someone has to wait on me, I believe that people should be allowed to act as human beings and not voiceless automatons.

When we got to my bedroom for the weekend, it was a terribly plush and gloomy old space. The bed was taller than I was, and every other wall was concealed by damask drapes, as if a child had taken a crayon to patches of the wallpaper and they didn't want anyone to notice. I changed and washed as quickly as I could, but Percy didn't settle down to sleep as I had hoped.

"It won't be any fun," I told him, and he stared back at me, unconvinced. "I'm serious. You'll have a much better time here asleep."

I knew there was no sense arguing with the creature, and, sure enough, when I left the room, he padded after me.

"Ah, you're still here." There was more than a note of surprise in my voice when I discovered that the butler was there waiting for me when I emerged.

"As I previously said, Mr Baines, I have been charged with showing you to the White Drawing Room." There was something mysterious about him, as if he knew any number of secrets that I would be lucky to discover.

With a nod, he turned back the way we had come and led me (and my persistent hound) through the house.

"Is Lord Darnley occupied at the moment?" I asked when I really couldn't stand the silence between us any longer.

"That is correct, sir. His Lordship is currently in the library with his assistant, Mr Lochtie, and his chief aide, Mr Castleton. They are preparing for the imminent arrival of the French Foreign Minister, Monsieur Briand. However, I'm sure that Lord Darnley will greet you at the earliest possible opportunity."

He clearly only spoke when spoken to and said no more as we glided through the Grand Hall. For a moment, it felt as though I were back in the British Museum, and so I seized Percy by the collar in case he decided to charge at one of the numerous treasures on display. The room in front of me was covered in what can only be described as artefacts. The place wasn't furnished so much as laid out for an exhibition. There were countless plinths holding an array of objects from grand inlaid chests and Moorish busts to ancient clocks and elaborate vases.

But it was the architecture that was the real star feature. Above us on the first floor, an arched gallery surrounded the enormous space. Three gilt lanterns hung from the glass ceiling, and I had the feeling of having abandoned the pleasant sights of Buckinghamshire only to reappear in an Italian courtyard.

I must have stopped to marvel at all of this, as the butler cleared his throat to get my attention.

"It's incredible," I said by way of apology.

In response, he offered another tantalising titbit. "The house formerly belonged to the Rothschild family. These are some of the items they sold to Lord Darnley when Mentmore Towers was put up for auction."

This was all he said before turning once more to leave the room. I was evidently required to follow him and, with one last look around the Grand Hall, I did just that. We walked under an open arch into another vestibule that gave onto the White Drawing Room itself, where, I was surprised to discover, a group of people were expecting me.

"You're Baines, I suppose," an exceedingly posh young gentleman announced, and it gave me a small thrill that he was both right and wrong at the same time. "We were told you were coming."

"And here I am," I replied, as I hadn't a clue what else to say.

He was a strange-looking fellow with bony cheeks and a sharply pointed nose. Although he was certainly dressed for the occasion, in a long black tailcoat and remarkably tight trousers, his gold watch chain and matching cufflinks made him look like the butler who had just disappeared.

"What are you drinking, Baines?" a woman with piled-high red hair asked me, and I was uncertain how to respond. The problem was not the question; that was simple enough to answer. It was her instantly friendly attitude that struck me. She stood beside a drinks cabinet and had a warm smile on her face as though we were dear old friends.

"I'll have a cognac, in honour of our foreign visitors."

There was one more man there, but he was hard at work. Sitting in the corner of the appropriately white room, he was writing in a journal, apparently oblivious to our discussion.

"We're all the cast-offs in here," the first man explained. "We're not important enough to be in with the diplomats, nor insignificant enough to be ignored entirely. That's why they deigned to organise this meeting for us. There were servants in here before, but I sent them away. It all gets so very tiring watching them wait upon you like dogs eager for a treat. You know?"

"Yes, of course, it must be terrible." I immediately felt stupid for bringing Percy, who had been cowering at my side ever since we'd entered.

"You are rude, Spencer," the girl said as she brought over my drink. "You haven't introduced yourself."

She was rather beautiful, despite the dimensions of her towering hair. She had freckled skin and hazel eyes. Her gaze was intense and lingered upon me as she handed me the glass so that I found myself both charmed and disarmed. I wasn't sure that I could trust her, but I was eager to find out whether I should.

"I'm Primrose and this is my brother Spencer." She was evidently a confident person and spoke as though I should know who they were. "Primrose and Spencer *Darnley*."

"Oh, how silly of me. Bella's told me all about you." This was a lie, and I now realised that it was not just Rider who had failed to prepare me for this encounter. Bella could have written a short booklet – preferably with diagrams – to explain the world into which I would be dipping my toe. She certainly hadn't informed me that Lord Darnley had children.

"Bella told you about us?" Primrose sounded surprised. "I'd like to have eavesdropped on that conversation."

"Ummm... well, I can assure you it was all nice things." Percy would have come up with a better response than this, and he is a dog.

The fiery-maned beauty did not react to my tentative utterance but added a significant detail as she glanced at her brother. "Spencer here has been in love with your dear sweet Bella since he was four years old."

Spencer helped himself to a glass of something strong and brown and sat down in a hard wooden chair. "How dare you, sis. I'll have you know that I was three when she first stole my heart, for all the good it did me. It turned out she already had her eye on some peasant boy from her village."

Primrose was clearly enjoying herself and told me more. "That's right. And as soon as that patriotic young man grew up and went off to war, Spencer here asked Bella to marry him."

It was unnerving to hear people talk about me as if I wasn't there. Of course, as far as they knew, I wasn't.

"In my defence, I was only sixteen at the time, and she turned me down most delicately," Spencer was quick to add. "In fact, my whole life has been devoted to chasing and failing to win the hand of your girlfriend, Baines, and now here you are."

"Here I am," I said once more, as I tried to make sense of what he might feel on the matter. A lowering look crossed his features, and I had to hope, for Gilbert's sake if not mine, that he'd recovered from the heartache of losing Bella. It was something of which I had some experience.

A voice that I knew only too well sounded from the doorway. "Oh, you rotters. Trust you two to rake over old history. I fully expected you to give Gilbert a thoroughly cold welcome."

Bella rushed over to hug Primrose and kiss Spencer on both cheeks, before coming to put her arm around me. "I'm glad you've met my Gilly, though." She squeezed me tightly, and I decided that I could get used to playing the part of her boyfriend. "Isn't he wonderful?"

"Just perfect," Primrose replied with a soft growl in her voice. There was definitely something feline about her. "It's not too late to marry Spencer if you'd like to pass this one my way."

"You've always been so funny, Primrose." Bella's eyes said something very different to her mouth just then, and I got my first hint that the two of them were less friendly than Bella's greeting had suggested.

Rather than continue the exchange, Bella detached herself from me to go over to the man in the corner. "My apologies, we haven't been introduced."

She held her hand out to the unnamed gentleman with the horn-rimmed glasses and terribly neat beard.

"I'm Lady Isabella Montague," Bella persevered. "And you are?"

He released an exhausted sigh, as though reluctant to be pulled from his scribbling. "My name it is Monsieur Vidocq. I am the aide to Monsieur Rochefort, who is the aide to Monsieur Briand." The tired-sounding Frenchman took her hand and proceeded to explain the one thing we already knew. "Monsieur Briand is the Foreign Minister of France. He will soon arrive for a meeting with your Lord Darnley."

"Oh, how interesting." Bella clearly had to do a lot of pretending in this refined world of lords and politicians.

With his part said, Vidocq nodded and returned to his work.

He didn't speak again for some time, which afforded us the opportunity to talk about him in hushed voices in the far corner of the room.

"What's the story with Monsieur Charmant?" I quipped once I was fairly confident he couldn't hear us.

"Oh, Vidocq's fine really. He's just a typical red-tapeworm." Spencer didn't stop looking at Bella as he spoke. "He came up here this morning to prepare for his boss's arrival ahead of everyone else. It was my job to accompany him as he saw to a lot of minor and terribly dull details."

"I don't like him," Primrose revealed. "He's as cold as a dead fish. A lot of Frenchmen are like that."

"You mean you don't like him because he hasn't knelt down at your feet and composed an ode to your beauty," her brother suggested. "You hate it when you're not the centre of attention."

Primrose looked at me as she replied, and I sensed she was worried about what I would think. "As I said, he's a cold fish."

I can only imagine what sort of argument would have erupted at this moment if another of the guests hadn't arrived.

"Ernie!" Spencer was immediately distracted and went to greet Castleton.

"Oh, my dear, dear Ernest. It's such a pleasure to see you." Primrose was just as excited by the sight of the newcomer and raced her brother to reach him. I was beginning to wonder whether there was anything over which they did not fight.

I lingered beside Bella, partly to be polite, but also because I couldn't remember if I was supposed to know Castleton or not. Spencer once again showed little desire to introduce me to anyone as he engaged his father's chief aide in conversation.

"We heard you'd had a spot of bother this week. Something to do with the police, wasn't it?"

Our ally on the case became circumspect. "I wouldn't say that. It was just a misunderstanding really, but it's all fine now."

He looked at Monsieur Vidocq in the corner before noticing us
and walking over.

Primrose did the honours. "This is Lady Isabella and her
new man, Gilbert Baines. Bella worked in Whitehall after the
war. Did you ever bump into one another?"

Ernest looked at us uncertainly. "I don't believe so. But then
it is a large place."

"No, I'm quite sure we never met," Bella replied, which
confirmed that we weren't supposed to know Castleton, and I
could now formally introduce myself.

"Baines," I told him with outstretched hand. "Banking's my
game. It's not much fun, but then neither am I."

Bella chose this moment to kick me in the back of the leg. I
have no doubt I deserved it.

"I'm Ernest Castleton." He was more convincing than I
was. If I hadn't known otherwise, I really would have believed
we'd never met. "I work for Lord Darnley."

"How's your little fiancée?" Primrose asked him before I
could say anything more. I was beginning to wonder whether
there was any man with whom she did not flirt.

"Hermione is very well, thank you. I've just come from
seeing her."

"What a shame she isn't here tonight." Primrose was even
more sarcastic than I was, and yet I really didn't mind it. She
was not just good-looking and evidently rather feisty. There was
a glimmer of mischievousness about her that I found most
appealing.

Something in our conversation finally caught Monsieur
Vidocq's attention, and he put away his journal and came over.
"So you're Castleton," he put to Castleton... obviously. "I've
been told to liaise with you on a few important matters. Would
now be a good time?"

"Very well, monsieur." He looked reluctant, but could
apparently see no way out of it, so turned to us to take his leave.

"Baines, ladies, I hope to continue this conversation a little later."

We nodded in agreement, and Spencer pointed us to the door. I had no idea of the timetable for the day, but it was already evening, and I could only assume that dinner would be starting soon. Bella put her arm through mine and the siblings led us to the Grand Hall.

"Have you any idea who the traitor could be?" she hung back to ask in a whisper.

"Yes, it's bound to be the butler."

"Really?" Her voice came out a little more loudly than she'd been intending.

"No, of course not. Although that's what Boyle thinks." I decided to stop teasing and tell her the truth. "I only got here a quarter of an hour ago. I've met a few potential culprits, of course, but there's no way of saying who's a spy."

"Then keep up the good work."

O, that smile of hers. It could still send a shiver through me and, as we followed the sound of buzz and bustle in a neighbouring room, I remembered what it was like to be on her arm aged seventeen. For just a moment or two, I remembered what it was like to be in love.

"You know," she murmured, "I think this is going to be a walkover. We don't even have to identify a murderer. We just have to look for the person who's acting suspiciously and call Rider to arrest him."

"What could be easier?" I asked, as we walked into a glittering dining room where approximately fifty potential suspects were enjoying their aperitifs.

"Ah," Bella said before correcting her previous statement. "Perhaps I spoke too soon."

We were immediately offered drinks and hors d'oeuvres by waiters in moss green waistcoats – one (or all) of whom could have been working for the Syndicate. A group of French diplomats had just arrived, too. The majority of them had thin moustaches and slicked back hair, which made me think that, should a member of a criminal organisation wish to get close to a key meeting between two of the most important men in Europe, it would be easy enough to blend in. There was a group of plummy folk I took to be members of the Darnley clan, but it was still possible that one of them had revealed state secrets in order to settle a family feud.

Including the household staff, there must have been at least eighty people at Mentmore who could be the traitor. It was impossible to know where to start looking.

"You were wrong, Bella. It's much harder to find a culprit without a body. Perhaps someone will keel over dead and then we can get to work."

I believe we both held our breath for a moment in case a shot were to ring out or someone should grasp his throat in horror as a drop of poison did its worst.

"You made me worried then, Marius." Bella castigated me with a harsh tone and her pointy elbow.

"Well, we need something to help us make sense of this mare's nest." I looked around the exquisitely decorated room in the hope I might spot someone skulking. Was it really too much to ask for the spy to use an unconvincingly false nose or oversized glasses to help us locate him? "We're outsiders. No matter what Rider and his bosses might have thought, we can't be much use unless we know exactly why the French are here this weekend."

Bella looked as nervous as I felt, but before she could reply, I caught the sound of a hubbub from the front entrance and, a few moments later, yet more people arrived. They were led by two men who couldn't have looked more different. Our Foreign Secretary, Lord Darnley, had a pale, shaven face, white hair in a sharp parting and blue eyes. The man next to him was dark with a bushy moustache. He reminded me of that physicist chappy, Albert Einstein, and yet I felt I'd seen him before some-where. Rider had mentioned that the French Foreign Minister's name was Aristide Briand, and it finally clicked why I knew him. Briand had been the Prime Minister through much of the war. As soon as he entered the room, significant cuttings from newspapers of the day popped into place in my head.

"There's Uncle Alistair." Bella waved to her godfather as the group moved past us into the centre of the room.

"Darnley's not really your uncle, is he?" I asked, though I realised I already knew the answer.

"Not by blood or marriage. It's just a friendly name I've always called him."

Darnley waved back over the heads of several other guests, but that was as close as we would get to him for some time. Percy had become overwhelmed by the sheer number of people there and gone to hide under a chair at the side of the room. I had warned him he wouldn't enjoy such a large party, but my beloved hound rarely listens to me. To save at least one of us from the uncomfortable evening ahead, I asked the nearest footman to take the poor canine to the kitchen and make sure he was well looked after.

This was one problem solved, but before I could suggest to Bella that we work our way through the crowd to be closer to Ernest Castleton and his colleagues, a huge man with a mess of curly grey hair accosted us. He looked rather like an opera singer and evidently knew Bella very well.

"My dear girl," he said whilst shaking her hand so violently that I thought her arm might be pulled from its socket. "What a pleasure to see you. It's been far too long. I don't remember the last time I saw your father. How is the old devil? Is your mother still keeping him in line? Are your brothers well? I remember when Freddy and I were at school together. Oh, the times we had. There was one occasion when..."

As you may have predicted from this burst of babbling, he

continued like this for some time. He didn't wait for answers to the numerous questions he posed but raced on with such energy and enthusiasm that it was quite mesmerising. I eventually came to understand that this man was not only Lord Darnley's brother, but also his advisor or confidant or some such.

After fifteen minutes of chatter, the gong sounded for dinner, which would surely give us the opportunity we needed to escape the cheerful windbag.

"Oh, Bella, my dear. It's been such a pleasure," he proclaimed with a wistful look in his eye. "I can't say how happy I am to talk to you again like this. I will speak to my brother to make sure that I can sit opposite you at dinner."

He went off to do just that as the mass of guests spilt out of the dining room. The Grand Hall had been transformed in the time since we'd passed through it. Gone was the display of priceless antiques and, in their place, three long banqueting tables had been laid out with everything we could need for our feast.

"This isn't going to work," I complained when we sat down in one corner, as far as it was possible to get from the key group of diplomats. "We're barely in the same room as the action, let alone at the same table."

Bella was presumably just as disappointed as I was, but she didn't let it show. "All in good time, Marius. If you'd ever been to a function like this, you'd know that nothing really happens before the bigwigs have gorged themselves."

I looked around at the eager faces and bulging waistlines and decided that she was probably right.

SIXTEEN

We were surrounded by members of Lord Darnley's family. On one side was his daughter Primrose – who took every opportunity to touch my sleeve and stare into my eyes. Opposite her was Spencer –who did more or less the same thing to Bella. Whereas just in front of us, their uncle dominated the conversation and seemed oblivious to everything around him bar the food on his plate and the wine in his glass. Oh and, as far as I could tell, the rest of the table was made up of various cousins, grandparents and, no doubt, love-children of that great family.

The only good thing about the Foreign Secretary's brother rambling on to Bella was that it gave me the chance to observe the goings-on in the room as a whole. Lord Darnley himself was seated with Monsieur Briand and his entourage. Castleton and a pair of his French equivalents were on one side, and the two men's wives were on the other. I found it odd that the hard-working Gaul we'd met in the White Drawing Room sat some distance from this main group. He was supposedly the assistant to Briand's assistant, but he was stuck at the end of the table.

The meal was truly appetising, filled as it was with rich

dishes. I ate everything from snails (no doubt chosen in defer-
ence to our foreign guests) to roast beef (similarly selected to
conform to their stereotype of us). I was only grateful that we
didn't have to eat frogs' legs. I'd had them once when I lived in
France and, perhaps it was down to my preconceptions rather
than the quality of the dish, but they were not to my taste.

It came as no surprise that the French delegation was far
quieter than the British. Though we may be famous for
being reserved, we Brits certainly know how to enjoy
ourselves around the dinner table. Once a glass or two of
wine had been consumed, the noise and animation in the
room really increased. With regards to our Gallic cousins, on
the other hand, I've been to more raucous funeral parlours
than French restaurants, and I've always wondered whether
it was a question of cuisine rather than manners. The
French take the time to contemplate the sophisticated food
they are consuming, whereas we British are happy so long as
dinner comes with potatoes, and no one chokes on a chicken
bone.

When the meal was over, the party split up into groups and
we were diverted accordingly into the various salons around the
Grand Hall. To my frustration, we ended up right back where
we started in the White Drawing Room. Bella was pulled away
by yet more of Darnley's relatives, and I was cornered by
Primrose.

"I've always thought that there is something very sensual
about banking," she lied, and I couldn't help laughing.

"You've clearly never met Gilbert Baines..." I realised my
mistake and quickly tacked on a significant addendum, "before.
You've clearly never met me before. I'm about as sensual as a
brick."

"Bricks can be sensual. You can... touch them." She would
not give up, and I found her persistence difficult to comprehend. Even if she and Bella were old enemies, it was frankly

uncouth to attempt to steal another woman's boyfriend so publicly.

"Spencer, what was that you were saying about the work you hope to do?" I turned to her brother to ask.

He was apparently capable of ignoring his sister's bad behaviour, or perhaps Bella's beauty had eclipsed all else. He looked perfectly jealous of the old lady to whom she was talking, and it took him a moment to realise what I'd asked.

"Oh, I suppose I'd like to follow Father into politics. Not that he ever notices me. I worked in his office once, determined to learn the ropes, and he palmed me off onto one of his assistants. It's maddening, it really is."

"Oh, poor little Spencer. It must be so hard being Daddy's golden boy." This was his sister mocking him. I was perfectly polite all evening, though it wasn't hard when compared to her.

My trying evening had at least provided the opportunity to accumulate theories on the people I had met. There was nothing to say that a member of the family hadn't become involved in the affair. Spencer might well have taken revenge on his father for his apparent negligence. Primrose was clearly the envious type, and even Darnley's brother – who, though he had gone into great detail on the interior decoration scheme of his nearby manor house, hadn't seen fit to share his Christian name – lived in his brother's shadow. All three of them seemed as if they were crying out for attention, and though I wasn't about to accuse them of collaborating with a sinister criminal gang just yet, the thought was firmly planted in my brain.

I rather wished that Percy had remained so that I could have had at least one ally at my side. It would have been nice to see him look around that busy room and decide whose feet would be best to occupy. I don't know exactly when I'd become such a dog lover, but, for all his sullenness and dramatic turns of mood, I sincerely loved my hairy companion.

The best thing about being with the family, though, was

that they were the first to leave. The politicians and their associates were staying at the house for the weekend, but as soon as ten o'clock struck, the wider family dispersed, which meant that I could finally do what I'd wished to do ever since I arrived: I had a good snoop about the place.

I made my excuses to Spencer and his sister, sacrificed Bella for the greater good – she was stuck with Darnley's ever so haughty wife – and then I hurried off to investigate. I couldn't just barge into whichever coloured drawing room the diplomats had requisitioned, but I had a fairly good idea of the layout of the staterooms by this point and wanted to explore the rest of the house. I soon located a vast imperial staircase which led off the Grand Hall up to the gallery. It was suitably impressive for such a house, with its green marble handrails and smoothly hewn matching white balusters, but the view from the top was even more magnificent.

Right, I'm going to stop there as I could go on for ever about that beautiful building.

I stood in the gallery overlooking the now empty hall and wondering into which of the many rooms that led off the square walkway it would be best to poke my head. I might just as well have used a child's picking game to select one, but before I could, I heard raised voices from below and hid behind a pillar to listen.

"It's not acceptable, Rochefort," an orotund yet musical French voice echoed about the hall. "You've let me down." This is my translation, and he didn't use that exact expression, but the literal equivalent *you abandoned me* doesn't quite have the same sense in English.

"I'm so sorry, Monsieur Briand," the second man said as he hurried to light the politician's cigar, and the other aides gathered around them. "I did everything I could to prepare for this evening. I understand if you wish to discharge of my services."

I inched around the pillar to watch the Foreign Minister's

reaction. I could see that he was debating with himself over the best course of action. When he finally spoke again, a puff of smoke came out of him, along with his reply. "That won't be necessary, but I don't understand why you interrupted the meeting like that. You made me look a fool in there. A total fool."

"I really can't say what came over me." Rochefort hung his head in apparent shame. "I will do my very best from this moment onwards."

I was hoping that their conversation would reveal more than this, but as Briand's advisor bowed like a Japanese servant, the English contingent spilt from the chamber, and I continued on my journey.

I found myself in the corridor that led to the guest bedrooms, one of which was mine. Now that I had the time to look more closely, I noticed that the whole wing was arranged around a square courtyard that was open to the elements. It seemed that the layout of the house was like a squared-off figure of eight. I had no wish to disturb any sleeping guests and had just decided to return to the Great Hall when the butler appeared.

"Sir, may I help you?"

"My dog," I blurted as he'd rather startled me.

"I beg your pardon?" He was apparently as surprised as I was.

"I'm looking for my dog. Can you direct me to the kitchen, by any chance?" There were so many excuses I could have summoned that were better than this one. Why do I always get so hot under the collar and utter the first thing that comes to me rather than taking my time to fashion a reasonable response? Why can't real life be more like writing a book?

His suspicious expression soon disappeared, and he looked worried about my sanity instead. "It's downstairs, sir. That is where kitchens tend to be. You can take the servants' stairs to your left if you so wish. It will save you returning to the Grand Hall and potentially getting lost again."

"Spiffing!" I muttered, as that's the kind of thing that idiots say. I certainly didn't want him thinking I had a brain or he might have questioned why I was poking about up there.

The butler retreated on quiet feet, and I wondered whether Boyle had been right about household staff making capable spies. Either way, the top domestic would remain on my list of suspects. The house was quiet, and so I decided that the time really had come to fetch Percy and go to bed. As the butler had suggested, the kitchen was located exactly where one would expect to find such a room in a large house. It was not the immense space I had imagined, though. In fact, with several maids and a cook there, it was quite packed. Two of them were washing dishes, one was slaving over the range, and the whole place felt like a Turkish bath.

I would like to say that Percy ran over when he saw me there, but he was half asleep beside the fireplace and barely opened his eyes.

"We love your dog," the nearest maid told me when I tried to pick him up, and he grew even floppier. "He's been so affectionate all evening. Thank you for bringing him. I reckon he's much better company than most of the guests we get here." She can't have been more than fourteen and was full of the joy and energy that I had possessed at her age.

I smiled to show my appreciation. "I can see that he's worn out. He must have made a real fuss of you all. Has he had his dinner?"

"I should say," the cook yelled through the steam of a boiling pail of water that she'd just emptied into a giant pot. "He's enjoyed his snails and his roast beef. Not to mention the pork medallions and—"

"I'm going to conclude that he ate more than I did." My laughter mingled with hers.

"I'm afraid we didn't have time to walk him, though," the young maid explained.

I looked down at the sleepy beast and tried to imagine how I could persuade him to walk to the garden of his own accord. After much cooing and encouragement, I realised the plan was a non-starter and carried him outside.

SEVENTEEN

The kitchen door gave onto a walled garden that was appealing even in the darkness. It was full of herbs, flowers and vegetables, so I kept on through a gate to the parkland beyond. That lazy dog was finally roused by the cool night air, and it felt nice to have the vast expanse of the estate to myself, having spent the evening surrounded by the great and good of England and France.

I looked back at the house and could make out most of the property thanks to the light spilling out of each window on the ground floor and the full moon overhead. Over by the south entrance, I could see the glow of a cigarette under the porch and, once Percy had concluded his business for the evening, I went to see who was there.

"My goodness, Marius!" Castleton was leaning against a Doric column that held up the small stone structure. "You gave me a fright appearing from the folds of darkness like that."

"I go by Gilbert these days," I told him, and he held out a cigarette case for me not to take one. "No, thank you. I was never particularly keen, and the noxious smoke I inhaled from other sources during the war only confirmed my opinion."

He took a further drag and stared off into the darkness as the smoke wafted around us. "Well, I'm glad you found me. I've been watching the French carefully since they got here, and something strange has just occurred."

"I got that impression myself."

"Oh, really?" He jerked his head back as he looked at me.

"I was in the Grand Hall not fifteen minutes ago and over-heard Aristide Briand's reaction to the meeting's premature end."

"It was very odd, I must say. We were all together in the room when Briand's aide, Clément Rochefort, suddenly brought the proceedings to a halt. It's remarkable, as we were just getting to the key moment."

"With regards to that," I said, "as Rider's not around, and you know I'm not involved in any of this, I think it's time you told me what everyone is really doing here this weekend."

He released a puff of smoke and a huff of laughter. "I'd love to. I really would, but—"

"Listen here, Ernest, I understand the need for secrecy, but if your bosses really were worried about my discovering too much, they shouldn't have sent me here."

I could see that I had put him in a difficult position, but I needed to know the truth.

"I can't tell you everything, but it's only right that you possess the basic facts." He pulled on the hem of his dinner jacket as if presenting himself for inspection. "A select group of the boys at the GC&CS, along with their counterparts in France, have been working on something that could secure international peace for decades."

"That sounds like it was worth the drive here."

"Yes, it's a truly daring project – top secret, of course. I didn't know anything about it until a few weeks ago. Have you heard of a place called Room 40?" He quickly read the answer on my face. "It housed the cryptanalysis division of the British navy. All the way back in 1914, they came into possession of three German code books, which we used for the next four years to make sense of the enemy's transmissions. It helped us learn their strategies, and it surely reduced Allied casualties, especially at sea."

"Yes, but we're not at war anymore," I felt I should point out. "What good would that do us now?"

"You're right. It's not the Germans who most concern us these days. But what if the Russians have the same idea as the Kaiser and decide to invade the rest of Europe? Do you like the thought of having to call your son Vladimir?"

Though I understood his thinking, this threat seemed like a minor one compared to the hundreds of thousands of people who would die before we got to that point.

"I see," I replied, to get us back to the facts. "But what has this got to do with world peace? Or the French, for that matter?"

"Over the last year, a project was put into motion to design a machine that could crack any codes and cyphers that our enemies could conceive. The French are only too happy to be a part of it if it means they can avoid another invasion. They're in the middle of everything on the continent. When our plan comes to fruition, there will be no sense in anyone challenging us to a war; their chances of winning will be greatly reduced from the outset."

"And you really think that whatever you're cooking up could ensure that?"

"I certainly hope so. More importantly, the Syndicate must believe it's a possibility. It would appear that they want to get hold of the machine more than anyone."

I had a question for him on that very point. "And do these criminals plan to sell it to our rivals? Or do they have even more nefarious plans of their own?"

"It's hard to say." He paused and flicked his cigarette so that the glowing ashes sailed through the air before fading to black on the stones beneath his feet. "Perhaps they'll sell it on to the highest bidder, or perhaps they'll destroy our research. There's a lot of money to be made from war. Plenty of people would be happy if such suffering and instability were never to end."

Another of my preoccupations rose to the surface. "You must know our own boys rather well. Do you think one of them could be the traitor?"

"I don't see it myself, but we can't rule it out entirely." There was an openness to Castleton that I had to admire. He was not the kind of person I would have expected to go into politics. He was far too honest for that. "Someone must have told them where the safe house in Hastings was. And they surely had their reasons for wanting to kidnap me."

"I've been wondering about that all day." I paused to choose the right words. "Can you imagine why they chose you rather than one of the technicians who created this machine of yours?"

He was just as careful but eventually answered the question. "I really can't. After all, I couldn't describe how the thing works, or even how the pieces fit together. I've only actually seen it once." He looked up at the stars for a moment, and in the silence that fell between us, I could hear poor sleepy Percy yawning. "If there is a traitor passing information to the Syndicate, it's Briand's chief aide I'm keeping my eye on, and you'd be wise to do the same. I can't get a sense of what drives Monsieur Rochefort, and I don't understand why he brought the meeting to an end early. We were supposed to be discussing the progress the project has made. From what I know, the French have a series of etched metal discs that go together with a similar collection of our own. They all slot onto a bar which itself is housed in a wooden box that is quite unlike anything I've seen before. When the machine is assembled, you feed in an encrypted sentence and, with a series of flashing lights, you get it back in plain English. If it works, it will be quite remarkable."

"So it interprets secret messages? I heard of a machine

when I was living in Germany that could create an unbreakable code, but this actually deciphers them?"

"That's correct." He sounded terribly proud. "There's no guarantee that it will function as designed, but we have high hopes. In fact, we were supposed to be testing it tonight."

"Until Rochefort had other ideas."

"Precisely." His face brightened for a moment as he took another drag on the glowing cigarette. "He called the meeting to a close just as we were getting started. It was most peculiar. Right out of the blue, as if he was the one in charge, he announced that it was too late to do anything tonight and that we should call it quits."

This sounded like a nightmare of mine in which I attend a meeting with important people from all over the world. The British Prime Minister, Stanley Baldwin, is about to introduce the President of the United States and, for some reason, I stand up and start singing a nursery rhyme.

Froggy went a courtin' and he did ride, mm-hmm.
Froggy went a courtin' and he did ride, mm-hmm.
Froggy went a courtin' and he did ride,
With a sword and a pistol by his side, mm-hmm, mm-hmm, mm-hmm.

Only, I don't stop after the first verse. I carry on through all nine of them as the world's leaders stare in open-jawed disbelief that some impertinent guttersnipe is still singing. So I can well imagine how Monsieur Rochefort had felt when he'd called a sudden halt to the proceedings.

"Did he give a reason for what he'd done?" I asked when the horror of this imagined scene had waned.

"He tried to make a joke of it. He said that we'd all drunk and eaten so much that it would be a good idea to go to bed and make a fresh start in the morning. It was incredibly awkward for all involved, but his boss is far from fluent in English and couldn't object."

"What do you think Rochefort was hoping to achieve?"

Even in the dim light of the porch, I could see Castleton's eyes dip in reflection. "I don't know. I really don't. What could he gain from delaying the meeting? It will only put it off for a few hours. And even if he is the one working for the Syndicate, I don't see what good it does."

I was about to share my thoughts on the matter when the door behind him opened and who should come through it but Rochefort himself. He was a rather compact fellow with the same short hair and pencil-thin moustache as many of his colleagues. If anything, he was the model for all the others as, one level below the top man, he was presumably responsible for the whole team of advisors.

"Good evening, gentlemen. It's certainly a mild one," he said in crisp, correct English. He still had a slight Gallic twang, but even from this brief opening statement, I could tell that his command of the language was far greater than most Frenchmen I had known.

His eyes were little more than shining black points in the darkness, and yet his stare was as penetrating as any owl's. I'd rarely felt so uncomfortable before another person. It was as if he could see through my body and deep into my mind. I wondered for a moment whether he knew that we'd been talking about him, but even if he'd been listening at the door, it was surely too thick for the sound to have carried.

"Good evening, Mr Rochefort. This is my friend Gilbert Baines."

"I'm very pleased to meet you, Mr Baines. Are you another member of Lord Darnley's staff?"

I must admit that I rather enjoy telling people that I write murder mysteries. I like seeing their reaction, and it's normally a pleasure to hear about their favourite writers and their ideas for future stories – although if they've read one of my books and not liked it, it is admittedly less enjoyable.

It therefore brought me no small amount of pain to have to say, "I'm a banker."

The French Foreign Minister's aide gave me a long, hard look, then seemed to dismiss me from his thoughts. He already had a cigar in his hand, and his English counterpart reached into his pocket for a match.

"I apologise, Mr Castleton, if my interruption in the meeting caused you or your colleagues any inconvenience. I could explain my reasons, but I doubt they would make a great deal of sense to you."

"Yes, of course," Ernest began, and I could see he was considering this careful response. "Although you could give it a go, as I'm terribly interested in what happened."

Rochefort appeared reluctant but could presumably see no other option. "It is Monsieur Briand." He paused to wave his cigar through the air, and the aroma instantly became stronger. "He would not like to admit it, but he is not as young as he once was. These meetings can continue so late sometimes, and I made a scene to prevent my superior from having to excuse himself."

From the conversation I'd overheard between the two Frenchmen, I knew this was a lie, but there was no way to communicate the fact to Ernest without Rochefort hearing. To be honest, I did try winking, but either he didn't notice in the low light or he concluded I had something in my eye. He certainly showed no sign of having understood.

There was a period of uneasy silence as the two men smoked, and it seemed that no one knew what to say. For his part, Percy had fallen asleep on my feet. The poor creature was exhausted.

"Well, gentlemen. I believe that any conversation you wish to have would be best conducted without me," Rochefort eventually exclaimed to break through the silence. "I will bid you goodnight."

He stubbed out his half-smoked cigar, nodded to each of us in turn and went back through the heavy oaken door.

"What a strange person!" Castleton was instantly animated. "Do you see what I mean now?"

"Yes, that was a little odd."

Castleton paused before replying, and I could see that he was excited to have fashioned a new theory. "I'm telling you, if anyone is up to something in the French delegation, it's him. And if he wasn't trying to prevent our project from coming to fruition, I can't begin to imagine his real motivation this evening."

"He was certainly lying." I looked back at the door as if this would reveal something about our visitor. "I heard Briand challenging him. Whatever the explanation for Rochefort's behaviour, the order to end the meeting early didn't come from his superior."

His cigarette was almost finished, and I thought he might abandon it and accompany me inside, but he immediately lit another. The life of a high-level political aide is no doubt a stressful one.

"I'm sorry, Ernest, but I think it's past my dog's bedtime," I told him. "I'm not feeling too spritely myself, to be quite honest. It must be the drugged champagne I drank finally catching up with me."

"You should take care of yourself, man." Perhaps he avoided saying my name, as it would have been silly to call me Gilbert when there was no one there but a bad idea to use my real name in case he slipped up later. "I have to say that it's made me more confident knowing that you're on the case."

"Then you have far too much faith in me."

"I mean it." The moonlight caught the curve of his smile.

"Rider told me about what you and Lady Isabella have achieved with this detective agency of yours. I'm glad you're here."

It was hard to know how to respond to this. I've never been the best at taking compliments, and so I simply said, "Goodnight, Ernest. Thank you for not bearing a grudge."

I picked up my dozing dog and stepped inside. I listened at the keyhole for a moment to see whether Rochefort would have heard anything, but the door was thick, as I'd predicted. I carried Percy through the house on my shoulder and he didn't open his eyes. He really could sleep anywhere, though he might have been pretending. Perhaps he'd been taking tips on subterfuge from all these spies and foreign agents. If he started wearing a trench coat with the collar raised, I would need to have a serious word with him.

The louder he snored, the more tired I felt – or perhaps it was the strain of carrying a four-stone animal that finally exhausted me. Either way, I found my way to our sleeping quarters for the evening and climbed swiftly into bed.

It had been a long day and, sadly, the night would be a short one.

EIGHTEEN

I woke to the sound of muffled cursing and instantly wished that I'd brought my service pistol with me.

"Who's there?" I demanded, though it was still dark in my room, and I couldn't tell from where the noise had come. "You should know that I have a gun under my pillow. Now, I'll ask one last time. Who's there?"

"If you've got a gun, then why don't you use it?" a soft voice came back to me and, for a moment, I thought it was Bella.

"Is that you..." I realised my mistake just in time. "... Primrose?"

She stepped into a thin slice of moonlight that broke through a crack in the curtains. "How did you guess?"

There was an almost manic smile on her face. It reminded me of the first moment I'd met her, but something had changed. She was no longer bound by the rules of a polite dinner party and evidently had no fear.

I didn't know what to say to her and so, as is my wont whenever attractive women show any interest in me, I decided to talk nonsense. "Is there something wrong with you?"

"I beg your pardon?" I had already insulted her, so that was good.

"I mean to say... how can I help you?" This was still poppy-cock, but slightly less offensive at least.

She took a few steps closer, and then perched on the side of the bed a short distance away. "I couldn't sleep for thinking of your handsome face." She sounded like a Shakespearean actress all of a sudden. There was something just a little too practised and precise about her delivery. "I'm here because I believe I'm in love with you."

This was ridiculous. I mean, I would have liked to believe what she was telling me but, well... "We only met a few hours ago. You can't possibly—"

She was wearing a peach silk dressing gown that wasn't quite closed at the neck and I watched the deep breath she took travel through her. "You clearly don't know what an effect you have on young ladies like me if you don't understand."

I looked at the door for a moment to check she was alone. It was left ajar but just as dark as much of the room. "I'm not sure that your father would approve of your being in here."

It was at this point that Percy, who had been asleep on the ottoman, stirred for a moment. He looked up at the strange woman in our bedroom and, being the expert guard dog that he isn't, instantly fell back asleep.

"Don't talk of my father. I only want to think of you." She put one hand to her chest and shuffled along the bed to be closer to me. "Can you tell me one reason why we shouldn't be together? Do you deny that you have felt an indescribable longing since the moment our eyes met?"

I would have denied all the above, but someone had dried my mouth with a towel whilst I was sleeping. I couldn't make a sound.

"I desire you, Marius! I need you."

"I need..." I managed. "I need a glass of water." I hopped

out of bed on the opposite side from her and ran to a tall wash-stand where a basin, glass and large ceramic pitcher were waiting for me. I poured myself a drink, tipped it straight down my throat and then poured another.

"You can't think of one reason!" she continued as I tried to get my thoughts in order. My eyes had adjusted to the darkness by now and her hair shone in that sliver of silvery light. "Not even your love for your girlfriend can divide us. So have me, Marius. Love me!"

It finally hit me. "That's the second time you've called me Marius."

She dropped the pretence and began to laugh. "So it is! You know you were rather slow there. I thought you'd realise straight away." She leaned back on her elbows and enjoyed another soft titter at my expense. "I thought you were supposed to be some sort of detective."

"Well, I'm a total amateur, which is certainly 'some sort of detective', as you put it." I confess that I was rather stunned by her act. "Would you like a glass of water yourself, or did you just come here to laugh at me?"

"I'd happily have something stronger if you've got it."

"I don't, as it happens." I looked into the jug and realised that there wasn't even any water left. "Would you care to reveal why you have disturbed my slumber?"

She turned in the light, and her face became a fraction more serious. "If I told you I was an insomniac, would you believe me?"

"It seems I am quite gullible this evening, so you never know."

I returned to the bed and climbed back under the covers. Though the days were warm, the nights in old houses like Mentmore could be ever so cold, and my flannel pyjamas did little to protect me.

"How do you know who I am?" I asked when she said no more.

"A mutual friend of Bella's and mine has met Gilbert Baines. She told me he was an empty-headed bore. You are neither stupid nor dull, and so I put two and two together." She bit her lip then, and I knew there was more to her story. "And then, admittedly, I remembered that I'd seen you in person as well."

"We'd met before last night?"

"Not exactly, but I was at the Mid-Surrey Crime Writer's Awards when you won the prize for best debut. I've always loved mystery novels. I read all the new books as soon as I can get my hands on them. But far more interestingly than my reading habits, tell me why you're pretending to be someone you're not."

"It's a very long story." I felt it had been years since I'd last spent any time at home, as opposed to two short days.

"And I am a very good listener." Now that she was no longer putting on a predatory act, I found her a great deal more charming. She may have been a little jealous of Bella, and more than a touch sensitive around her brother, but her appeal was hard to ignore. Of course, this didn't change the fact that there was no way I could reveal why I'd come to Mentmore Towers, or why I'd had to pretend to be an empty-headed bore.

"Why don't you tell me about yourself?" I said to worm out of it. "We didn't have much of a chance to talk over dinner, what with your uncle dominating the conversation."

She sidled closer to me once more, and it seemed that my ploy to distract her had worked. "What is there to tell? I'm the daughter of a powerful man. My father was a promising politician, and my mother had a lot of money. They wed and had two perfectly spoilt children. I'm sure you know how such stories go."

"I do, but I have a feeling that your version of it might be worth hearing."

Her voice fell to a whisper. "What are you suggesting?"

"I'm suggesting that you're an intriguing person. I knew when I entered the drawing room last night that you were a woman with something to say for yourself, and that's terribly rare."

She punched me then. She actually punched me right in the chest. And let me tell you, it hurt!

"Why on earth did you do that?" I asked in a moan. "I was trying to be nice."

"You just said that a woman with something to say for herself is a rare phenomenon. What did you expect me to do?"

"I should have said *a person*!" I rubbed the bruise. "I meant that finding a person with anything in his *or her* head these days is rare. I wasn't trying to insult womankind..."

"Just humankind in general," she said to point out the flaw in this argument.

"Precisely." I couldn't help but laugh at my own decidedly misanthropic view of the world.

"You're a curious man, Marius Quin." Those huge hazel eyes caught hold of me again and might not have let go if it weren't for the scream that cut the air and made us both flinch.

At first, I thought it was the shriek of a fox on the grounds of the estate, but there was something too human about it. I expected it to be followed by relieved laughter or perhaps the sound of feet stamping down the corridor, but there was nothing.

"What did that—" Primrose began, but I was already out of bed and off to investigate. "Wait, Marius. It might not be safe."

She was right, but that had never stopped me before. At least I wouldn't catch a cold, though, as I took the time to seize a flannel dressing gown from the back of the open door before disappearing out into the hall with Percy just behind me. We padded along the corridor, moving swiftly but trying to remain quiet so as to... Well, I'm not certain that I knew what I was doing, but I had a sense that it would be wise not to make too much noise.

I heard nothing from the bedrooms I passed. The sky was only just beginning to lighten above the second courtyard and, except for the odd maid or footman charged with heating water for the household or baking bread, there was no reason for anyone to be awake yet.

I followed the path I'd walked the night before and came to the Grand Hall as my dog overtook me. He may have been a sleepy creature, but he was an infinitely curious one and was just as eager as I was to find out from where the scream had emanated. Well, it was either that or he was sniffing his way back to his friends in the kitchen.

I approached the marble balustrade of the arched gallery and found what I was looking for. There in the hall below was a man in a black suit laid out face down on the carpet. It must have been a twenty-foot fall if he'd gone over the handrail, and it was unlikely he would have survived. I was about to descend the elegant staircase when something caught my attention on the other side of the hall. There was a figure in black moving calmly along the walkway. I don't believe he saw me at first, but when Percy heard him and scampered faster, he picked up the pace.

"Stop," I called, as Primrose, Castleton and a number of Lord Darnley's assistants appeared in the corridor behind me.

Leaving the new arrivals to see to the fallen man, I bolted after the figure around the walkway to the dark corridor into which he'd disappeared. I stopped to listen before quietly navigating the narrow hallway myself. Percy is smarter than me and stayed behind in the comparative brightness of the gallery.

I listened at every tall dark rectangle which I took to be a door, but there wasn't a sound. I couldn't imagine a killer trapping himself in one of the bedrooms, so I assumed he was hiding in the darkness to jump out on me, but when I got to the end of the hallway, there was no one there. And that was when I spotted his escape route. There was a concealed entrance to a set of servants' stairs that was flush with the wall. Before I could find a light switch, or at least a candle to inspect it, someone appeared from behind me.

"Qui est là?" an (inevitably) French voice demanded. "Dites-moi tout de suite, qui est là?" Which means, *Who's there? Tell me right now, who's there?* in case you didn't know.

He was silhouetted against the light, and I couldn't make out much as I walked back towards him.

"It's me, Monsieur Vidocq," I told the frightened Frenchman as he seized a candlestick for protection. "Gilbert Baines. We met last night before dinner."

I believe it took him a moment to make sense of this reply, but then his knitted brow unravelled just a touch. "What is happening? I heard a scream and people were running past. And now I find you here."

"I can't tell you yet." I was already walking back towards the gallery to reach the vast staircase. He seemed uncertain whether to grab hold of the potential troublemaker, or accompany me, but he eventually followed along to see where I would take him. When we made it downstairs, the others were waiting a few feet from the body.

"I think he's dead." The four words were so distant that they didn't sound as if Primrose had spoken to them. I would have put my arm around her shoulders to comfort her, but Castleton was there to do the job.

"How can this have happened?" Vidocq said as he peered up at the obvious point on the gallery from which the unlucky soul before us must have fallen.

I didn't answer but knelt to look at the figure on the ground. His hands were palm down and his face was twisted to the side, looking away from me. I recognised Monsieur Briand's chief aide at the very moment that Primrose spoke.

"Is he alive?" she demanded, suddenly panicking at the sight before us. "Tell me, is Monsieur Rochefort alive?"

There was nothing I could say to make it better, and so I just shook my head. The pool of blood around his head was still expanding. He would have died the moment he hit the floor.

NINETEEN

The noise of the chase had woken other members of the household. Several French diplomats appeared from the corridor where I'd met Vidocq, and he broke the news in a calm whisper, as, one after another, they came to inspect their fallen comrade.

There was no sign of the French Foreign Minister, and except for Primrose, none of the Darnley clan appeared. Bella watched from the gallery, as if too frightened to come any closer. She saw Primrose sobbing on my shoulder and gave me a typically disapproving glance. So that was good.

I wanted to inspect the corridor upstairs again to see where the servants' stairs led, but with Castleton now attending to his duties, the young lady needed my support. It's a terrible thing to become inured to death. My time on the front line in France had started that process, and our cases over the last year had proven just how much it takes to unnerve me.

A key international diplomat was dead before me, and all I could think of was the mystery it presented. *Did he fall or was he pushed? Was the man I saw fleeing the scene even the killer?*

Should I have woken up every last person there and searched out the culprit?

"The police will have to be called," I eventually said aloud, as the Mentmore staff arrived to assist with whatever came next.

"Yes, sir," the no longer quite so superior butler replied in a demure murmur.

"Not yet." Vidocq was suddenly more commanding since we'd found his boss there, and his colleagues clearly held him in high esteem.

"Be serious." I released Primrose in order to march over to him. "A man is dead. We must inform the police so that they can investigate."

"I am with the police," he said, and several heads turned to look at him. "That's right. I have been working incognito to ensure the security of Monsieur Briand and his staff."

My first reaction to this was, *Well, you haven't done a very good job.* I managed to keep such thoughts to myself, though, and Vidocq continued.

"I am an inspector for the Sûreté de Paris. My superiors they learnt of a threat to the Foreign Minister and his British counterpart. This is why I arrived early yesterday to make sure of the arrangements here at Mentmore." His accent was far stronger than Rochefort's, and though the odd mistake cropped up in his English, the confidence with which he delivered his speech made everyone listen.

"You're not going to call the local police?" I felt I had to confirm.

"I will when I have the permission of the aforementioned gentlemen. There are important matters being discussed this weekend. Perhaps whoever killed Monsieur Rochefort he wishes us to bring the police here. Perhaps all this is a diversion from his main objective."

I couldn't disagree with him entirely, especially as I knew exactly which matters were being discussed.

"Then we should have a look at the body while we wait for the Foreign Secretary to arrive," I suggested to break the impasse.

Bella had found her nerve and come to take a closer look, but as there was an actual policeman at hand, he took precedence over us two meddlers.

"There's a mark on his neck," I said, nevertheless. "I don't see how it could have been caused by the fall. It looks to me as though someone tried to throttle him. When that failed, they must have pushed him over the balustrade to his death."

Vidocq said nothing. His eyes swept over the corpse from one point to another as though he were sketching the dead man in his mind. I was impressed by his efficiency and felt I could learn a lot from him. He moved around the body without touching it and finally crouched to inspect something.

"There's a piece of paper in his hand." Bella pointed to show where she meant, but I felt that Vidocq had already seen it.

"Thank you, madam," he replied, in a tone which suggested that great detectives like himself were not awarded the time, space and silence they deserved. "If you stand back and leave me to my task..." The request faded out, and he leaned forward to extract the piece of paper just as Aristide Briand arrived.

It was strange to have the Foreign Minister there without his entourage, and even stranger to see him in a long velvet smoking jacket and matching sleeping cap. He looked around the bystanders as if trying to make sense of the scene, but he betrayed no emotion over his advisor's fate.

"What have you found?" he asked the detective in their native language, and Vidocq swiftly answered his superior.

"It looks like a torn page." He held up the triangle of ripped paper and I tried to read the scribbled words it bore, but the distinctive French style of cursive writing had always confounded me, and I could make nothing of it.

Briand's face turned quite pale then, and he shouted to his underlings, who had by now retreated to the dining room where breakfast was being laid out despite the tragedy.

"Menier! Lemoine!" the minister exclaimed. "Come here quickly, men. It's worse than we believed."

Bella was standing beside Primrose and her newly arrived brother. Although I had no doubt they had all studied French in their youth, even if they hadn't, the panic Briand exhibited was unmistakable.

When the two aides arrived – one young, dark and handsome, the other stately, grey and stooped – he barked a clear order at them. "Go to my bedroom. Check that the case is still there. Check all the papers. Check the discs."

The two men nodded and hurried towards the imperial staircase in order to reach the corridor through which the presumed killer had escaped. Whilst the others waited for the men to return, I sat beside Inspector Vidocq and examined the body a little more closely.

"Do you know who could have done this to him?"

"I have an idea." As he spoke, he pulled up the man's sleeves to study his fingernails in case a fibre or hair had become lodged there in the struggle that had preceded Rochefort's death. "I was sent here to prevent a criminal gang from achieving their aims. The question more significant, however, is not who is to blame, but why they would choose to kill Monsieur Rochefort."

Again, his eyes traced over the scene, and they soon came to a rest. "There are marks on his wrist. I believe you were right in your conclusion, Mr Baines." Vidocq nodded his approval, then set about searching the various pockets of the dead man's jacket. It wasn't until he reached the last one that he discovered a key on a short chain which he held up to the light. It was the small, flat kind used on briefcases, and I had to wonder whether this was why he'd been killed. Briand had mentioned a case to his assistants. Perhaps Rochefort had refused to hand over the key to the killer and paid the price.

"What's going on here?" A confident voice travelled down the corridor that led to the White Drawing Room, and I turned to see Lord Darnley. He was already dressed in a cream suit with a beige cravat. He didn't wait for an answer but dashed over to us.

"Lord Darnley," Vidocq began, but Bella was too quick and caught the Foreign Secretary's attention.

"Uncle Alistair, it's terrible. Monsieur Rochefort is dead."

As my friend spoke, Spencer Darnley emitted a gasp and turned on his heel to leave the scene. I might have paid him more attention but, in the very next moment, his sister rushed past me towards their father. Primrose remained the most nervous person there and evidently needed the comfort he could provide.

For his part, our host was more concerned with the tragedy that had unfolded that morning than his daughter's emotions.

"Monsieur Briand, I'm so sorry this has happened." Even though his French was first rate, Darnley spoke to his guest of honour in that slightly patronising, over-pronounced manner in which we Brits tend to talk to foreigners. "The poor man must have got up in the night and fallen."

"Don't be so naïve, Daddy," Primrose growled in response. "He was murdered. A man has been murdered here in our home."

Briand may not have spoken a great deal of English, but he clearly knew enough to understand the young woman's comment. He raised one hand to his mouth in silent dismay, and things were about to get worse.

"Monsieur Briand," the younger of the returning advisors said in a soft voice as he approached. He was a handsome Spanish-looking fellow, with black hair, deep brown eyes and the posture of a Victorian debutante. "I'm afraid it's just as you suspected. Everything's been taken."

I believe that Briand looked about for something to support his weight at that moment, as he could no longer bear to stand. The room had been returned to its usual state after dinner the previous evening and, though it was full of those fascinating items I have already described, there was not a sofa or armchair to be seen.

"What's happened?" Darnley had lost his confidence and the muscles in his face pulled taut as he awaited the bad news.

Standing just beside him, Castleton interpreted the scene for his superior. "It's the French code-book and discs, sir. Whoever killed Rochefort has stolen them."

TWENTY

It was at this point that things really went to blazes.

Darnley issued instructions to every aide, servant and member of his family to search for the material that the murderer had taken. The French themselves were up in arms, and no one could decide whether it was a good idea to call the police or shut down the house to make sure that neither the culprit nor the stolen items could leave the estate. It seemed perfectly obvious that it would be best to do both, but a fact that I should have long since realised had finally dawned on me: nobody trusted anyone else.

The French didn't trust the English and vice versa. Darnley and Briand didn't trust their staff or families and, as no one was particularly interested in what we were doing, it was the perfect time for Bella and me to put our detectives' nous to the test.

"It's all very sad," was all she would say when we managed to slink away from the others. She was understandably distant and wouldn't look at me as we spoke.

We'd finally found the Green Drawing Room, and it was certainly the advertised colour. Everything from the curtains to the carpet (and the ceiling to the walls) was wonderfully verdant. Walking through the elegant space felt as if we were exploring a forest.

"It's more than sad," I corrected her. "We're in the middle of an international disaster. Wars have started over less than this, and I can't help feeling that we should have done more to stop it." This may sound melodramatic, but having fought and nearly died in one, I did not take the possibility lightly.

"What could we have done?" She finally turned to me, and her expression bordered on the distraught.

"Well, I spoke to him last night. Mr Rochefort, I mean. Castleton and I were smoking on the porch of the south entrance, and he came out to us."

"You don't smoke," she said, focusing on entirely the wrong point.

"Oh, very well. I was taking Percy for a walk and Castleton was smoking, but then Rochefort came out to us and just lingered there."

"Don't be so hard on yourself, Marius. That doesn't mean you let him die."

I looked for the right words, as I was clearly making a hash of things. "That's not what worries me. Now that I know what happened later, I believe that Rochefort wanted to talk to us. You see, when he came out of the house, there was a peculiar air about him. It's hard to describe, but I think that he wished to confide in us but couldn't."

"So he knew his life was in danger? Is that what you're suggesting?"

"Perhaps." I considered her point for a moment. "Yes, perhaps he was afraid what would happen to him and was looking for help. Or maybe he simply needed a confidant to share his burden."

"What did he actually say?"

I sat down in an armchair beside the immense unlit fireplace, and Bella took the one opposite. Percy had not had a full night's rest and fell instantly asleep on her feet.

"Very little. He told us that he'd broken up the meeting last night because Monsieur Briand got tired working late. That was a lie. I overheard the two of them talking, and Briand barracked his subordinate for the interruption. So what was going through his head?"

"How bizarre." Her gaze travelled off through the window for a moment. "You wouldn't think that an aide would have the authority to do such a thing. Perhaps Briand was too polite to contradict him."

"What I do know is that the biggest calamity for everyone here is not the man lying dead in the Grand Hall, but the papers and discs that his death enabled the killer to steal."

She looked a little confused, but Bella wasn't the type to be beaten even by such a complicated case as this one. "I heard Briand mention discs. I thought perhaps it was code for something, but there really were physical discs taken?"

"Yes, Castleton explained why the French came this weekend. The two countries have created a machine which contains several etched discs with different elements on each for decrypting cyphers. The French had half of them, and the British have the rest."

"Rochefort must have known about the threat. He surely stopped the meeting before the traitor could glean too much information."

"It's possible." I leaned back in the chair and looked up at the ceiling in the hope that some revelation might come to me. "But even if he'd identified the culprit and feared that he would try to steal the discs, that doesn't explain why he didn't tell anyone. The meeting finished at around ten o'clock, and I heard the scream as he fell from the gallery at a quarter past six this morning. What happened in the meantime?"

She was just as baffled as I was, and it was clear that we still couldn't answer such questions.

"Why are we here, Marius?" she eventually asked, to add another mystery to the collection we'd accumulated.

"Is that a rhetorical question?"

"I'm not asking why Rider told us we had to come. He said that they needed us here because I was the only one who could secure an invitation. But I've turned that idea over in my head ever since, and it never made sense to me. His organisation could surely have explained to Uncle Alistair that they felt it would be in the best interests of his family's security to have one of their men embedded here. They could have probably passed Snipe or Boyle off as diplomats."

"I very much doubt it," I replied. "It would be hard to pass those two off as anything but white rhinos."

"Be serious, Marius." She paused to gather her thoughts. "The fact is that we are not spies. We've had some success in our investigations, and I greatly enjoy what we do, but it doesn't make sense that the government would allow us to come here when they could have sent trained investigators. I accept that I have personal access to the Darnley family that they do not, but the least they could do was send one of their men in your stead."

"Thank you very much." I tried not to sound offended by the idea I was so replaceable. I failed.

She smirked at me for being sensitive. "I meant that no one here knows what Gilbert looks like."

"Actually, that's only partially true. Primrose had heard reports of your beau and realised I wasn't him. That's why she came to my room this morning."

This minor detail evidently shocked her. "She came to your room? My goodness, Marius. What will people say about you? What will they say about me?"

"Do calm down, Bella. For one thing, I'm not really your boyfriend."

She got to her feet then and crossed the room to stand as far away from me as possible. "Fine, it's none of my business, but please try not to cause a scandal."

It was hard to know what had most alarmed her, the idea of my being alone in a bedroom with her beautiful adversary, or the looming threat to the nation. "The point I was trying to make before you started on about pretty Primrose..." Even coming from her own mouth, this name upset her, and she had to start again. "The point I was trying to make is that I think I might know why Rider sent us here instead of imposing one of his men on the party."

"Oh, yes?"

She turned away to look out of the window at the sun rising over the great lawn. "The only thing that makes sense is that the men at CG&CS, or whatever it's called, don't trust Lord Darnley."

It was my turn to be taken aback. "Your godfather, Lord Darnley?"

"There literally isn't any other person with that name in the world."

"Yes, but he's the Foreign Secretary, and you've known him your whole life. Do you really believe he could be working for this criminal gang that we keep hearing about?"

"No, of course I don't." She was more sure of herself now and walked closer to address me. "But maybe Rider does... or perhaps he's just being careful, but he clearly chose not to telephone Uncle Alistair to explain what was happening, and he didn't risk involving one of his men in case someone recognised him."

"It rather fits with what I was thinking when we came in here. In this sordid world of spies and espionage, it's impossible to trust anyone."

My comment seemed to ignite something in her, and she clicked her fingers excitedly. "You're right! The coded discs are split between the two countries! That means that the British can't use the machine without the French and vice versa. They don't trust one another to have all the power consolidated in one place."

"Or perhaps they're afraid of one nation spying on the other."

Her eyebrows travelled a half inch up her forehead. "I'm ever so glad that I'm not a spy. Everyday, ordinary murder suspects are far easier to trust than all these horrible politicians."

"I can't disagree with you there." We exchanged cautious smiles, and then I asked the key question. "But what do we do next?"

"I would say that was obvious." She made me wait a few seconds for the answer before we both spoke at the same time.

"We have to change out of our pyjamas," I said, but she went for, "We have to speak to Lord Darnley."

"Very well." I considered the two options. "We'll start with my plan and then move on to yours."

TWENTY-ONE

Along with dressing like a civilised day-dweller, I thought it wise to make my toilette, consume a French pastry or two – while Bella couldn't tell me off – and escort my dog to his favourite room in the house. The kitchen staff were overjoyed to have him back. I'm certain that all thoughts of murder went clean from their heads when they saw the irrepressible hound waddle in there with his tail swishing.

"You'll be all right here, won't you, boy?" I asked, but he had more interesting things to distract him, and so I started my search for Bella.

Though Mentmore Towers was simply vast, and I'd yet to visit the towers themselves, everything important seemed to happen in and around the Grand Hall. Dinners, arguments, murders! It was the hub and heart of the building, and I went straight back there. In the end, a compromise had been reached, and the local police had come to inspect the scene of the crime before being stationed outside to guard the perimeter. With this done, Monsieur Rochefort had been moved somewhere cooler to preserve the corpse. The alternative was to leave him in the direct sunlight that poured through the leaded skylight above him. I could well understand why they went with the first option.

"Gilbert!" a voice called as I crossed the hall, but that wasn't my name, so I kept walking. "Old chap, I'm over here."

I realised my mistake and turned to see Spencer propping up the colossal fireplace. It looked as if it had been hewn from obsidian, and it was adorned with rams' heads, trailing flowers and overly complicated cherubs in white marble. I'd rarely seen such an ugly piece.

"It's beautiful, isn't it?" the young man asked in a dejected tone. "It was designed by Rubens and imported to England by the original owners of the house. And to think, it may have been the last thing that poor Monsieur Rochefort saw before he died."

A truly sorry way to go, I thought but didn't say. Instead, I nodded and muttered, "How very sad. I don't suppose you've seen Bella, have you? We're going to talk to your father." I'm aware that I changed the topic rather callously, but I spied his verbose uncle approaching and couldn't afford to be trapped there.

"I can't say for certain, but his office is in the Amber Room. It's just through the library."

"Wonderful."

When I didn't move, he understood the problem and pointed me in the right direction. "The library's just over there."

"You're very kind. I hope we can talk again soon." I managed to say this quickly enough to escape from his approaching relative with little more than a wave.

The cheerful figure was laughing through the sadness. "Terrible business with the Frenchman, eh?"

"I would love to stay and chat," I called back over my shoulder, "but..." My words trailed off and his melancholy guffaw travelled across the hall as I made my exit. The last glimpse I had of Spencer suggested that he wished he'd come with me rather than being cornered by his uncle.

I found myself before the imperial staircase once more, but I had never heard of a library being located anywhere but the ground floor of a property and so, rather than mounting the stairs, I took a dark passageway off the vestibule and soon found the room I required.

I knocked, heard a soft, "Come in," and did just that.

"I'm glad you found us," Bella told me, as though she'd provided even the vaguest instructions for where I was supposed to meet her.

I did not answer but took a moment to examine the library. It was suitably dry and dusty for an old place like Mentmore, though the shelves were arranged in a curious octagonal formation and covered every wall. The only problem with this was that there were no doors to go through. How could we reach the Amber Room if there was no Amber Room to find?

I was mulling over this question when one of the bookcases swung outwards and Ernest Castleton came through the hidden doorway.

"Hello, Gilbert. It's good to see you again." From the way he spoke, I came to the conclusion that his boss was in the neighbouring room. After all, my half-hearted claim to be someone that I wasn't was largely for Darnley's benefit.

"Have you discovered anything more about what happened to Monsieur Rochefort?" Bella asked before I could say anything.

"I'm afraid I haven't, but Inspector Vidocq is investigating." Castleton displayed a certain hesitancy that was quite different from what we'd seen of him the day before, and I wondered whether it was the murder that was troubling him or something more. "He's been interviewing Rochefort's colleagues and seems confident that we will recover the stolen items and find the guilty party."

I was about to ask whether it had been Rochefort's responsibility to protect the discs, but that would have to wait as there was a call from the antechamber beyond the false bookcase and Castleton motioned for us to go through. The Amber Room was small compared to many of the others I'd seen in Mentmore, but it was a good place to hide from everyone, so perhaps that was why the Foreign Secretary had chosen it as his office.

"Isabella and your young gentleman." Lord Darnley beamed as he rose from his desk. I doubt I'd ever met a man with such a smooth, confident voice before. It came out with the consistency of fresh toffee. "I'm so sorry that I've neglected you. It was unfortunate that your visit coincided with my meeting." He cleared his throat then, perhaps to acknowledge the morning's events without actually saying anything about them.

There was something else that had not been acknowledged. His daughter was lying on a chaise longue against the far wall. Primrose held a white handkerchief to her mouth and looked truly disconsolate. She gave no sign of having noticed us but stared into the middle distance, which was a tricky thing to do in such a small room.

"It's very kind of you to host us here at all, Uncle Alistair," Bella replied with her usual grace. "I'm sure that after all that you've been through this weekend, we are your least concern."

He sat down and motioned for us to do the same. "Frankly, my dear, I wish that were not true. I would like nothing more than to spend a pleasant morning conversing with the two of you, but everything here is in disarray. There is no sense in my pretending otherwise."

"That's rather what we've come to discuss," she continued, and, if I'd had a pad and pencil about my person, I would have noted down this careful phrase for use in future interviews.

She really was the most wonderfully discreet human being when it was required. Bella could communicate complex thoughts and instructions with just the flick of her eyes or the flex of a muscle. In fact, that was exactly what she did now. She took a swift glance towards the tearful redhead on the sofa, and Lord Darnley knew just what she meant.

"Don't worry about Prim. She already knows all my secrets. There's nothing we can't say in front of her."

My companion nodded and, the line of her mouth perfectly straight, she began in earnest. "Perhaps most importantly, we were wondering why Scotland Yard haven't been called about the murder of Monsieur Rochefort."

Lord Darnley's face became oddly crinkled as he considered this thorny question and its unlikely source. "Now, now, Isabella. For one thing, we don't even know that he was murdered. He might well have had too much to drink and fallen in the night."

He died this morning at a little after six o'clock, I decided it was better not to say, but Bella was feeling courageous.

"He died this morning at a little after six o'clock. Considering the importance of your meeting, it seems unlikely that the French Foreign Minister's chief aide would have been up all night drinking."

"And there were bruises on his body," I added, as she had now paved the way for such a statement. "I heard the scream when he fell and saw a man running from the scene. I believe that he escaped through a set of servants' stairs before I could catch him."

"Have you told Inspector Vidocq all this?"

When Darnley looked at me with those fiercely blue eyes, it was easy to understand how he had risen to such a lofty position. The man had an innate power and knew how to wield it.

"Not in any detail. I'm afraid we were busy with..." I decided it would be wise not to finish that sentence. "Vidocq has yet to interview us, but he saw me just after the killer escaped, and I believe he caught the gist of what took place."

He looked at me for a few seconds longer than I would have

expected, and I knew he was trying to get the measure of me. It was the first time that weekend that I was happy to be incognito. Assuming his daughter hadn't given away my secret, that is.

When he'd inflicted that silence upon us for long enough, he straightened in his chair. "I appreciate your concern, but I have discussed the matter with Monsieur Briand, and he does not wish to involve Scotland Yard at this stage."

"Then what about Mr Rider?" Bella replied, her indignation seeping through. "Don't you think he should be informed of what's happened?"

If he'd been surprised by her attitude before, he was positively shocked now. "Isabella, how do you know that name? In what exactly have you got yourself tangled up?"

She didn't answer but looked across at me. It was the wrong thing to do and gave away just what a weak position we held. Darnley was a clever man, and I don't say that because of the newspaper articles I'd read which praised his statesmanship, decision making and political bravery. I could feel it in his presence. He knew how to talk to people, and he knew when he had the upper hand.

"We're not tangled up in anything," I said in the hope he would overlook her misstep. "We are merely two concerned British subjects, and I happen to be a friend of Rider's." A hint of confidence and contempt can work wonders in any argument, and I spread them both thick. "I believe that he would be the person to tell if the situation here has got out of hand."

"I see." His voice fell, and Primrose looked up at us for the first time. "Well, I'm genuinely glad that you feel you can talk to me like this. But do you really think that I haven't considered everything you've just suggested?"

Bella's face clouded over, and I got the sense that she regretted speaking out of turn. "I would never wish to offend you, Uncle Alistair. It's simply that Gilbert knows what happens in situations such as—"

He'd heard enough and wouldn't let her finish. "Do all bankers have your experience, Mr Barnes?"

"It's Baines," I replied, a little sanctimoniously considering that it wasn't even my name. At this point, I might just as well have told him who I really was, but I didn't want him getting any angrier. "But Barnes is fine."

He seemed to relax then. Perhaps my easy-going manner had put him at ease as he put his hand across the table to hold Bella's and spoke more softly. "Your father has told me all about the adventures you've been having with that mystery novelist friend of yours, and I greatly enjoyed Marius Quin's first novel that you sent me last Christmas."

Oh, joy! He got my name right but Gilbert's wrong. It is hard to express just how happy this made me. I should probably mention that I'm not normally a petty person... except when it comes to Bella's truly unexceptional boyfriend.

As Lord Darnley had come to a sudden halt, Bella continued for him. "I believe you're about to qualify that statement."

His smile widened. "You are a wonderful person, Isabella, but you mustn't worry yourself about what's happening here. There are other people who can do that for you. So once you've told Inspector Vidocq all you know, I imagine you'll be free to leave."

I thought she would say thank you and allow us to be ushered away, but she begged another favour. "I understand all that. Of course I do. However, I would be immensely grateful if you could set my mind at ease on a few key matters."

He sat back again, and I felt that, with every word that was spoken, he was re-evaluating the situation. "Are they matters to which you as a member of the public should be privy?"

"For the most part, no. But we do know about them, and so that no longer matters."

He sat motionless for a few long seconds before nodding and accepting her request. "Very well. You have three minutes."

She didn't need to think up her first question. Everything was there in her head, ready to begin.

"Was it Rochefort's job to look after the French half of the code-breaking equipment? Is that why he was killed?"

To my surprise, he turned to his daughter. "Primrose, I was wrong. I think perhaps you should leave us."

The young woman looked from her father to Bella, and it was clear which of the two she blamed for her imminent ejection. Without a word, she got to her feet and sloped from the room.

Her father waited until she had gone and then, even though he had given us permission to discuss the topic, he answered Bella's question in a reluctant tone. "Monsieur Rochefort was the Foreign Minister's chief aide. He certainly had access to the stolen items." This was his diplomatic way of saying yes without saying yes. "As to why he was killed, it would seem a logical conclusion to think that his death was down to the codes, but it is too early to say with any certainty."

Bella swiftly moved on to the next point. "Why do you think he stopped the meeting last night? Monsieur Briand was unhappy with him for doing so."

Darnley smoothed his eyebrows self-consciously with the tips of his fingers. "I cannot speak for Briand. All I know is that the meeting was cut short."

"Uncle Alistair, you didn't answer my question." I'm sure that she summoned the spirt of the little girl she'd once been. She couldn't have sounded more innocent, but then her tone became firmer. "Why do *you* think it occurred?"

He spread his fingers out on the desk before him. "It's pure speculation, of course, but I assumed that there was a problem in the French camp. They'd come all this way to see the culmination of a secret project that our experts have been working on for months, and then it was called off at the last moment."

It was my turn to say something. I knew I wouldn't be as careful in my choice of words as these two diplomats, and so I didn't try. "I find it particularly interesting that the discs for the world-changing code-breaking machine are split between London and Paris."

"Then you are a bright man, Mr Baines."

I crossed my legs beneath the desk and continued. "Evidently you don't trust them, and they don't trust you. You used one another's resources to create this machine, but you couldn't have it in just one place or even make one for each of you because you would be afraid that France would spy on Britain and vice versa."

"That may be true, but you haven't asked a question." He was frighteningly good at... well, talking. I was very glad that we weren't interviewing him as a suspect in the killing, as we wouldn't have stood a chance against such a capable and confident individual – not on our third case at least.

"My question is, do you already know of a threat that exists between our two countries? Is that why you went to such lengths to ensure that the machine could not be used without our knowledge?"

He looked at Bella and then back at me. It was hard to know what he was thinking, as he had added an extra sheen of inscrutability to his hard-shelled exterior. "We are always wary of our foes, and over the years we have learnt to distrust our allies, too. I'm sure you know your European history. We've been bosom pals and sworn enemies of practically every country on the continent. My great-grandfather fought in the battle of Waterloo, and people in my family discussed it so often that it almost seemed like a recent event. It would be foolish to throw caution to the wind, and I do not blame France for taking the same approach."

"So you admit that it is best not to trust anyone?" Bella put to him.

"That's one way of saying it."

"Do you trust your own staff?"

He looked across the room at a painting of a pack of hounds ripping into a fox. "As much as I can."

"Should they trust you?"

He instantly turned back to her, and I was glad not to be the object of his gaze at that moment. I suppose that you don't get to be one of the most important politicians in the country without a certain strength of character. But the intensity of the man was unparalleled; he looked like a bomb waiting to explode.

Luckily, Bella knew how to defuse him. "I'm not suggesting for one moment that you were involved in Rochefort's death. I remember you dandling me on your knee when I was tiny." This was a rather clever inversion of the very thing that family friends say to younger generations. "But we came here for reassurance, and you've yet to offer any."

His demeanour softened then. It was impossible to say whether this was the natural reaction to his beloved goddaughter's words or a more cynical ploy to get rid of us. "You have no reason to worry. I would never do something to harm a project that could offer great benefits to the country I love. A man has died in my home this morning. I have no doubt that the press will discover what happened here and it will create a terrible scandal. My family may be tainted by the event, but I had nothing to do with it."

He looked back up at that hunting scene on the wall, and I had to wonder why it had caught his attention. It was a Gainsborough, if I was not mistaken, and it struck me as being far too large for the small room. It covered almost entirely the space between the window and the door.

"I never doubted it, Uncle Alistair. Thank you so much for

talking to us." As she rose to leave, Bella looked disturbed by the encounter.

"You're very welcome. It really has been lovely to see you, my dear. I hope that the next time we come together will be in happier circumstances."

She nodded but said no more.

"Who knows, Gilbert, perhaps it will be at a wedding." As he said this, I felt as though my every internal organ had started to cringe.

"I certainly hope not," I replied without thinking and then struggled to summon an explanation. "Or rather... Or rather I hope we meet again before any such happy occasion."

TWENTY-TWO

"So you don't like the idea of marriage at all these days?"

I believe that, even if we'd identified Darnley as the traitor and discovered that he was working with a criminal organisation to sell secrets to foreign rivals, Bella would still have been angrier with me for implying that I didn't want to get married.

"I never said that I don't like the idea," I began, before realising that the natural conclusion to this sentence was *it's the thought of your marrying Gilbert to which I object.* That would not have been well received, and so I searched for a way to conceal my true feelings. "It's just that... well, I recently heard a story of a fellow who was set to marry the love of his life when he discovered she was a manipulative murderer. The woman was quite mad, and it all came to blows at the altar."

This did absolutely nothing to resolve the situation. "Oh really. So what you're saying is that no woman can be trusted and—"

As we walked into the Grand Hall, our conversation was ever so unfortunately interrupted by Lord Darnley's brother – whose name, I was about to find out, was Arthur.

"Terrible business, don't you agree, Isabella? I can only

wonder at the strain it will have on poor Alistair. He has enough
to deal with without a death here. And to think, I've heard whis-
pers that the man was pushed! A murder at Mentmore Towers.
Can you imagine such a thing?"

I felt quite happy ten minutes later when the loquacious
chap was still rabbiting. "Of course, I've never been to Norfolk
myself, though I do hear that it's a pleasant destination."

Twenty minutes in, I was starting to question whether the
tetchy discussion with Bella would have been preferable to
having to listen to the man's endless chatter. "I've always been
fond of French cheeses myself, so you might say I have an
affinity for our continental cousins."

By the time thirty minutes had passed, I was sure it would
have been. "Modern printing processes are just wonderful,
don't you agree? Just think of the innovations we've seen in our
lifetime!"

So you can imagine what a relief it was when he finally
declared, "I can't stand here all day talking. I'm on my way to
see my brother and won't keep you any longer." And with that,
he bowed rather foppishly and marched past us as if he'd barely
spoken two words.

"It's not exactly a surprise that only one of the brothers
made a name for himself," I dared venture.

Bella is far more generous than I am. "Poor old Arthur. He's
a very kind man, but he does have a lot to say."

There was no obvious reply to this, and so I turned my mind
back to the discussion we'd had with Lord Darnley.

"You know there was something which went unsaid in the
Amber Room."

"Oh, yes?" Bella pulled me towards the corner of the hall,
and we stood pretending to admire an alabaster bust.

"I assumed at first that Briand wouldn't want to call in
Rider's men or the Yard because he wouldn't know who to
trust."

"Or he felt that the French would be outnumbered. That's not so strange, is it?"

"Yes and no." It sometimes feels as though my ideas are stored in neat files in my head, and it sometimes feels as though a poorly behaved monkey has gone in there and thrown them about willy-nilly. Right then, it was an out-and-out simian invasion, and I had to search for what I wanted to say. "It's understandable, but it might also hide something sinister. What if Briand refused to call anyone more knowledgeable than the local police because he was the one who killed his aide? After all, the case was stolen from his room as he was supposed to be in there asleep. Perhaps he took it and then killed Rochefort to confuse things."

Bella clearly wasn't convinced. "You're suggesting that a former Prime Minister of France is working for a criminal gang and turned to murder to gain access to a briefcase that was already in his possession. You do realise that the man won the Nobel Peace Prize two years ago? I really don't think he's to blame."

I let out a groan of frustration. "Oh, you're probably right. The problem now is that we can talk to Castleton and Darnley until the pigs fly home, but that gets us no closer to understanding how the French see things. I think we should talk to Inspector Vidocq as your godfather suggested."

"Do you think he'll be willing to discuss his findings?"

"I believe it's quite possible," I told her, and we set off across the hall to poke our heads into the dining room. "When we found the body, he seemed open to my assistance. He pointed out certain findings as he studied the scene and was happy to listen to my ideas."

"He wasn't interested in what I had to say." She was evidently appalled by the idea that anyone could be so rude, which put me in mind of someone else who was less than polite to my beloved Lady Isabella.

"Why aren't you and Primrose friends?" I asked as we continued to fail to find anyone from the French camp.

She became a touch defensive. "It's not that we aren't friends, it's more that we don't get on well together and have a rather low opinion of—" She stopped herself as reality dawned on her. "Gosh, you're right. We really aren't friends."

I clapped my hands together in mock celebration. "What a surprise. So could you now take a guess at the reason for the animosity between you?"

She considered the answer for a moment as we walked towards the main entrance. "I suppose it's because of the closeness I share with her father. She was a needy child and never wanted anyone to outshine her."

"And you shone so brightly that she just couldn't stand you, I suppose?" I was at least half teasing, and before she could reply we reached the front door, where a rather large footman blocked our way.

"I'm sorry, sir, madam. I have instructions not to let anyone leave the house."

"We were just going for a walk," Bella presumably lied. I didn't know why she'd taken us to that part of the house in the first place.

"I'm sure you were, madam, but I have my orders from Lord Darnley himself."

"We were just with Lord Darnley. He suggested that we'd soon be able to leave altogether."

"I have been told that I must stand by this door and not let anyone through it," he explained for the third time.

"And what if we were to climb out of a window?" I asked because, as we've already established, I tend to say things that I shouldn't.

His smile disappeared, his polite manner went into hiding, and he took a step closer to intimidate me. "Then one of the police officers who is patrolling the perimeter of the house would grab you by the collar and put you in handcuffs."

I was surprised he didn't wave his fist in my direction, not that I needed any more persuading.

"Of course, forgive me." I put my arm through my friend's to steer her away. "Let's go somewhere a little less... angry, shall we?"

We took the servants' stairs that I'd noticed earlier to the first floor. Up in the still fairly dark corridor, we finally located the French delegation. As soon as we came out of the concealed doorway, I heard the murmur of their raised voices and rushed to the nearest door to try to hear what was being said.

"It's no good. I can't make it out," I told Bella, who did not look impressed by my scheming.

"Is this your plan? To listen at keyholes?"

"Not at all." I may have blushed just a fraction, so it was a good thing it was dark there. "Admittedly, that *was* going to be my plan, but these cursed doors are all too thick. It doesn't help that I haven't spoken French in some years, but it's very hard to eavesdrop in an old house like this at the best of times."

"You don't need to tell me that. I grew up in one." She looked both sad and nostalgic at the same time. "I never managed to listen in on any of my parents' conversations as a child. It made my mischief-making with my brothers far more difficult." She sighed melodramatically but soon recovered her usual vim. "So what do we do now? We don't know why our victim was murdered. The suspects are all hiding somewhere. The police officer investigating isn't as friendly as on our previous cases, and we still don't have a clear idea of how to find the traitor."

I walked to the spot where Inspector Vidocq had been when he'd challenged me that morning. "We're here at the behest of the British intelligence services, isn't that right?"

"I suppose so."

I put my hand against the door. "I mean, there's no doubt this time."

"I don't see how there can be."

"Then it's about time we started acting like spies." I gave the door a cautious push, and it creaked open far more noisily than I'd been expecting.

The space inside looked much like my own and no doubt countless other guestrooms in the house. There were eighteenth-century pastoral tapestries on the wall, and the furniture was far more elaborate than it needed to be. Most importantly for us, however, was the fact that there was no one else there.

From the shoes arranged in a perfect line beneath the bed, and the tidy way the pens, pencils and books were aligned on the desk, I had no doubt that this was Inspector Vidocq's room. That was not the reason we had entered it, though, and I made my way quietly over to the far wall, then pushed up the sash window to peer outside.

"When you spoke before about climbing outside, I assumed you meant on the ground floor," Bella informed me, and sure enough, I could see a few bobbies of the Buckinghamshire Constabulary patrolling the property in their smart black uniforms. I just had to hope they wouldn't look up.

"You're not going to do something foolish, are you?" she asked when I leaned out to look at the gap between that room and the next.

"No, I'm going to do something awfully dangerous, and it's your job to keep an eye out in case anyone spots me."

There was a stone ridge protruding from the building a few feet below the window and so I climbed out of the room and, as if such risky endeavours were an everyday occurrence, lowered myself down on little more than my fingertips.

Bella stuck her head out to whisper angrily at me. "I thought you said this wasn't foolish."

"Fine. It is also foolish, but it's primarily dangerous, which is why you shouldn't be distracting me."

I soon realised that this was a very poorly thought-out plan indeed. Real spies were forever engaging in daring deeds in adventure novels, but perhaps they had no fear of heights. More than the physical difficulty of the task, it was the risk of falling that most unnerved me.

"Of all the stupid things you've done in your life, this has to be the stupidest." This wasn't my internal monologue, but my wise companion, who continued to call down to me in a crabby whisper from the window above.

"What other stupid things have I done?" I knew I shouldn't have posed this question, but as I shuffled along the ledge at the approximate speed of a millipede, that's exactly what I did.

"Buying that inconceivably expensive flat in St James's for one thing. You are not a prince, Marius, and you have no need to live like one."

"Admittedly, that is a decision that I have lived to regret." *Much like lowering myself out of a window to navigate a brick wall*, I thought but didn't say. "However, I don't believe I've done anything else quite so idiotic."

"Oh really? Then what about when we were younger?" she was quick to ask. "Just before you went off to war, you had every chance to—" Her furious susurration came to a sudden halt, and she added in an even quieter voice. "Marius, don't move."

My head was flat against the wall, and I couldn't see what she'd spotted, but I took her advice, nonetheless. I stood perfectly still and could hear someone walking in the garden just underneath me. There was a crunch-crunch-crunching of feet on gravel, which was nearly drowned out by the racket that my heart was making. After a very long minute, I spotted one of the constables skirting the side of the building and, when I felt sure that he was far enough away not to hear, I moved again.

"In my defence," I said, to return us to the unhappy topic,

"I'm a mystery novelist, not a spy novelist. I don't know what I'm supposed to be doing, but this is exactly the kind of thing that happens in Richard Hannay books, so please blame whoever it was that wrote them."

"Buchan."

"I beg your pardon?"

"John Buchan writes the Richard Hannay books," she replied matter-of-factly as I reached the first window in the neighbouring room.

"Well, forgive me for not remembering, but I'm a little distracted at the moment." I contemplated shooting her a sardonic look, but that would have involved turning my head, and I didn't want to lean out any further from the wall than was necessary.

For all my apprehension (and her derision), I was now in a prime spot to hear what was happening in the neighbouring room to the one I had just exited. The windows weren't nearly so thick as the doors, and the figures inside were making quite a din. I had to stand on tiptoe, but the curtains were half drawn, and so I could look in without being noticed. The Foreign Minister was standing by the mantelpiece with his back to the room as his advisors bickered.

"We can't trust the British," the eldest of the aides exclaimed. He was older than the rest, with lines of grey in his hair and a crooked posture like the old man in the nursery rhyme. "I've always said it. They cannot be trusted. How do we know that our trip here isn't an elaborate trap?"

There were some mumbles of agreement before the dark-haired man I'd seen in the Grand Hall stepped forward to make the counter-argument. "Monsieur Menier, with all due respect, I believe you are too rash in your judgement. The British are our allies. Without them, we would have fallen under the imperialist yoke of a foreign power once already this century. What reason would they have for tricking us?"

"Rash?" was possibly all that the older man had heard of his colleague's response. "Am I rash to suspect the worst after our compatriot has been murdered?"

"There's nothing to say we won't be next," an anonymous figure in the shadows proclaimed.

"I just believe we should wait to see what Inspector Vidocq discovers before jumping to conclusions." There was a certain nobility to the way the young man spoke before his elders.

The belligerent Monsieur Menier raised one finger as if beginning a speech in Parliament. "And if the British have seized the discs and are now rewarded with an advantage over the rest of the world, what then?"

Briand had been silent this whole time but turned to his colleagues with an impassive expression on his face. As they raged, the top man actually looked rather calm about the situation.

"The discs!" Menier continued. "Darnley's men had their discs here last night. We should locate them and take them for France. At least that would prevent anyone else from using the machine."

He appeared to be the senior advisor now that Rochefort was dead, and his opinion certainly carried weight with the others, but Briand finally reacted to his bellicose attitude.

"Are you suggesting that we break in to Lord Darnley's office? Or perhaps you were thinking of his private apartment? Why not go a step further and take his children hostage, just to be safe?"

This brought about another burst of discussion as the various underlings argued against one another.

"There's nothing to say that one of you is not the killer," the younger aide cut through the chatter. "Perhaps there is a traitor in our midst."

"You insult us, Lemoine," Menier suddenly yelled, and I thought, *Hello! We could have a late entry into the contest to see who the culprit will be!* If Menier was secretly working for the Syndicate and killed Briand's chief aide, he would certainly wish to dismiss the idea that the threat was close at hand. "I know every last person in this room personally and cannot conceive that one of us would betray our mother country."

"We thought we knew Vidocq, and he turned out to be a *copper*." Obviously, Monsieur Lemoine did not use the English slang word *copper*, but it's a better translation of the French *flic* than *policeman* would have been.

"What are they saying?" Bella asked at that moment, and I glanced away from the drama to respond.

"I'm sorry, but I can't listen if I'm talking to you."

I had no fear that one of the Frenchmen would hear me. They were shouting so loudly I could have been inside the room with them, and they wouldn't have noticed. Slightly more worryingly though, when I peeped back over the windowsill, Briand was right there, looking out across the estate. It was a minor miracle he hadn't noticed me.

"I'd like to know how you can be so relaxed, monsieur?" I heard his elderly colleague put to him. "You do realise what it will mean if our enemies gain control of the machine that our experts helped create."

Aristide Briand had been a mainstay of French politics for decades. He'd been the Prime Minister of France on more than one occasion and was not intimidated by this challenge. In fact, as he stood with his back to the room, I saw a half-smile on his face.

"I deeply regret what happened to poor Clément Rochefort," he turned around to reveal, and I could breathe once more. "He did not deserve to die as he did. However, I will not allow the missing discs to influence my thinking on other matters. As far as I'm concerned, Lord Darnley can be trusted, and the British are our friends. They would not have invited us to participate in the creation of this machine in the first place if they had ulterior motives."

I didn't dare look into the room as before, but I imagined Menier walking closer to his superior to plead with him. "We might at least contact army intelligence or the police back in Paris to aid Vidocq in the investigation."

"I have made my decision," Briand said in his usual calm yet expressive tone.

"But, monsieur—"

"I have made..." he said a little more sternly and paused pointedly between words, "my decision."

The room fell quiet, and I decided that the time had come for me to return to Bella. Even as I came to this conclusion, I heard someone walking in the garden and froze again. Thirty seconds can feel like a lifetime in the right (or perhaps that should be wrong) circumstances. The man on patrol whistled a slow, mournful tune, and it was easy to imagine that he knew I was there and was mocking me with a funeral dirge. And yet he eventually passed by, just as his colleague had a few minutes earlier. I wouldn't judge the local bobbies too harshly. I very much doubt that anyone had instructed them to watch for spies scaling the upper floors of the building.

Whatever their instructions were, the officers failed to spot my derring-do, and I shuffled back to the other window without incident.

"Bella?" I whispered, hoping she might give me a hand up. When she didn't reply, I scrambled over the windowsill myself. It felt much higher going up than it had been coming down, but I must say that this whole miniature adventure had worked out rather well. Perhaps I really was cut out to be a spy, and I couldn't help reflecting how far I'd come since the winter. Gone was the frustrated, uncertain person I'd been when I bumped into Bella on a frozen pavement in Bloomsbury. I was a man of action now.

Well, that's what I thought for approximately fifteen seconds before I closed the window and heard a voice that certainly wasn't Bella's.

"Hello, Mr Quin."

I didn't turn around immediately. I needed to think of an excuse first.

"Inspector Vidocq," I said brightly. "You're probably wondering what I'm doing in your bedroom." I spoke in the singular as there was no sign of my accomplice.

"Not really," he replied with all the pride you might expect from a Gallic detective who believes he has caught his prey. "I saw your impression of a spider from down in the garden. It was most adventurous, but your fun is now over." He pulled out a revolver that had apparently been stored rather carelessly in his trench coat pocket. "Marius Quin, you are under arrest for the murder of Monsieur Clément Rochefort."

TWENTY-THREE

Of course, I should have accepted that things looked bleak when (once again) someone had used my real name. The problem was that I hadn't actually noticed. I'd gone by Marius Quin my whole life and only pretended to be Gilbert Baines that weekend. I'm sure that, should anyone decide to compose a novel or two about the early adventures of Sherlock Holmes or Arsène Lupin, they would have been guilty of just such a faux pas.

"Where's Lady Isabella?" I asked, partly because I wanted to make sure she was safe, but also because I was still trying to devise an explanation for why I was spying on the French Foreign Minister.

"She is not the one with who you must be worried." His English was not quite perfect, but at least I no longer had to expend any energy thinking up translations. "Not least because she is waiting safely outside this room."

"I'm not a killer," I told him, though, since the war, this was not entirely true. It was not the moment to go into technicalities, though, and I left it at that.

"You're here under false pretences, under a false name." He

waved the pistol towards an armchair and I took the hint. "Why should I believe anything you say?"

It was a valid question, and one I would have asked in his position. I could have told him that Rochefort's killer would never be so foolhardy as to climb around the façade of a building in the daylight. I even considered saying that it would make a truly awful ending to a story if the culprit were to give himself away in such a manner. Neither of these were particularly strong arguments, though, and so I opted for something else entirely.

"Until this morning, you were also here incognito."

"This is true, Mr Quin. But this does not change the fact you look incredibly guilty." With his free hand, he pinched each collar of his plain white shirt to ensure that they were neat. I should have known the first moment I saw him that he wasn't a diplomat. His cheap brown suit could only have belonged to a policeman.

I had at least delayed my arrest for a few seconds longer and so I kept going. "How long have you been a police officer, Inspector?"

"I am the one asking these questions," he replied most insistently, then answered all the same. "But I had my start at twenty-one and have been doing this job for two decades." It surprised me to hear that he was in his early forties. There was something old-fashioned about him, and I would have guessed he was at least a decade older. "I began as a regular officer in the countryside – a *gendarme*, if you will – before moving to Paris to work for the Sûreté de Paris – that is the Parisian civil police."

There was something pleasantly pernickety about him and I decided it would be best to tell the truth. "I am not here to cause you or your countrymen harm." Of course, the story of that week was so fantastical that it was hard to know how to tell it, and so I started with, "My name is Marius Quin."

"Yes, I know this." He was perplexed by my stupidity. "I

just used your name twice to show that I know this and that your little ruse pretending to be Gilbert Baines it was not a success."

"My name is Marius Quin," I said once more, as he had interrupted, and I really didn't want him to think I was an idiot. "I am an author, not a spy. I write books – mysteries, in fact."

"And yet you were just on a ledge outside the sleeping quarters of the Foreign Minister of France. What were you doing out there? Watching the birds, perhaps?" He was very expressive with his hands. It seemed that each word he spoke had its own gesture. The fact he was holding a gun at the time made every new sentence potentially the last I would hear.

I shifted in my seat. "Well, I admit I was spying, but not for the reason you think. I had nothing to do with Rochefort's death."

"Oh, yes." The gun waved through the air, and I flinched for the fifteenth time. "You just happened to be running away from the place where the chief aide to the French Foreign Minister fell to his death? Is this so?"

"Not exactly. I was in my room when Monsieur Rochefort died. Ask Lord Darnley's daughter." I suddenly realised what a scandal there would be if the press discovered that such a high-born lady had visited a young gentleman's room in the night. Of course, being French, Vidocq barely reacted, and I continued my account. "We heard a scream and, as I approached the scene, I caught sight of another man who disappeared into the dark corridor where you and your countrymen have your rooms."

"I know all of this, Mr Quin." He was becoming more impatient. "It does not explain what it is that you are doing here."

"I'm here for the same reason you are. I know about the Syndicate, and I've been sent by the British government to stop them obtaining the machine that our two countries have designed together."

His expression changed from angry to cynical with the movement of a scarce few muscles. "I see. The British government, they send a writer of mysteries to stop one of the most dangerous criminal organisations I have encountered in my career. Was Beatrix Potter not available this weekend?"

He was funnier than I'd expected, and I couldn't hide a grin. "I know how it sounds, but you must understand that I'm not the important one here."

"Oh, do not preoccupy yourself, Mr Quin. That fact is becoming increasingly clear."

"What I mean is that the group of people who sent me only did so because my friend Lady Isabella is Lord Darnley's goddaughter." He clearly didn't grasp my meaning and so I continued. "She was able to get an invitation at the last minute, whereas there was no way for a police officer or spy to come without raising suspicion."

"In which case, you also have failed in that respect." Any attempts at humour were now forgotten, and he seethed as he spoke. "You are wasting my time with this ridiculous excuse. Now, tell me for who do you work, or I will have you deported to France to face charges for your conduct."

I very much doubt this could happen to a British subject on British soil, but I was quick to answer just in case. "I'm telling the truth. Lady Isabella and I are helping a man named Rider at the Government Code and Cypher School."

"A school? You are a student?"

"No, that's just what they call it to obscure the truth. Well, actually, they also pretend to be a lawnmower manufacturer..." Why was I making everything unnecessarily complicated? I cursed under my breath and started again. "It's hard to explain, but I only stepped out onto that windowsill in the hope of finding Monsieur Rochefort's real killer. Over the course of the morning, I've come to question whether a member of the French delegation could be working for the Syndicate. I climbed outside to listen to your countrymen as they discussed today's disastrous events."

He became more contemplative and took a few moments to deliver a response. "This is something about which I have myself been curious." He touched his hair affectedly then, and I noticed there was something terribly correct about him. Much like the tidy room in which we sat, Vidocq was well groomed, and though his well-pressed clothes were not expensive, not a hair on his head was out of place. "Monsieur Briand he has known my identity from the beginning and provided me with the information I require, but as an outsider, it is hard for me to know what is really happening between the Foreign Minister and his staff. What would you say is their current thinking?"

I felt more confident now. We'd moved away from my possible complicity to the details of the case. "There appear to be two factions in Briand's group of advisors. Monsieur Lemoine is preaching caution, whereas Monsieur Menier and his followers believe that the English are to blame for Rochefort's death and that you are all at risk. The fear that the code-breaking machine could be assembled by a foreign nation is strong on both sides."

"Ah, Menier." If anything, he looked more troubled now that I was talking sense than he had before. "I have had my eye on him, and I still do not know whether this man he can be trusted." He drummed the fingers of his free hand on the arm of his chair as he spoke, and I was relieved when he finally laid the gun down in his lap. "This house has certainly been divided in two since this morning. It is my belief that this Monsieur Menier may be, as we say in French, a dirty type."

"I think you mean a bad egg," I suggested with a smile.

"No, Mr Quin. I talk not of eggs." He showed no amusement at the misunderstanding. "I mean that Menier could be the traitor. The question is what part Rochefort played. Remember that it was Rochefort himself to whom I reported when in disguise as a political aide-de-camp. Did he stop the meeting because Menier made him do so? Was this in the belief that it would be possible last night to take the discs in the confusion that resulted? I would like to believe that the stolen case it is still hidden somewhere in this house."

"That sounds like wishful thinking to me. But even if you're right, Mentmore is as big as most villages. It could take you days to find it."

He absent-mindedly ran his fingers along the thick silver chain around his neck. "That does not concern me, Mr Quin. I have yet to find a problem that can defeat the great Serge Vidocq."

He was certainly sure of himself, and I rather wished that I possessed such confidence.

"So you believe me now?" I had to ask.

He put the revolver back in his pocket. "Oh, yes, of course. I did not really think you were the spy. You are too... what is the English word?" I was about to suggest impulsive or perhaps foolhardy, but he opted for, "Bumbling! Yes, that is the one. You bumble about the place knocking things over and drawing attention to yourself. A real spy, he works in the shadows. We may have known one our whole lives and never realised it. You are not that person."

"Steady on, man." I took exception to the idea that I had knocked anything over. I thought I'd been rather smart since I'd arrived in Mentmore.

"I have another question for you which the British they would not entrust me with the answer." He paused then and locked his fingers together. "If we are to prevent a disaster, I must stop the killer from taking the English part of the machine. Can you tell me whether Lord Darnley has taken the necessary precautions to assure that this does not come to pass?"

I had to think for a moment. "I'm afraid I don't know. But then I'm not part of his inner circle. As far as he knows, I'm his goddaughter's dull, banker boyfriend. I know nothing of the machine or its protection."

"I see. Then you have told me everything that you know." He rose to his feet in that oddly smooth manner of his. There was nothing rash about Vidocq. I would have readily believed that his every movement had been planned out weeks in advance. "I wish you luck, Mr Quin."

He glided over to the door and would have passed right through it if I hadn't interrupted him.

"Wait one moment. What about some quo for my quid? The least you can do is answer a few questions."

He shook his head unambiguously. "No, it is not. The least I can do is nothing at all." Despite this, he stayed right where he was, and so I put my first point to him.

"Do you believe that Menier killed Rochefort?"

"I do not say this. You see, I have a list of suspects. I have weighed up the potential for each man in the orbit of Lord Darnley and Monsieur Briand. I have carefully pieced together what I can about them, and I am eliminating their names each one separately."

I thought his answer a fudge, but it was clear that he wouldn't tell me anything more, so I tried a different question. "Very well, you're not willing to share your theories, then tell me why you accompanied Briand to Britain in the first place."

His usually resolute mien softened a fraction. "I see no reason not to answer this, as I have already told you as much. My superiors had received word that someone intended to steal the machine that our countries have been building. I was despatched incognito in order to monitor Briand's entourage and make sense of the threat which France now faces."

"You're a good man, Vidocq." Flattery is often maligned, but it sometimes does the job. "and perhaps you'll afford me one final enquiry. Will you tell me how you discovered my true identity?"

"Trust me, Mr Quin. That certain people in this building know who you really are is less significant than the fact that one of them has betrayed his country and may kill again." He opened the door and peered out of it. "I will bid you a good day. You must leave Monsieur Briand alone from now on, or I really will have you arrested."

He tipped his hat to me, slid through the narrow gap in the doorway, and left me with my thoughts.

TWENTY-FOUR

A range of emotions flooded over me. Foolishness was obviously high on the list – that was a given. I'd never felt such an amateur as when coming face to face with that evidently superior detective. I was rather coming to believe that I was a half-competent sleuth until he managed to disabuse me of the idea.

It was not so much what he'd said as the way that he said it. I had the feeling that he'd dismissed my opinions before the conversation had even begun. And I might well have turned over such dark thoughts for some time longer had Bella not come to check on me.

"What happened, Marius? Are you quite all right?"

"I should ask you the same thing," I murmured before finally breaking free of my thoughts. "What did Vidocq do when he found you?"

"Don't worry. He was perfectly reasonable. He pointed his gun at me and told me to wait in the corridor until he left. I was terrified that he was going to turn you over to the police, or worse, shoot you from the ledge to stop you listening to the conversation next door."

It was this gloomy prospect that propelled me to my feet

and out to the corridor. "Then it's lucky Vidocq's not the hasty type. Instead of shooting me, he waited until I'd climbed back through the window, and then hauled me over the coals. He knew who I was and made me prove that I wasn't a traitor."

"Excellent." Any fear she'd had was gone, and she instantly sought a silver lining. "So what did you learn in return?"

"Very little indeed."

"Oh, come along, there must have been something in what he said."

"He asked most of the questions." I thought over my interrogation as we walked towards the centre of the house. "Well, there was one thing, but he's a clever sort, and I don't know if it's true."

She didn't need to say, *Hurry up, Marius. I'm waiting to know what it was*, as her silent expression communicated all that and more.

"He told me that he has his eye on one of Briand's senior advisors. There's a tall grey-haired chap by the name of Menier, and Vidocq suspects that he's the one who's trying to steal the machine."

"And of killing Rochefort, too?"

I had to consider the answer, as nothing was clear in my head anymore. "No, he didn't say that. But he did imply that Rochefort interrupted the meeting last night at Menier's request."

As we walked down the corridor, I could see how happy Bella was to have a theory to explore. "Perhaps Rochefort stole the discs, and then Menier killed him for them?"

"It's possible." I'd been turning the question over in my head for some time. "And if true, it suggests that the Syndicate has more tentacles in more pies than we previously knew."

"In what sense?"

"In the sense that we may be dealing with more culprits than we'd imagined. Almost anyone here could be responsible for the murder or the theft or both. There's nothing to say we're on the hunt for just one man."

Bella chewed the matter over before responding. "If Inspector Vidocq is correct, then perhaps Rochefort broke up the meeting for... some reason. He got up before dawn to pinch the case from Briand's bedroom and... and after that, all he had to do was leave the estate, but Menier got to him first... for some reason."

"That is an imprecise yet plausible theory, except for two things."

She was all curiosity now and smiled as she spoke. "Oh, please tell me, wise one."

"Well, first, the man I saw fleeing the scene of the murder couldn't have been Monsieur Menier. He was too sprightly and young. And second, if Rochefort is the thief, he only drew attention to himself when he interrupted the meeting."

We'd come to the very spot in the gallery from where Rochefort had fallen, and a new idea struck Bella. "Which strengthens the possibility that we are looking for a whole team of people, rather than one killer."

"It certainly chimes with what we know of the Syndicate; they've already done something similar to us," I told her as we moved around the walkway. "They hired us to retrieve Castleton from the police in order to keep their hands clean. Then, when we'd achieved our goal, they paid Inspector Ordinary to kill us and cover their tracks. It's certainly one way for them to maintain anonymity. They rely on contractors and saps like us to influence the world from a distance. It's a clever scheme when it works."

"You almost sound impressed," Bella suggested as we took the stairs down to the Grand Hall.

I took a deep breath to consider the possibility. "I don't mean it like that, but if the Syndicate really is capable of recruiting spies in high-up places and undermining the covert plans of two major nations, they must be good at what they do."

She stopped walking and turned back to look at me. "What concerns me is that Vidocq discovered your real name."

"Well, quite. Out of everyone here, only Castleton knows who I—" I realised that this was wrong even before she interrupted me.

"Castleton and Primrose."

I don't know whether she'd intentionally guided us there, but we were standing in one corner of the courtyard in front of a dark hallway. Bella went ahead of me, and we found ourselves climbing yet another staircase. I couldn't understand at first why we had come downstairs only to go back up again, but we were clearly in one of the towers which gave the house its name, and the rooms we navigated were not accessible from the upper floors. We passed through a nursery, which didn't look as if anyone had played in it in a decade, then a dressing room, before coming out on a landing at the top.

"I assume she still lives here," Bella explained as she approached the door in front of us and raised her hand to knock.

A morose sound travelled out to us, and we entered an ornately decorated bedroom. The walls were hand-painted with delicate murals, and I quickly saw that each one represented a different season. Bare trees framed the windows that looked over the front of the property whilst, just opposite, cherry blossom bloomed right up to the ceiling. This was all very pretty, but it didn't compare to Primrose herself, nor the strange ornament by which she stood in the middle of the room.

"What do you want, Bella?" Unlike the previous evening, she only had eyes for her enemy.

"We've come to check that you're all right, old friend." *My old friend* was a good actress when she needed to be, and her voice was full of compassion. "You looked so distraught in your father's office that we thought we had better talk to you."

Primrose turned a switch on the silver box in front of her, and a mechanism whirred. On the top of it was a delicately constructed orange tree and, after a few moments, a white dove rose up in its centre and began to sing a lilting melody. The bird rocked back and forth as it turned in a circle but, when the song was over, it hid in the metal leaves once more. I'd never seen anything quite like it. It was almost astonishing enough to distract us from Bella's question.

"How do you expect me to feel?" Primrose asked when the room fell silent again. "A man was murdered in my family home. Do I not have the right to be a little glum?"

I decided that any comforting might come better from me, and so I stepped past Bella to do just that. "We're not questioning your emotions. We just wanted to make sure that you weren't suffering."

She smiled then, which I considered a good thing until it turned into a sneer. "Oh, I've no doubt that you've come here out of the goodness of your heart."

There wasn't much hope of my ending a feud that had been raging for years, and Bella asked another question. "Why do you think so poorly of me? I don't understand what I've done in my life to make you angry, but I wish you'd come out and say it."

Primrose turned away completely as her tears returned. This was in marked contrast to the carefree young lady who had visited me in my room that morning.

"Come on, Bella. You know you've looked down on me your whole life. If it wasn't bad enough that I have a useless brother whom my father worships for the letters B-O-Y on his birth certificate, I've had to live in your shadow too. You're the daughter my parents wanted."

I thought this a tragic thing to say about oneself. It was almost as if she wished to be erased from the family. Perhaps it was just an act, but I genuinely felt sorry for her.

"I'm sure that's not true," I replied. "Lord Darnley said when we visited him that he trusts you with all his secrets."

She turned back to look at me over her shoulder. "You mean he thinks so little of me that he barely notices when I'm there. Just as some families chatter away about every secret and scandal in front of their servants, he couldn't care less what I hear of the inner workings of the British government."

"Then do something about it." Unable to suppress her anger, Bella practically bared her teeth. "Your whole life you've complained about the hand you've been dealt when, as far as I can see, you have every luxury and opportunity. You're rich and beautiful, and I wish you would stop pretending otherwise."

I was a mite impressed with not just her passion, but the directness of her words. From my experience mingling with the upper echelons of society, avoiding saying what you really think is considered quite the art form. For Bella to come out with this raw truth was refreshing.

"It's so easy for you," Primrose replied in a mumble, but she was on shaky ground there.

"No, it isn't. I've spent the last few years supporting my father in his illness when no one else would. My mother refuses to stoop to such a task, my brothers claim to be too busy to help most of the time and, if I were to leave his care to the staff at Hurtwood House, I feel quite certain that my father would descend into depression." Her beautiful sea-green eyes seemed to burn and flare. "So, no, Prim. My life is not easy, and as the only girl in a family of four brainy, competitive siblings, it never has been."

Primrose finally looked at her with something other than loathing. I thought at first that her expression was one of pity, but I was mistaken. Perhaps it didn't last, but in that moment she was a little amazed by the girl she had held in contempt for so long.

She dropped into the chair behind her before speaking

again. "How can you put up with it? How does anyone accept this world for what it is?"

Bella's arms hung limply at her sides, and her shoulders relaxed as though she'd forced herself to stand up straight all day and could take it no more.

"I don't have any answers." She walked across the room and sat on the arm of the chair. "I wish I did. I wish life wasn't so hard, but it is, and that means people like us have to work harder for our families to take notice."

"People like us?" Primrose's voice was just as hollow as before. It sounded as if she was repeating words from a language that she didn't speak.

Bella smiled down at her and moved the fringe from her face. "I've always assumed that was our problem. We're just too similar." She paused and took a deep, troubled breath. "Perhaps there is a Primrose or a Bella in every famous family. Perhaps elder daughters are born to take the weight on our shoulders and feel hard done by. I've always hoped that we can forge our own paths, regardless of what our siblings do or how much attention our parents afford us."

I finally understood the contradiction in Primrose. She came across as capable and independent, but she remained very much a child. I'd seen it in her clashes with her brother, and she held onto her grudge against Bella as if they were still fourteen. In contrast to my friend, who managed to find positivity in the darkest moments, Lord Darnley's daughter led a charmed life, but she could only see the worst. A man had died, and yet she couldn't help feeling sorry for herself.

It isn't always easy to sympathise with such people, but Bella did her best. "I'm sorry that you feel the way you do, Prim. I really hope you can see that we are not rivals and never have been." She paused as though it would be unkind to change the topic so quickly, and when she spoke again, her manner had a bluntness to it. "But we need your help to solve Monsieur Rochefort's murder."

"So it's true," Primrose said in a faint voice. "You've come here to play detectives."

"That's not quite the expression I'd use," I had to respond. "We believe that we can help your father to resolve the situation in which he and his colleagues find themselves. From what we've been able to ascertain, the French are just as confused by Monsieur Rochefort's death as the rest of us. But the fact remains that whoever killed him and took the discs must still be in Mentmore. When I saw Rochefort last night before he died, it was as if he had a secret to share. I've come to believe that he knew his life was in danger."

Rather than express vague sentiments as I had, Bella got straight to the point. "Is there anything you can tell us that might be important?"

Primrose's body stiffened as she replied. "I was with Marius when the man fell over the balcony. I'd never spoken to Rochefort or even paid him much attention."

"We're not accusing you of anything, my dear." By this stage, Bella's attitude towards her had become positively maternal. "We just wish to know whether you overheard anything that could help us."

One key word in this sentence sent Primrose's eyes darting around the room. "Overheard?"

"That's right. When you sit in your father's office with him. We thought you might have heard some significant detail that we wouldn't be able to discover."

The answer when it came was oddly wooden, as though Primrose had practised it in advance. "I don't pay a lot of attention to my father's work; I just like to spend time with him when he's here. He rarely comes to stay when Parliament is sitting."

I considered telling her of our encounter with the intelligence services and the mission Rider had given us, but something held me back. Rather than take her into our confidences, I flipped a switch and viewed her as a suspect once more.

"It is rather convenient that you came into my room just minutes before Rochefort was killed." I allowed this point to sit between us for a moment so that she could imagine the worst. "I wondered whether you had been woken by a noise in the house. The killer walking past your room, perhaps?"

"No, it's nothing like that." She would need another moment to consider her answer. "I told you this morning, I suffer from insomnia. I often wake early and, as I had nothing else to do, I decided to have some fun. I knew you weren't Gilbert Baines, and six in the morning seemed as good a time to tease you as any."

As soon as her response was delivered, she slumped once more in her chair. She was not the only one who looked troubled. My puritanical friend frowned at the idea that the unmarried daughter of a lord should enter a young(ish) man's bedroom. Or perhaps it was the fact that, whilst pretending to be her boyfriend, I'd been targeted by another woman. Although I often tried to guess Bella's thoughts, there was no guarantee I was anywhere close.

What I can say is that she reacted to this with a question of her own. "What were you thinking, going into Marius's bedroom?"

Any truce that had been forged between them was now forgotten. "What difference does it make to you? He's not really your boyfriend and you have no claim on him."

Bella was so offended by the implications of this statement that she had to move back across the room. She stood in front of the winter mural, looking as fierce as a Boadicea.

The offence she felt only spurred her on. "My friend here won't ask the most important question, and so I'll do it. Did you know that Rochefort was going to die? Did you go to Marius's room to make sure he wouldn't interfere?"

Primrose screwed her eyes tightly shut and balled up her fists as though she hoped we'd leave and never return. It was a poor plan and, when she looked again, Bella was still just as furious.

"Tell me the truth."

"I don't know anything about my father's work or the French. I don't know what was taken or why it was important. The first time I heard of these codes or discs, or whatever they are, was when Rochefort's body was found. Whatever you think of me, I'm not a criminal."

"Did you tell Vidocq Marius's real name?" she batted back.

"Who's Vidocq?" Primrose's teeth ground together in indignation. "I know less than nothing, and it's not as if I could have killed the poor Frenchman. I was with you at the time, Marius, and I don't understand why you're talking to me like this."

Bella had heard enough. She took one last look around the room and stormed out. I stayed for a moment to make sure that Primrose was not too disheartened, but I shouldn't have worried. She got to her feet and walked back to the silver automaton as though nothing had happened. I watched as she cranked a handle and turned the switch for the dove to emerge. It sang its mournful song and then returned to its hiding place for its owner to tempt it into the open once more.

TWENTY-FIVE

"Well, that was... inconclusive," I said when I found Bella waiting for me on the ground floor.

"I don't trust her. She's selfish and unreliable, and it's impossible to know whether anything she told us is true."

She was still on edge from her encounter with Primrose. She leaned against a plain white wall but couldn't quite stop moving. Her hands were restless at her sides, and she kept shaking her head as if trying to come to terms with what we'd seen and heard.

"I know the history you both share is a complicated one, but there's nothing to say she's connected to the Syndicate or involved in Rochefort's death. The fact she came to see me at the same time could just be a coincidence."

"So we should rule her out as a suspect? Is that what you mean?" Her agitation was clear in the uneven tone of her voice.

"Of course not. I'm saying that her attitude towards you is not proof that she is a criminal. You're hardly an impartial interviewer."

"Oh, please, Marius. Be reasonable. She turned up at dawn, and that just happened to be the moment at which Rochefort was murdered. Oh, and the death conveniently happened within earshot of your room. Are you so blinded by her charms that you deny she could have set the whole thing up and used you as her alibi?"

I couldn't imagine how to answer such a question, and so I didn't try. "I just think that I should have gone to speak to her on my own."

"So now it's my fault?" She gasped and, though it was dark in the little vestibule at the bottom of the stairs, I could see the anger colouring her cheeks. "Really, Marius, you can be quite insufferable."

She pulled away, but I caught her hand in mine and wouldn't let go. "That's not what I mean, Bella, and you know it." I kept my voice stern and steady. I didn't want to upset her further. "You're letting her get under your skin, but you're smarter than that. All I meant was that the two of you don't get on well, and we can't use the way she spoke to you as evidence of her complicity in a crime."

Bella stared right through me, even as she relented. "Oh, maybe you're right, but there's something about Primrose that always riles me. I lose my head around her every time we're together."

"Then we'll need to think of a way to take your mind off it," I replied and started the walk back to that elegant museum in the centre of the four towers.

"How do you plan to do that?"

I spotted other wind-up automatons in the Grand Hall, including an intricately constructed peacock whose immense painted tail must have come to life just like the bird in Primrose's room. However, I had a far less extravagant diversion in mind. "We're going for a stroll."

I think we both realised at this moment that we did not normally hold one another's hands when sleuthing – or at any other time for that matter – and I dropped hers as though it had scalded me. In return, she widened the gap between us, and we walked side by side in silence. Perhaps this wasn't the warmest gesture on my part, but it was bad enough that I had to pretend to be her boyfriend in front of people, without acting like one in private.

She didn't appear to take it too personally, at least, and by the time we reached the kitchen, I believe she had recovered from her run-in with Primrose. It must have been the mid-morning lull between breakfast and lunch as, rather than attending to their duties, the kitchen staff had placed Percy on a chair and gathered around to feed him scraps.

"Who's a lovely boy?" the schoolmarmish cook asked as she dangled a chipolata above his nose. Percy acknowledged that he was, indeed, a lovely boy, and one of the maids took her turn to spoil him.

When this had gone on for over a minute, I cleared my throat loudly to make sure they noticed us.

"Ah, Mr Baines, sir." The cook became flustered and shot to her feet to see to whatever was steaming on the range. "We were just giving your dog a spot of elevenses."

"That's right, sir," her colleague confirmed. "Flopsy-Pup has a very healthy appetite."

"Flopsy-Pup?" I asked, a little perplexed.

Cook smiled broadly as she dried her hands on a tea towel. "You didn't tell us his name, sir, so we made one up for him."

Flopsy-Pup looked ever so cheerful and evidently didn't mind his whimsical new moniker. Personally, I was not so keen on it, but then the name Percy had been foisted on him by my uncle and I hadn't complained then either.

"I'm here to take Percy for a walk," I told them, and they looked a touch guilty and bowed their heads as if I'd repri-manded them.

Bella was on hand to make them feel better. "We truly

appreciate all the attention you've given him. He's clearly been ever so well looked after."

They curtseyed, and we escorted Percy to the door that gave onto the kitchen gardens. We closed it behind us, and there was a gentle burst of laughter as the dog-spoilers went about their usual business. I didn't mind them overindulging him, though it was probably a good thing we interrupted his (at least) second meal of the day. He was heavy enough already, and I would surely have to carry him again soon.

"Excuse me, sir, madam," another brawny footman called to us when he saw that we had dared set foot outside the building, "I'm on strict instructions not to allow anyone through that door."

"Fine, then I'll have to tell my dog to do his business in the Limoges room. Or perhaps the entrance hall would be preferable?"

He looked uncertain how to tackle the problem, and so I offered a solution.

"I'll tell you what. You can stand at your post by the door, and Lady Isabella and I will take Percy here to the edge of the forest. Your superiors know who we are, and you can watch us the whole time. I can assure you that I am not concealing any stolen items about my person nor has my dog eaten them."

He was less than convinced by the plan but shrugged and looked away, as though to say, *Very well, but I don't wish to hear any more about your creature's filthy habits.*

"You're very kind," Bella replied with no little sarcasm evident.

Once we'd left the walled garden, we continued through the wide archway to the main lawn. The footman watched us suspiciously the whole time we were out there, which only strengthened my belief that it had been a good idea to bring Percy that weekend. Bella and I could speak without fear of being overheard, even if we were interviewed twice more by patrolling constables before we got to Percy's latrine.

"Now perhaps you can tell me why we're out here," Bella said once we'd reached the treeline.

"To view things from a different perspective."

The dog once known as Flopsy-Pup sniffed about the place as I turned to look back at the house. In swathes of sunlight, Mentmore Towers looked like a temple from some eastern land. I'd never got much further than Germany in my travels but, just for a moment, the towers reminded me of Turkish minarets, and the building itself, with its sandy ashlar stone, of a great Egyptian pyramid. This would not help me solve the puzzle before us, but it put me in mind of what I wanted to say.

"I think we should imagine for a moment that we are actors in a play who have only been given half of the script. The fact is that Rider and his associates were happy to send us to Mentmore, but unwilling to tell us of the machine that we ultimately came here to protect. Castleton was almost kidnapped for that same knowledge, and any number of sinister forces will evidently stop at nothing to possess it."

Bella reflected on this for a good few seconds before responding with a question. "Are you saying that we've been manipulated in some way?"

"Oh, undoubtedly." I watched Percy scrabbling about at the bottom of the trees, and I decided it wasn't so different from what we ourselves had been doing that weekend. "I'm not saying that the spies who saved us from Inspector Ordinary have intentionally tricked us, but they certainly haven't made our task any easier. We're supposed to crack an uncrackable problem in a world of politics and deception with which we're in no way familiar."

"It is hardly a perfect situation. I'll give you that," she agreed. "So how can we resolve it?"

"I really can't say," I answered unhelpfully, but she was too busy thinking through the problem to listen to my answer.

"Perhaps the enigma we must solve concerns not just the events we have witnessed here at Mentmore but the whole uncanny weekend. Perhaps Inspector Ordinary's visit to your flat could be the real clue to uncovering everything. Or maybe there's something we've missed in the trail we followed to Hastings that could help us understand who stole the French discs."

"Another problem we face is that this is no ordinary case of elimination," I replied as I considered her point. "I could make a list of names, but unlike in our previous investigations, we can't even interview half of them to rule out potential culprits. The French diplomats aren't available to us, and we haven't even excluded the possibility that a member of the Darnley family is involved. Primrose can't be the killer, but she might well have stolen the discs and then come to my room while someone else dealt with Rochefort. There's still her brother to consider, and who knows what Lady Darnley and her brother-in-law were doing at the time of the murder."

She bit her lip as she considered this stark possibility. "I would love to dismiss the idea that people I've known my whole life could betray our country, but I have already learnt once this year that it's best not to rely on opinions we have held since childhood." She leaned back against the trunk of a tree and tipped her head to look at the branches above. "I just have to hope that the culprit turns out to be someone who means nothing to me."

"Monsieur Briand's advisors would fall into that category, and they're certainly manipulative enough. In addition to Vidocq's chief suspect, Monsieur Menier, there's a handsome young fellow with very dark features by the name of Lemoine. They were swift to appear at the scene of the crime after the killer had got away, and I overheard Menier suggesting that Lord Darnley organised this weekend in order to steal the other half of the machine." I paused before adding a small caveat. "Briand wouldn't hear a word against his British counterpart, but he remains a suspect himself – especially as he argued with the man who we found dead this morning."

She stared into space as the information I had just unloaded filtered through her brain. "This really is very different from our previous cases. And you're right that simply naming the potential killers won't help us narrow the field." I was about to ask what the solution was when she told me just that. "What we need to do is consider the questions that remain and work backwards from there. I don't just mean the identity of the traitor, or why Rochefort was murdered, but all the minor points that could lead us to the truth."

I never found my former love so blazingly beautiful as when she was discussing one of our mysteries. Her jet-black hair took on a silvery gleam in the daylight and her eyes were so bright that the sun was surely jealous. Despite all of that, it was the challenge before us that excited me most.

"First, I'd like to know exactly why Rochefort interrupted the meeting. If he was the thief, and he planned to steal the various parts of the machine, it would have been better to see how it operated. Even if he was following someone else's orders, it was a strange thing to do."

Bella crouched down to stroke a relieved-looking Percy. "Yes, but, if the Syndicate wished to gain information on the French, as Briand's chief aide, Rochefort would be the best person to recruit. He's surely the most likely thief."

I kept switching between feeling certain that we were on the right path to doubting everything we concluded. "Perhaps, but anyone who knew where the Foreign Minister kept the discs could have taken them."

"Oh, this is hopeless. We're going around in circles. We'll have to ask Ernest," Bella said, looking back once more to the house. "He must know more about the interaction between the

French and English camps than we do. It's even possible that Inspector Vidocq has entrusted him with more details of his findings."

"Yes!" I clapped my hands together and startled my dog. "That's exactly what we'll do, but there's plenty more we need to discover, too. It's as you were saying a moment ago; the events that preceded our arrival could be just as relevant as what we've seen here. And what I'd most like to ask about is the moment that started this whole spiralling tale. We need to ask Castleton about the first attempt that was made to kidnap him."

Energised by this resolution, I was about to march back to the house when she called to me.

"Wait, Marius. I still don't understand why we came out here."

"Because, my dear friend..." I stopped to look back at her. "...no one else was going to walk Percy, and I didn't want him to spoil the carpets."

TWENTY-SIX

It was not just Percy who had benefited from our time in the gardens. Our turn in the fresh air provided a change of pace for all three of us. I finally felt that, even if I couldn't yet identify the thief, the killer and the traitor – or say whether they were one, two or three separate people – I at least now knew which questions we needed to ask.

Inside the house, there was a hustle and bustle to Mentmore. Maids and footmen dashed about preparing for the coming meal. I noticed that the French diplomats had dispersed, and several had decamped to the White Drawing Room, where the discussion I had overheard appeared to still be raging. There was no sign of their boss, but when we went in search of Castleton in the library, Lord Darnley was in the antechamber beyond, dictating a letter to a young chap whom I took to be his personal secretary.

Bella closed the door to the Amber Room so that our conversation would not disturb her godfather. Castleton himself, meanwhile, looked as though he was approximately a week behind in his work. He was desperately organising papers into piles and didn't have the time to glance up at us.

I should probably have left it to Bella to say something discreet, but I finally had a theory for the mystery we were supposed to be solving and so I did what I could to get his attention.

"Here we are," I tried, but that sounded terrible, so I added an equally incongruous, "What a day!"

He finally looked at us, but his eyes soon darted away again. "I'm sorry, both. I really am. I don't mean to ignore you, but Lord Darnley is about to have a tête-à-tête with Monsieur Briand. The two of them are meeting in the du Barry Room, and I'm barely ready for it."

He was quite nervous as he bundled the main pile of papers into a manila folder.

"You poor thing, Ernest," Bella tried. "You'll do yourself an injury if you continue like this."

I assumed she meant a heart attack before he reached forty – although a paper cut was surely the most immediate danger.

He seized two more piles from the shelf on the wall and ran them into his superior's office. A moment later, Darnley's young secretary came out carrying the files. Our host was only a little way behind, dressed in the same cream suit that he'd worn when we found Rochefort's body. He walked past with a rather grave air and was apparently too preoccupied to notice us. Judging by this hectic scene, I could only imagine that the events of the weekend were coming to a head.

His work now done, Castleton hurried back to the desk and collapsed in his chair.

"What can I do for you?" he asked once he'd poured himself a tumbler of whisky and swallowed a slug of the stuff. "I'm sorry that you've seen me in such a state, but I can't tell you how important this meeting is. Even if we've lost half the machine that our experts have spent so long designing, the continuing co-operation of our two nations is vital."

I could see just how nervous he was from the bulging vein

in his neck. To put him at ease, I pulled back a chair from the other side of the desk and offered it to Bella before taking another for myself. I can't stand it when people hover unnecessarily, and I hoped this would calm him somewhat. I needed him to know we were in no hurry and that he could take his time – even if this wasn't true.

"You've evidently had quite the morning, and we don't want to put any more on your plate, but we have some questions for you."

He let out a sigh of relief and his usual cheery smile returned to his face. "Please, fire away. I feel a lot better now that my work is done."

It was customary for me to let Bella speak first and so I signalled for her to do so.

"First, we'd like to know where the French were keeping their half of the machine. Could anyone have taken it, or was it in a safe of some description?"

Castleton peered first at the door, then through the window to see whether anyone could hear. This wasn't enough to reassure him, and so he pulled shut the thick blue velvet curtains to cut out the blinding sunlight and dampen his words.

"Monsieur Briand told Lord Darnley that they were in a case beneath his bed. The case had been with him wherever he went, but he hadn't expected anyone to risk coming into his bedroom to steal it in the night."

"So the case itself was taken?" Bella pronounced each word as though precision was of the utmost importance. "If so, the thief would have had to break it open elsewhere."

"You're absolutely right. In fact, it has since been found on a staircase that leads to the wing where you both have your rooms. The mechanism had been forced and the contents removed. From what I understand, Rochefort had the keys to the case on him when he was killed. I rather wondered whether he was pushed over the balcony when he wouldn't give them to the thief. No doubt the killer would have retrieved them, but you turned up and disturbed the plan."

"I see." I doubt I sounded convinced. "That is certainly a possibility. Though it wouldn't explain what Rochefort was doing up before the dawn, fully clothed. His behaviour since he arrived strikes me as suspicious."

Bella added a touch more mystery to an already puzzling scenario. "And if he was the one who stole the discs, then there must be a second traitor."

"I suppose it's unlikely that he simply fell over the balcony in the process of stealing his prize?" Castleton posited before swiftly dismissing this potential solution. "No, that doesn't make sense. If he was the only one involved, the discs would have turned up elsewhere."

"There were bruises on his wrists, too," I added. "I'm fairly confident that he was intentionally pushed over the handrail after a struggle with the killer. He died on impact with the floor."

We'd gone back to where we'd started, and so I shifted the discussion on to my main concern. "Bella raised a point earlier that I believe could be important. The answer to this riddle may not be in what we've seen this weekend, but the events that brought us here. I don't mean the theatrical treasure trail that the Syndicate laid out for us to follow – that was a ruse to make us believe we were brilliant detectives who would have no trouble saving an innocent man from his burly captors. We should look at the parts of the story that we know are genuine. The first attempt they made to kidnap you could be essential."

Bella allowed herself a soft laugh at the idea that we were brilliant detectives, but Castleton had fallen quiet.

"To be frank, I'd rather not remember it, but I'll tell you what you need to know if you think it will help." He required another long sip of his drink before he could begin. "I'd finished work at 54 Broadway and was walking through the park on my way home. There was a dark stretch of path without street-lights, but I didn't think anything of it. A man came at me from the shadows with a gun. He told me I'd have to go with him if I wanted to live. I assumed at first that he was a common robber, but then he called me by name. Before I could decide what to do, a colleague of mine happened upon the scene."

"So it was your colleague who shot the man dead?" I had never been clear on exactly how he'd been saved.

"That's right, but my assailant gave Lieutenant Snipe no option. He lifted his gun and was about to pull the trigger when Snipe fired. I don't mind telling you how frightened I was."

Percy was sitting on *my* feet for once and yawned to show that he had heard of far more frightening scenarios... or perhaps he was just tired.

"I can only imagine how horrible that must have been for you." Bella spoke in her usual compassionate tone.

"Not as bad as it was for the dead man. Still, it's a blasted shame that we couldn't interview him. If the Syndicate are as cunning as my superiors believe, it would have been a rare opportunity to gain information on them, but their agent took his secrets to the grave."

I tipped my head to one side to think. "And that was the point at which Rider decided to send you off to Hastings?"

He nodded. "Yes, Mr Rider didn't dare take any risks. He increased security around Lord Darnley's office, and I was always supposed to come to Mentmore yesterday. You and Lady Isabella merely brought forward my travel plans."

We exchanged a warm look as he summarised our interference with this pretty euphemism.

"Is it possible that the criminal in the park was there to recruit you to the Syndicate?" Bella suggested.

He frowned as he considered the question. "I suppose it is. Though I would say it was a bit late for that. They evidently have at least one infiltrator here and, to me, Rochefort's death suggests that the Syndicate's plan has been in place for some time."

It felt as though our ideas were finally flowing and, even if we hadn't landed on the right one yet, we were getting closer with every try.

"What about the time you spent in my flat?" I put to him. "After he left us unconscious, what did Inspector Ordinary actually say to you?"

His gaze fixed onto me as he cast his mind back. "He said that the two of you had gone to buy food for a feast to celebrate my rescue. That was when he gave me the champagne. He looked so much like Rider that I wondered whether he was one of our men that I hadn't met before. However, he didn't give me his name, which I found strange, and then his plying me with alcohol was the final straw. My hackles were already up from your intervention in Hastings, so you can imagine what I thought of him. I didn't risk drinking the champagne, and I got out of the car just as soon as I could."

"Of course, the real question is what the Syndicate hoped to achieve by kidnapping you." This was Bella's neat summation rather than mine.

"That's the thing. I don't believe I know anything in particular." Castleton dropped his head into his hands at the very thought of the interrogation he'd avoided. "I'm just a messenger boy, really. I assist Lord Darnley in his work and liaise with the GC&CS. But I wasn't involved in designing the machine and don't know how it works."

"They evidently thought you did," I replied. "I suppose their own intelligence let them down. They didn't go about your abduction in the most professional manner. A man in a park with a gun is not the subtlest tool they could have used."

"Nor are a pair of amateur detectives with only two previous cases under our belts." Bella seemed to enjoy emphasising our inexperience.

"Whoever these criminals are," Castleton began, "they clearly don't wish us to uncover their identities."

"Yes, but relying on outside contractors for this sort of thing must be a haphazard way to go about one's business." I tapped the desk a few times as I considered what we knew. "I suppose that no one would expect such a powerful organisation to use amateurs, and they have more experienced men like Inspector Ordinary to pull the strings and tidy up problems whenever they arise. The first attempt to kidnap you didn't go to plan, and so Ordinary stepped in and hired us. When we succeeded in retrieving you from Hastings, he came to claim his prize."

"The Syndicate didn't reckon on your suspicious mind and quick thinking, Ernest," Bella told him with an appreciative smile. I realised then that, had she fallen in love with a capable fellow like Castleton, I would have wished them both luck. It really wasn't the time to be thinking about her inferior boyfriend, but that's what I was doing.

Ernest Castleton, it turned out, was not just capable but terribly modest. He changed the subject rather than acknowledging Bella's high praise. "So we know a little more about the blighters we're up against, but where does that put us?"

"How do you mean?" I asked in reply.

"Briand and his party are to leave Mentmore this afternoon. Are we to assume that, if one of them is working for the Syndicate, he will attempt to secure the other half of the machine today?"

Bella offered her perspective. "That must be it. It will be far easier for the traitor to achieve his goals this weekend than once the discs have returned to London. Lord Darnley must be warned."

Castleton sank lower in his chair with the same fatalistic expression he'd worn when we arrived. "There can be no disturbing him while he's engaged. He's given me strict instructions that, even if the Russians have invaded or London is burning again, he won't open the door until his meeting with Monsieur Briand is finished."

As they'd been speaking, something dawned on me that I felt I should have realised before. I wasn't ready to express my thoughts just yet, but I knew that, much as Bella had concluded, the final stages of our enemy's plan were already in play.

"I'll tell you what," Castleton said as he pushed his chair back from his desk and rose to standing. "I'll go to the du Barry Room and wait outside. That way, I'll be able to warn him of the trouble we're facing as soon as he emerges."

"That's the most any of us can do," Bella said with a grateful nod. "And we'll be selfish and unhelpful by having lunch. At least it will keep us occupied."

"I don't blame you for wanting to recover some energy." A brief look of amusement shaped his features, but it died away again as the reality sank in for all of us. "And it's a good idea to keep an eye on as many different suspects as possible."

They said a friendly goodbye, but I hardly heard a word of it. Over the last minute or so, the most monumental shift had occurred as various pieces of the evidence had been shaken up. My mind was consumed with a troubling idea, and I felt certain that it would only be a matter of time before I discovered the truth.

TWENTY-SEVEN

I know that we dropped Percy off at his regular haunt, but I don't remember our journey from the kitchen to the dining room. I was lost in a fog, and only emerged into the light when someone addressed me over the luncheon table.

I repeated the question before recalling that "Hargreaves Bank" was where Gilbert worked and that I was supposed to be him. "Yes, that's where I work."

"I know it's where you work," Lady Darnley replied a little irritably. "I was asking whether you know James."

"Oh... James." I had a good theatrical scratch of the head. "No, I can't say the name rings a bell."

Her chin pulled in closer to her neck. "But James Hargreaves owns the whole institution. Surely you know him. Bella's mother told me that you were the head of investment banking or some sort."

"Oh, James!" I replied, as if I finally understood the word we had both now uttered more than once. "I didn't know who you meant because I always call him Jimmy."

"You call Lord Hargreaves Jimmy?" Her pupils grew in an instant.

"That's right." It was too late to retreat from this nonsense. I'd told the lie, and I would have to make the most of it.

"Viscount Hargreaves of Totterdown allows his employees to call him by such an informal epithet?"

"No, of course not," I responded through gritted teeth. "The very idea is quite unthinkable. We only call him Jimmy behind his back."

I had hoped this would be preferable to the prior implication, but she looked even more horrified. I could only imagine how she would have reacted if I'd told her that I was actually not a banker but, in truth, a liar and a feckless author.

"This is all very interesting," the woman's brother-in-law intervened. I was once more grateful for Arthur Darnley's loquacious tendencies. "But I was talking about the continuing potential for the Garden City Movement to transform Britain and solve our long-term housing shortage. Did you know that Letchworth Garden City had the very first roundabout twenty years before the word entered common parlance?"

He continued chattering like this for most of the meal, which, much like the night before, gave me the perfect opportunity to observe my dining companions. Lord Darnley's whole family was there. Primrose looked just as miserable as when we'd seen her in the east tower, and her brother wasn't a great deal chirpier. He stirred his dessert with his spoon as though searching for something deep inside his bowl.

There was also a large cohort of Darnley's colleagues at the neighbouring table. I noticed that the private secretary we'd seen in his office was looking about the place, much like me. Our eyes met through the lines of diners, but then he immediately glanced down at his plate. I really didn't like the thought of yet another suspect presenting himself at this late stage. I feel that all potential killers should be introduced early on in a case so that everyone has the chance to consider their guilt.

Bella did her best to broaden the conversation to include

anyone other than Uncle Arthur, but whenever she seemed to have found a foothold within it, he would seize control once more. Even Lady Darnley, a tall, powerful woman who still possessed traces of her daughter's red hair and comely looks, sat there in meek amusement as the chatter continued.

At one point, Inspector Vidocq poked his head through the doorway and appeared to count the people inside, much as a schoolteacher will when taking the morning register. I would love to have known all he'd been up to that weekend, but he was the sort of detective who knew how to keep his mouth shut. I can't say I blamed him; he was clearly a competent sleuth and didn't need meddlers like me getting in his way.

"I'm sorry. I can't do this," Primrose announced to break into the scene. I don't believe it was the food – or even her uncle's blathering – that she could no longer tolerate, so much as the polite pretence she was expected to maintain. "A man was killed in the room next door, and we're sitting here as though nothing is wrong. Fruit salad and light confabulation can't cover the tragedy we've all witnessed. I can't..." She looked to the door and, on the point of tears, found what she wanted to say. "I can't just act as though everything will be all right."

She flew from the room, her long silken skirt billowing around her as she went, but hardly anyone reacted to her dramatic exit. A few of the English civil servants grimaced at these inappropriately emotional words, but our hostess laid down her spoon and smiled as if she hadn't noticed anything was amiss.

"Arthur, that was very interesting what you were saying about Ebenezer Howard." Thanks to this calm response from Lady Darnley, the scene continued much as it had before. Spencer was the only person whose demeanour changed. He suddenly became alert and talkative, and he even managed a nervy laugh.

"Dear old Prim," he said with a rub of the hands over his

empty bowl. "She does love to make theatre out of everyday life. When we were children, she would make us dress up as famous characters from Shakespeare or ancient history. The number of times I had to play Julius Caesar to her Cleopatra! It was... well, I lost count."

"I remember that." Bella was apparently happy to go along with this switch in mood. "You used to put on a real spectacle for me."

I could see the toll it was taking on the man to maintain his jovial tone, and I had to assume he felt much the same as his sister. "Oh, that's right. You were here too. What times we had. What larks."

There was something not quite right about the way he spoke. It was more than nerves or Primrose's outburst that had upset him. I wondered for a moment whether he knew more about the events of that weekend than we'd previously envisioned. Perhaps we'd interviewed the wrong sibling, and it was Spencer who could guide us to the killer. I thought back over his behaviour that day and began to notice a pattern.

"Father never had time to watch us, of course," he continued in that same excitable manner. "He had more important things to do than being with his children."

This sudden outpouring of emotion resulted in a most unprecedented occurrence. Spencer's uncle suddenly stopped talking. I don't think I'd been in a room with the man for longer than a minute without him blurting out a burst of verbiage, but he was now silent. The drop in volume was uncanny as, even though his nephew continued to bewail his misfortune, the chatter that had previously accompanied him was now absent.

"There's no need to discuss such things, dear boy," Lady Darnley told him as she squeezed his shoulder. It might have looked like an affectionate gesture, but I was sitting just opposite them, and I could tell that she dug her nails in. It would not be enough to keep him quiet, though, and he looked at her as though she was just as much to blame as his neglectful father.

"You know that I'm telling the truth, Mother. Daddy barely saw us even when we were in the same room. The only way he would have paid me any attention is if I had covered myself in government reports and budgetary statements."

In the low voice people use when they're trying to prevent their children from making a scene, she rebutted his claims. "Your sister says that your father was only interested in you and had no time for her because she was a girl. So which is it? Was Daddy unfairly biased towards you or entirely ignorant of your existence?"

"A little of both, no doubt." He was full of spite and fury, and his mother's protestations only served to rile him. "There's no sense denying it. I doubt that any senior politician in the history of this country has been a particularly good father, and mine certainly hasn't defied convention on that score."

Lady Darnley glanced about the room to see how her guests would react, but it was too early to tell. They were staring mutely, waiting to discover what came next.

"Your father has made any number of sacrifices for this family," she said when the silence had lasted several days – or at least, that was how it felt to me as an increasingly uncomfortable onlooker. "He's given his life to politics so that you could grow up with every advantage, not just because of the wealth of this estate, but the name you bear. Even his enemies respect him, and it's easy to understand why."

I don't know if it had come on suddenly or I'd only just noticed it, but Spencer's eyes were streaked with jagged red lines. It looked as if someone had taken a hammer and shattered them.

"Be honest, Mother. We already had the name and the money. He didn't have to join the government to keep a roof over our heads. Why didn't he devote his time to being a good father? Why do men like him never consider that to be a grand achievement?"

This was when the gentle hubbub from the neighbouring table finally started. It is not every day that you get to see your boss's family airing their dirty linen, but Lord Darnley's colleagues had front row – well, second row, maybe – seats to watch the action, and they all seemed to have an opinion about the revelations they'd heard.

"You're being selfish," was all Lady Darnley could say in response, but it was clear that her usual confidence was waver-ing. "You've always been a needy child. Perhaps we spoilt you. Perhaps we were too kind, and that's why you're acting this way."

"What a brilliant argument," the young man said and, for a moment, the curl of his lip and the defiance in his stare made me think of his sister. "I accuse Father of negligence and you say that you spoiled me. It's lucky I didn't say he had a violent nature, or it would have been proof of my self-destructive urges."

"That's enough, Spencer." Her words seemed to echo about the room despite the fact they'd been delivered in a furious whisper. "I won't hear another word from you. It's one thing to blame us for your misfortune, but it's quite another to do so when we are joined by important guests." She turned to the other table to wince apologetically, as if this could correct what the clerks, aides and secretaries there had heard.

"That's all you care about, Mother: keeping up appear-ances. Never mind your children's suffering. Never mind how it feels to be an afterthought in the family. Just as long as everyone thinks Father is a great man, nothing else matters."

I thought he would follow his sister from the room, but when he threw down his napkin and got up from the table, he stayed right where he was to hear her response.

"Why would you say any of this now?" Her voice finally

broke, and she stared at her son accusingly. "What's got into you, boy?"

I'd been wondering much the same thing.

Spencer opened his mouth to answer but presumably couldn't bear the thought of the words he had to utter and changed his mind. "You wouldn't agree even if I told you. You're as much a believer in the myth you've helped establish as any of Daddy's acolytes."

He cast his eyes around the room then to wallow in that sad moment and see himself reflected back in the faces of those present. A few eyes dipped in embarrassed silence, but most were beyond superficial politeness now and looked straight back at him. I've often found that our famous British manners have a limit, and we'd clearly passed it some time ago.

With a shake of his head, he was gone. His mother reached after him, as if he'd fallen from her grasp, but no one dared speak. Decorum returned to the room, and with it, our shyness. In fact, there was only one person there rude enough to react to Spencer's departure, and that was me. I ran after him before he could disappear entirely. It wasn't just for the sake of the mystery we were investigating or because I believed he could provide an insight into his father's behaviour. I followed him because I knew that no one else would.

He'd crossed the Grand Hall by the time I reached it, and I was just in time to see where he was going. Primrose's bedroom was in the east tower, and Spencer lived opposite in the western one. I shot across the hall and up an identical staircase to the one we'd mounted before. This time, in place of a nursery and dressing room, the middle floors of the tower housed a study packed with worthy academic texts and a room that held all sorts of sporting equipment – as long as those sports involved killing animals. There were rifles and fishing rods, knives and traps. If I'm honest, I think I preferred the display of toys in the nursery.

"What do you want?" Spencer shouted through the door when I knocked.

I couldn't think how to explain why I had followed him, and so I simply turned the handle and entered the room.

"What do *you* want?" he asked again, with the emphasis very much on the pronoun.

"I've come to tell you not to worry," I said without knowing why. "I imagine this weekend has been harder for your family than most other people here, but you mustn't be so bleak. For one thing, everyone will be leaving in a few hours and, for another, I genuinely don't believe that your father is a murderer."

I hadn't meant to shock him, but that's what happened. He had to sit down on the immense cast iron radiator under the window to make sense of what I was saying. He was lucky it was summer, or he would have had a nasty burn.

"How did you know what I was thinking?" he asked in some amazement.

"It's just logic, really. The way you were speaking made it sound as though you wanted to be angry with your father but couldn't quite manage it. Tell me to keep my opinion to myself, but I know how hard it can be to grow up in the shadow of our parents. Bella has certainly struggled, and though my father wasn't a lord or a politician, he set a high bar. I've never told anyone this before, but I very much doubt I've lived up to his example."

He turned to look out of the window over the gardens, and I felt that was probably it for the conversation. I possessed no psychic abilities. I hadn't really read his mind and, as a total stranger, I had no right to be up there with him.

Spencer didn't have anyone else to talk to, though, so I would have to do.

"I saw him," he said in a distant voice, and I understood now why he'd turned away. "I saw my father this morning when the Frenchman died."

I had to sigh then as I considered all the painful thoughts that must have passed through his mind that day. "I assumed that was the case. You were there one moment, gone the next, and it coincided with Lord Darnley's arrival."

He needed a deep breath just to continue. "He was coming out of a corridor on the far side of the Grand Hall, and I couldn't understand why he would be there at that time, already dressed. I didn't hear about the man who fled the scene until later, but as soon as I did, I realised that it could have been Father. There's a set of servants' stairs that connect the corridor that you inspected this morning with the rooms where he had been."

"I'm sure that's all true," I said in as sincere a tone as I could muster. "But that doesn't make him guilty. Do you have any particular reason to think that he's capable of murder?"

He looked away again and his voice fell. "Father is the most determined person I've ever met. He's all charm in public, of course, and people think that he's an honest sort, but the truth is that he'd do anything to achieve his aims. The furtive expression on his face when he saw the body set me wondering, what if he did it? As the day has progressed, I became more sure with every passing moment that he would kill if someone got in his way."

There was an elaborate golden chariot clock on the desk, and I could hear it tick, tick, ticking, as the silence fell between us.

"I don't believe your father or the French Foreign Minister are to blame," I said to put the matter to rest. "For one thing, whoever stole from the French and killed Monsieur Rochefort was working for a criminal gang. The chances of such an organisation converting a high-level cabinet minister to their cause must be slim. What's more, your father has direct access to the British intelligence services. If he wished to betray our secrets, he could have done so without the need for skullduggery and murder."

He cast a glance back to me over his shoulder, just as his sister had, and I realised how young he really was. Spencer was probably only a few years my junior, and yet there could have been a century between us. I'd noticed this before with the generation that followed my own – the one which had only barely missed out on being sent to war. While men my age had returned from the continent feeling hollow and alone, those who had stayed behind had to suffer through another kind of torment altogether. They were left with a mix of shame for not having done their part and relief that they hadn't had to go in the first place. When added to the problems that clearly existed within his family, this left Spencer more than just lost; he was cut adrift.

"I hope you're telling the truth," he said, and his tone was one of supplication rather than doubt. "I want to believe that my father is as good as everyone says, but when I realised that he was a suspect in the murder, just like the rest of us, I felt indescribably empty. It was as if my whole philosophy was built on a lie."

"I have a good idea who the killer is," I said out loud for the first time and, as soon the words had left my lips, I felt more confident. "If your only worry is that your father is a traitor, then I truly believe I can set your mind at ease."

His cheeks flushed with colour as he came to accept that I meant what I was saying. He was so happy in that moment, and I was proud that I'd had such an effect on him. I should have known, of course, that life's balance would not allow for any such joy without its accompanying sorrow. And just a few moments later, the house came alive. I didn't hear the scream myself. We were too far away for that, but I caught a sound like elephants storming the hallway just below the tower, and I immediately ran to see what the commotion was.

Even before I'd made my way through the crowd of Mentmore staff and civil servants who had gathered in a bedroom on the first floor, I had a sense of what had happened. Bella was there and buried her head in my shoulder as I came to stand next to her. There was a body on the floor at the foot of the bed, and I now knew that Inspector Vidocq of the Paris Sûreté would not be filing his report on that weekend's misadventures.

TWENTY-EIGHT

"Who found him?" I demanded as my friend summoned the courage to look at the dead man once more.

"I did, sir. I was up here making the beds," one of the maids revealed in a small voice.

I noticed that several of the key suspects had not shown their faces. There was no sign of Primrose or the two top politicians, who I could only assume were still in their meeting. Briand's chief advisors, Menier and Lemoine, were similarly absent.

Of the selection of political aides, house servants and footmen there, none of them looked interested in taking charge of the situation. As for the police, our one representative of that profession was propped up against his bed. It was instantly apparent that the thick silver chain he wore around his neck had been used to choke him to death.

I walked closer, and the sight was quite unbearable. A dead body is a story that you don't necessarily want to read, but as soon as my eyes latched onto his own bulging blue orbs, it was hard to look away again. There was a band of bright red where the metal had cut into him, and his face had taken on an oddly purple hue. From the marks I could see, it was clear that he had scratched at the chain as the killer tightened the ligature against his windpipe. They made him look as though he'd been savaged by a cat. And those are all the gory details I feel compelled to share.

One thing I did not see, however, was his gun. He'd had it on him earlier that morning, so what happened to it in the meantime?

"I should never have come in here," the maid said as she sobbed into a handkerchief. "I should have dealt with another room."

No doubt grateful for the distraction, Bella went to place a consoling hand on the poor girl's back. "You were doing your job, Cathy. You mustn't feel bad for one moment." How on earth did she already know the girl's name?

"And it's better that we found him as soon as possible," I added. "I saw Inspector Vidocq in the dining room less than half an hour ago, which might help us rule out certain suspects."

This seemed to cheer poor Cathy a little, though her cries sobs continued. "Thank you, sir. The thing is, I'd heard shouting a few minutes before, and I should have known to stay well out of it." She turned back and forth to address us. "I'm not the type to go looking for trouble, madam, but it had all gone quiet well before I came in here."

"You've done a wonderful job. And if you fetch the police who are patrolling the grounds, I'll tell them just that."

It was at this point that one of the girl's colleagues stepped forward to escort her out, which the other onlookers took as a sign to follow.

I needed to know something before the group of identically dressed diplomats disbanded and addressed the gang of advisors. "Where has Lord Darnley been keeping our part of the machine?"

Darnley's secretary looked at me with the appropriate level

of suspicion, but the cheery fellow next to him came straight out with the answer.

"It's behind a painting in his office." He received an elbow to the ribs for his trouble.

"Why did you tell him that?" the first replied. "He could be the killer for all we know, and you've just told him where the machine is!"

"Sorry, Lochtie. I didn't mean to—"

"I despair of you, Coupland. I really do."

They moved to leave, and I tried to make it up to poor, spectacled Coupland. "Go to the Amber Room directly and see that the machine is safe. I must admit that I fear the worst."

The two men departed in a hurry. I remembered Lord Darnley staring up at the gigantic Gainsborough painting and now knew why. His safe must have been just behind it.

As soon as we were alone, Bella reeled off a list of questions, only some of which I could answer.

"Do you think Vidocq had identified the killer and that's why he was killed? Can you imagine how his death relates to—"

"Wait just one moment," I said before my brain was so befuddled with what we didn't know that I couldn't concentrate on what we did. "Before we discuss any theories, let's start with the facts. Who was still in the dining room when you left? Is there anyone we can finally rule out?"

I hadn't known that there would be another killing, but I'd had a sense since we'd spoken to Castleton, and perhaps even his boss earlier in the morning, that the plot before us was more complicated than we'd at first imagined. The inspector's death only increased the possibility.

Bella took a ribbon from her pocket and tied back her long hair as though the time had come to be serious. Her bearing took on a poise and focus that very much suited her. And so, rather than firing more questions at me, she provided the information we needed.

"A few members of the party left the dining room shortly after you did. Uncle Arthur was the first to go. I believe that he was quite shaken by his niece and nephew's outbursts, but he was soon followed by a whole group of Lord Darnley's men from the Foreign Office."

"How much time passed between their leaving and the discovery of Vidocq's body?" I was trying to work out how long I'd been in the tower with Spencer, but my head was a mess of conflicting thoughts.

"Around five minutes." She came over to kneel next to me as if she was more worried about me than the dead man. "It couldn't have been a great deal longer."

I touched Vidocq's forehead with the back of my hand to see what warmth remained in him. He'd been killed very recently, but I was only a novice in such matters, and I couldn't say exactly when he'd died.

"The timing doesn't rule out anyone for certain then," I concluded before Bella set me straight.

"Except for Lady Darnley – she stayed in the dining room until I got up from the table. I was just leaving the Grand Hall when I heard the maid's scream."

"And I was with Spencer, so that's one more." I should probably have been happy to eliminate our first suspects, but it was only a minor achievement. "It's time to tell Rider. He should be here already, though I now understand why he isn't."

I got to my feet and drifted across to the door. This was the room where Vidocq had interrogated me. I'd found him terribly superior, but I'd still have preferred to see him alive than in that terrible state. I took one last look at him before I left, though the emotion of the scene was yet to hit me. He'd been killed doing his job, and that was sad by anyone's reckoning, but I needed to comprehend how his death fitted into the wider criminal plot.

Apparently aware that I was not quite with her as we left the room, Bella spoke softly. "I'll tell a footman to call around the local pubs to find Rider and his men. And then together we'll talk to Lord Darnley. This whole thing should have been brought to a halt when Rochefort was killed."

"That wouldn't have been possible," I mumbled in reply, but I couldn't explain my thoughts just yet.

Bella guided us back downstairs and all the way to the du Barry Room, which I had yet to enter, but she apparently knew well from her time there as a child. Castleton was still at the door, evidently torn over the best course of action.

"Have they been in there the whole time?" she asked, and he replied with a swift nod of the head.

"Nothing would draw them out, and the door is locked from the inside. I heard the ruckus though, and the butler told me what happened." If he'd looked sick and anxious when we'd last seen him, he was quite overwrought by now.

"You've done what you could, man." I gave his shoulder a reassuring squeeze, which seemed to buck him up a little.

"We should wait for Rider." Bella's words served to anchor us both to the spot.

So rather than bursting into the room in dramatic fashion and detailing everything that we knew – and a few things we were yet to uncover – we stood there, just like Castleton, and waited for something to happen.

In the end, Lord Darnley and Monsieur Briand finished their meeting a few moments before Rider and his two square-jawed colleagues made an appearance.

"What was the trouble, Castleton?" Darnley asked, eyeing the big brutes distastefully as they blocked his exit.

"There's been another murder, sir," his aide began, but the director of the Government Code and Cypher School had arrived to take charge of things.

"I'm sorry to appear uninvited, Lord Darnley, but my men will assume control of the situation." Rider turned to issue orders to Snipe and Boyle, and they bumbled off to look at the second victim. "We'll get to the bottom of all this, even if it takes a month."

"That won't be necessary," I told him. "I know what happened... Well, most of it, anyway."

I spotted Monsieur Briand hanging in the background as Darnley observed the scene with a curious expression that suggested he might yet change his opinion of me.

"Well..." He paused, as though uncertain what his reaction should be. "I suppose you should come inside."

He opened the door wider and the four of us entered the room. The Foreign Secretary issued a brief explanation in French for his counterpart, who raised his hand to show that he'd caught the gist and would need no more translation. This was the closest I'd got to Briand all weekend, and I now realised just how cautious a person he was. He did not utter a word for some time, as if the sound of his voice was a secret he wished to preserve.

Once Bella, Castleton and Rider had each chosen a spot in the comfortable lounge, I did my best to explain.

"A maid just found Inspector Vidocq's body in his bedroom on the first floor. He was killed within the last half an hour, and I believe that I have identified the killer." I didn't pause for effect then so much as to reassure myself that I knew what I was saying. "It was you, wasn't it, Castleton?"

TWENTY-NINE

The du Barry Room at Mentmore Towers was not as large as many of the elegant spaces we'd visited, but it was almost indescribably opulent. Everything was either green or gold. The virid wallpaper bore a dark embossed pattern of boughs and foliage, while the ceiling rose, egg-and-dart dentils and coving around the top of the room were covered in brightly glinting gilt. It was as pretty a room as I could imagine and took its name from an immense portrait of Madame du Barry herself, the lowly prostitute who rose to become Louis XV's official mistress (before meeting a most aristocratic fate beneath the guillotine).

It was not *her* neck that concerned me as I stood before the small congregation. Ernest Castleton had turned to stone. He stood before the comparatively simple marble fireplace and was no longer able to express a single emotion.

"You killed Inspector Vidocq to prevent him from killing you," I tried again. "I assume that's the case, isn't it?"

He released a breath that he'd evidently been holding for some time and rushed to explain what happened. "I did, but it really was self-defence, and I'll swear on whatever you wish me to swear that I did not harm Monsieur Rochefort."

He addressed this comment to Darnley and Briand, though I couldn't say how much of the hurried account the French Foreign Minister was able to follow.

Castleton turned back to Bella and me. "As you suggested, Lady Isabella, I came here to warn Lord Darnley of the threat to the English half of the machine. He was still in conversation with Monsieur Briand, so I went upstairs to look for the pair of you. I was walking along the corridor to the Grand Hall when Vidocq accosted me. He spoke in fast, insistent French, and I didn't understand everything he said, but he had a gun and I realised I was in trouble. He forced me into a bedroom there, and I managed to knock the weapon from his hand and tip him off balance. He fell to his knees, so I grabbed the chain around his neck and choked the life out of him before he could do the same to me."

"What had got into the man?" Lord Darnley enquired most perplexedly, but Castleton could only guess.

"As I said, he seemed quite out of his senses. I assumed the pressure to find the killer had got to him, and he'd lost his mind."

"I think I might be able to explain," I began, but our host was confused why I should be the one to say anything.

"I'm sorry, Mr Baines, but I don't understand your role in all of this. Rider, is he something to do with you?"

"I'm afraid so, M'Lord." Rider adopted that humble demeanour I'd seen him employ in London. "We knew there was a threat from a criminal organisation this week – the same organisation that attempted to kidnap Mr Castleton. I couldn't risk the traitor learning of our plan to catch him, and so I asked for Lady Isabella's help in the matter. Her friend Mr Marius Quin here is something of an amateur sleuth."

"Quin? You mean he's the novelist?" Lord Darnley's tone was not particularly happy as he discovered our ruse.

"That's right, my lord," I replied, and I can't tell you how happy I was to be myself again. "We became entangled with the Syndicate when a member of the gang hired Bella and me to find Ernest. We didn't realise that he'd been hidden for his own protection, and we made a bad situation worse."

"Though it all worked out for the best in the end," Bella was quick to clarify, and I decided to have a sit down and let her explain this bit. "We followed a trail of clues that had been laid out across London for us. It all seemed like such an adventure, and we soon found ourselves in Hastings where we did our best to 'liberate', in inverted commas, Ernest from his captors."

Rider winced as she told this part of the story. I can't say it reflected particularly well on any of us.

"And then, when we got back to the city, the man from the Syndicate left us unconscious and attempted to kidnap Ernest for the second time."

"Only, this time, I got away of my own accord," Ernest added with a more relaxed air about him now that the truth had come to light. In fact, he sounded rather proud as he described his most daring act. "I jumped out of the back of his car as we were speeding down the Mall."

Darnley muttered a few words in French to Briand, then turned to the man from British Intelligence. "This is all rather hard to believe, especially as I knew nothing about it until now."

Rider cleared his throat, adjusted his tie, and then cleared his throat once more for good measure. "We couldn't take the risk that someone in your immediate circle was a spy, sir."

The Foreign Secretary had certainly caught the underlying meaning. "You mean to say that you couldn't even trust Monsieur Briand or myself."

"Well now... You see..." Rider was in an impossible situation and chose his words with great care. "We never suspected you, M'Lord. But we knew that the Syndicate had twice tried to extract the information they required from Mr Castleton and, when that failed, we were afraid that they would make another attempt here at Mentmore."

"So what about Inspector Vidocq? How was he involved?" Lord Darnley addressed this question to me, and I felt this was one area where I was on firmer ground.

"I believe that he was a real police officer. If not, he would never have been able to book himself a place on this trip. However, it is now evident that he was working for the Syndicate. I have little doubt that he killed Monsieur Rochefort and obtained the French code discs. After that, he had the freedom to move about Mentmore to investigate the crime. Of course, what he was really looking for was the place where Lord Darnley and his associates had stored the English part of the machine."

"The blackguard..." Castleton muttered this brief but fair judgement as I continued the tale.

"My suspicions towards him were first aroused when we inspected Rochefort's body together. He seemed to accept me as a fellow investigator, although, as far as he was supposed to know, I was a dry, boring, largely charmless banker."

Rather than react to my not so veiled criticism of her boyfriend, Bella formed a conclusion. "The Syndicate knew who we were. They must have told Vidocq about the part we'd played, and so he saw through Marius's false identity immediately."

"That's right," I confirmed. "Primrose was the only other person here who knew my real name, and there is nothing to suggest she told anyone. But that's not all. When Vidocq interviewed me, he showed little interest in the identity of Rochefort's killer. He suggested that Monsieur Menier was the likely culprit, but only to deflect suspicion away from himself. Instead, he asked me about the machine, and I believe it was his goal all along to get his hands on it."

As I spoke, Rider leaned forward to listen in his (appropriately located) Louis XV chair. Although Bella and Castleton looked cheered to know that the traitor was dead, and the case solved, Lord Darnley's face was increasingly grey and grim.

"This is terrible. To think that someone could get so close to us without anyone suspecting him. Did you have no idea, Briand?"

The French Foreign Minister once more looked reluctant to reveal anything and so, rather than respond, he gave a wonderfully nonchalant shrug of his shoulders and lit a cigar from a box on the small marquetry table beside his chair. Madame du Barry looked on disapprovingly as the air in front of her portrait filled with filthy grey smoke.

There was a knock on the door at this moment and Lord Darnley's private secretary came into the room. I was surprised to see that he didn't address his superior from the Foreign Office but walked up to Rider and whispered something in his ear.

"Lochtie, what's happened?" Darnley immediately asked, but the discreet young man in the unremarkable black suit just nodded to the Foreign Secretary and slipped from the room as quietly as he'd entered.

"It's the discs, code books and housing for the machine, sir," Rider explained. "The safe in your office appears to have been compromised, and the contents removed."

Darnley was out of his chair in a second, but it was Briand who calmed him back down. "There is nothing to worry about, Lord Darnley," he promised in his own language. "The thief is dead; he cannot smuggle his prize from Mentmore."

"And what if it has already gone?"

"It won't have." Briand was typically close-fisted with the information he shared, but he spoke to encourage me to continue. "Tell me more of Rochefort, Monsieur Quin? How did Vidocq get our codes from him?"

It felt rude to continue in English, and so I changed to French so that the others would have to follow suit. I doubt that my grammar was as good as some of the others', but it certainly wasn't the worst.

"Before I could discover the answer to that question, I had to understand more about the Syndicate. I believe that whoever is in charge of the organisation has a network of agents of different ranks and responsibilities. There are those, like the first man who confronted Castleton in Hyde Park, who will know very little about the organisation. They are expendable, mere mercenaries who will be given the details of an assignment and a sufficient reward for their service.

"As you go higher up through the structure, you find men with more understanding of its workings. I believe that Inspector Ordinary..." Evidently this childish moniker needed explaining for those not in the know. "That's what I called the man who recruited Lady Isabella and me. I believe that the imposter Inspector Ordinary and the real Inspector Vidocq operated at a similar level. They appear to have possessed more knowledge of the Syndicate's workings, but it is impossible to say whether they were connected to the kingpins at the very top."

I must have gone into more detail than anyone needed, as Bella picked this moment to make an important point. "Ordinary hired us to do one small part of the work, and so it stands to reason that Vidocq would have hired agents of his own."

"Rochefort..." Briand whispered.

"Indeed." I smiled because it is not every day one gets the chance to impress a man like the Foreign Minister of France. "He was almost certainly the one who stole the briefcase from under Monsieur Briand's bed. He was fully dressed when he died, which suggested that he had a reason to get up and ready so early in the day, and he would have known where to find it. If my theory is true, he had arranged to meet Vidocq to hand over the case. When he'd done his part of the job, he was no longer of any use which is why we found his body on the floor of the Grand Hall."

"And the paper in his hand?" Darnley asked.

"That was nothing of any great significance," Briand saw fit to reveal. "It was merely a note from my desk that I assume Rochefort took in case it was important. When I saw it, I knew someone had been into my quarters and stolen from me."

"This is terrible," Darnley repeated, and he glanced down at the rich green carpet of the bi-coloured room. "We've come so close to disaster."

Bella evidently took pity on her godfather as she walked over to stand beside his chair and placed one hand on the back of it. "Yes, but thanks to the work of many people here, the danger has been averted. For all their guile and influence, the Syndicate were unsuccessful."

"That's marvellous!" Castleton beamed and, if there had been champagne to hand, I'm certain that friendly chap would have proposed a toast.

"I don't know how I can thank you," Darnley continued. "I really don't. It's all quite beyond my comprehension."

"Wait!" Rider's sudden interruption was like an exclamation mark without a sentence to proceed it, and we turned to look at him. "That's only half the story. Unless I'm very much mistaken, there's more to come."

"You know, Henry, you're not as dull as you pretend," I said, to pique him just a little, and test if I could guess his name correctly. So that was two points to me... I think. "And you're quite right, of course. Every scheme the Syndicate has employed had a backstop. If Bella and I had failed in our task in Hastings, Inspector Ordinary would have found someone else to do the job. Here at Mentmore, Vidocq was the man who oversaw the operation. He wouldn't have got his hands dirty breaking into the safe in the Amber Room, which means there must be another spy in our midst."

"Spit it out, man," Rider demanded. "Who was it? Who betrayed us?"

The tension in the room mounted at this moment. It was not just psychological – brought on by the heightened emotions of that tense and dramatic day – it was physical. The atmosphere changed much as it does before a rain shower. It prickled against the skin of every last one of us, and my eyes darted about the room to observe their reactions before I revealed what I now knew for certain.

"It was your job to get the discs, wasn't it, Castleton?"

The few heartbeats before he replied seemed to take hours. "You're talking rot. I would never betray my—"

That was as much as I would allow him by way of a defence. "I can't say exactly why you did it, but I know that you're to blame." I paused then and, for a moment, the only sound in that room was his loud and laboured breath. "I believe that your contact from the Syndicate came to see you in the park on Monday night, but Lieutenant Snipe happened upon you. Rather than risk exposing yourself to suspicion, you shouted that the man had accosted you and Snipe drew his gun. Your contact raised his weapon but was too slow. You sacrificed him to save yourself. Am I far off the truth?"

"You're a thousand miles away." The same nervousness that he'd displayed for much of the day had returned. "I'm no traitor."

I continued as if I hadn't heard. "You accompanied me out of the house in Hastings and all the way back to London because you believed that the Syndicate had sent me to get you. As soon as we were unconscious, you told Inspector Ordinary whatever he wanted to know, and then pretended to escape from him. You said you hurt your shoulder when you jumped out of the car, but I gave it a good squeeze before we came in here and it has miraculously recovered."

"This is wrong, sir," he protested, glancing from Darnley to

Rider and back again. "He's got it all wrong. You've no reason to trust him."

His fingers dug into the armrests of his chair. If he'd really been innocent, I doubt he would have panicked like that. I saw him eye the door, but he was not yet ready to make his move.

"You can say whatever you like. That doesn't make it true." I stayed where I was. It was a perfectly comfortable seat and I very much doubted that he'd be able to escape if he tried. "You've just admitted to killing Vidocq, although you evidently had a good reason. He'd already killed Rochefort, and as soon as you handed over the discs, you would have been next. Isn't that right?"

He didn't say anything, so I continued. "But what really gave it away was what you told us before in the library. You said you knew next to nothing about the machine, and if that was the case, it wasn't for what you knew that the Syndicate was after you, but what you could do for them. What did they offer in exchange for betraying your country?"

In some ways, he was terribly convincing. He screwed his face up, breathed out loudly, and I thought he would shout at me, but he put on a big show of calming himself down to appear more reasonable. "I don't know anything about this. I don't even know why I'm—"

His words faded out as the door creaked open and he caught sight of the newest arrivals. His last hope of escape was snuffed out when those brilliantly brawny brutes, Snipe and Boyle, appeared. In that moment, it must have dawned on Castleton that his goose was not just cooked but burnt to a crisp.

The cuckoo in the nest pulled Vidocq's gun from his pocket and, rather than waving it around the room in the vain hope he could force his way off the property, he pointed it at himself. "I must admit, Mr Quin, and you too, Lady Isabella. I underesti-mated you."

"Come along, man," Rider shouted. "Don't be a fool."

"I wish things could have ended differently." As if he had found some peace in the inevitability of his situation, Castleton's voice was calmer, slower, clearer now. "Please tell my fiancée, Hermione, that she is quite the most wonderful person I've ever known. Whatever my crimes, she doesn't deserve to be associated with a criminal, and that's why there's only one thing left to do."

"Don't do this, Ernest," Darnley begged him, but I could see that such pleas would achieve nothing.

"You don't understand. This isn't suicide; I'm doing it for the people I love. No one in this room will mention my name to the press if I'm dead. If I live, though, I will have to go to trial. My family's name will be dragged through the mud, and I will forever be remembered as a traitor. So if you don't mind, I'll take the other option."

"You've got it all wrong." Rider's voice went higher as he desperately tried to prevent the inevitable. "You'll never face a trial. The government wouldn't want the publicity. If you tell us all you know, we'll keep you somewhere out of the way and no one will ever hear from you again. There are worse fates."

His words clearly would not have the desired effect. Castleton cocked the hammer on the revolver, and I knew this would be my last chance. I grabbed the nearest thing to hand and threw it with all my might across the room. The grand blue and brown porcelain vase missed him by an inch, but it was enough of a distraction to allow Rider to rush from his seat to knock the scoundrel to the carpet. The vase smashed, the gun fell to the floor, and Snipe and Boyle were on their prey in a second.

"Curse you," he protested as they pinned down one of his arms each. He struggled and wriggled, but he would not break free, and I'd never seen the two lugs so happy. "You should have let me die."

"Don't make such a fuss." Rider was nursing the fist which had made contact with Castleton's jaw. "If you tell us all you know about the Syndicate and whoever hired them, you'll be fine. Oh yes, matey. I think you'll be a valuable little asset."

I hated having to watch what happened to him. It wasn't just the knowledge that a young man had thrown his life away that I found so unpleasant; it was the fact I had genuinely liked him. Discovering that someone as solid and amiable as Ernest Castleton could turn his back on his homeland made it harder to trust anyone.

"How could you do it?" Bella asked so that I didn't have to. "How could you betray us?"

These two simple questions cut through everything else. They wiped the bitter grin from his face and, in a moment, the fight went out of him. There were twenty questions I wish I'd asked, but I couldn't bear to look at him any longer.

The lieutenants pulled him from the room, and Rider stopped for a moment to talk to us. "Exceptional work, you two. I must admit, I didn't think for one minute that you'd manage it. We mainly sent you here as a decoy. I fully expected you to bumble about the place, distracting the traitor from the real agent we'd embedded with Lord Darnley. Thank you so much for going one better."

He left with a wink, which did not make me feel particularly good about this fresh revelation.

"Bumble?" I called as I chased after him. "Why would you think such a thing?"

THIRTY

It wasn't long before the house was overrun with police officers of various stripes. Chief Inspector Darrington led a contingent from Scotland Yard, though there was no sign of my friend Lovebrook. More of Rider's men had appeared, too, and I was coming to see why Darnley's private secretary was the one to give them their orders.

"That was the only part I worked out with any confidence," Bella revealed as we stood with Percy in the dining room watching the men take the house to pieces in their search for evidence of Rochefort, Vidocq and Castleton's conspiracy. "It occurred to me back in London just how strange it was that Rider changed his tune so rapidly. One moment he was furious with us, then, before we knew it, he was all charm and wanted us to take a trip to Mentmore. I wondered why he didn't simply get in touch with Lord Darnley or place one of his men here covertly."

"It was clearly because we were the best people for the job," I said, approximately one per cent seriously.

"Oh, without a doubt. But we didn't have any training for

the task we were given, and we certainly weren't informed of all the details we needed to know."

"And that told you that we were just a sideshow, did it? A distraction to keep the traitors on their toes."

"Well... not until a short time ago," she replied, "but I knew that we were not the sort of people whom a clandestine government department would normally despatch for such a mission. I assumed that Castleton himself was reporting back to them, though it now turns out that Lord Darnley's secretary was the man they recruited to identify the traitor."

I grumbled for a few moments, as I wasn't happy with Rider for thinking so little of our skills. He'd sent a more experienced, better trained and, let's be honest, far more competent agent to do the job, and it rankled in me, though I really shouldn't have given it a second thought.

"Still," I said for my own benefit as much as hers, "we solved the case and brought the villains to justice before the real spy could."

"We didn't stop the discs being taken, though. And, in all honesty, two of those villains were killed."

I was about to inform her of an enlightening theory of my own when Lord Darnley came to watch us watch other people work. He had something to tell us, too, but for a few seconds, he was content to observe.

"I thought you might like to join me for afternoon tea," he said. I could only assume that he wished to spend time with his goddaughter, but actually he was interested in me. "I'd like to ask you a few questions about your first book, Mr Quin. The denouement in *A Killer in the Wings* caught me totally off guard. I've heard you have a new one due in the shops any day."

"I do, indeed," I replied with a little less composure than I'd intended. "I'll have to send you a copy."

He put one hand on my shoulder and led me from the room. Well, Percy went first, actually, but he didn't know where he was going, so he had to keep stopping to wait for us. With Bella running after the silly hound, we walked through the hall and the White Drawing Room all the way to the Blarenberghe room in the far corner of the main wing. It was so called for the impressive collection of Flemish art on all four walls. There was a huge panorama of Paris that was particularly charming, but I was not there to appreciate the paintings.

Arranged upon a selection of Mentmore's very best antique furniture were several of that weekend's suspects. Monsieur Briand had pride of place in the centre, whereas his two senior advisors were way off in a corner. The Darnley siblings appeared far more chipper than before – I suppose that finding out your father isn't a murderer will do that – and the party was rounded off by Mr H. Rider, who was heaping scones and sandwiches onto a plate. His two henchmen looked very uncomfortable in such refined surroundings but played their part by standing next to the door in surly silence.

There was any amount of polite chit-chatting (and tea) to get through before the group splintered and Bella and I were able to put some of our outstanding questions to the men with the answers. Percy was already asleep under a table by this point and would miss out on a fascinating conversation – not that he cared because... well, you know why.

"We never discovered the reason Monsieur Rochefort interrupted the meeting last night," Bella began, though over the course of the last hour or so, I'd formed an opinion on that matter. Oh, and she asked this in French and her accent was extremely good, as expected.

"He interrupted the meeting because I told him to do so," Briand explained. "I reprimanded him for it so that no one would know the truth, but I had already instructed him that I was feeling my age and didn't want a late night."

"Which was not true," my oldest friend rightly concluded.

"No, it was not." With his usual, slightly infuriating sense of discretion, Briand would have said no more, but I wouldn't let him get away with such evasion.

"You called off the meeting because the machine that we've spent this weekend trying to protect is a fake. Isn't that right?"

He had hamster-like cheeks that puffed up even more when he smiled. "You are a smart man, Mr Quin. How did you know?"

"Well, for one thing, although your acting sufficed after the discs had disappeared from your room, you seemed positively indifferent today when we discovered that the whole machine had been taken. I've seen men get more worked up at having to retie their shoelaces than you did at the thought of our enemies gaining such a major advantage over us."

"How is it possible?" Lord Darnley was not as well-informed as I had expected.

"I think I can explain some part of this," Rider shuffled forward to say. And yes, he could speak French and, no, his accent was not up to scratch. "You see, we knew there was at least one person within our organisation who had been leaking confidential information. A trusted friend of mine in the French police believed they had a similar problem. He said the only man he trusted to worm out the individual was Monsieur Briand himself, and so I called up the Foreign Minister in order to devise a plan."

The rather petit, unimposing former Prime Minister had helped guide France through a war and won the Nobel Prize. He had done so much in his life and no doubt had more to achieve, but his only reply to this comment was a humble bow. He would say no more to admit the part he had played, though it was clear he had masterminded the whole thing.

"You mean to say that you planned this weekend in order to find the traitor and you didn't think of telling me?" Darnley's voice had risen a few notes higher and now echoed about the room. His family paid him no attention. They were evidently used to it.

"I'm afraid that we couldn't take the risk," Rider hurriedly explained in English once more. "We didn't know whether the man we were looking for was in your office which, as it turned out, he was."

Darnley still looked put out, and I concluded that Rider had at least entertained the idea that the Foreign Secretary himself had been recruited by the Syndicate. Now that the real traitor had been uncovered, though, it was safe to discuss the details.

"You know, there were several key pieces of evidence that only occurred to me when I knew what had really happened," I told the group of interested parties. "When Rochefort came out of the house last night to talk to Castleton and me, it must have been a prearranged meeting between them. I got in their way, but Rochefort could have gone back just as soon as I left. The funny thing is, Castleton tried to convince me that Rochefort was the traitor, so he was evidently happy to let him take the blame for both of their crimes."

"These sorts of things are so obvious once you know who the guilty party is." Bella offered a kind glance, and I was once more amazed that our run of success had continued unbroken. "What else did we miss?"

"More or less everything about Vidocq." I shook my head at the very thought of it. "He surely pushed his compatriot over the balcony. I caught sight of the killer running from the scene of the crime, and I should have realised that Vidocq had slipped into his own bedroom, leaving me to wander along the corridor straight past him."

"He advised me only to call the local police and leave the main investigation to him," Monsieur Briand admitted. "He told me it was better for everyone if we kept the matter between ourselves, and I convinced Lord Darnley of the same thing, as I didn't want the weekend to end until we'd captured the traitor. I failed to consider the possibility that Vidocq was trying to save his own skin. He's a respected investigator, and I never imagined he could be to blame."

Lord Darnley set aside these topics to return to matters of state. "What of the machine? How long will it be before it does the job it was designed to do?"

Rider became yet more nervous and tightened his tie again. I doubted he would be able to breathe for much longer. "Well, you see, the thing with that is..."

"It was never meant to work." Bella revealed the big secret we'd apparently both divined. "The whole invention was just that: a figment of the imagination that Monsieur Briand and Mr Rider conjured up to ensure that the traitors would expose themselves."

The more agitated Rider became, the more Briand smiled, and he was soon tittering away at the spy's discomfort.

"It was a *bon plan*," the Foreign Minister proclaimed, mixing the two languages. "And it worked well. I must apologise for keeping you in the dark, Lord Darnley, but we achieved our objectives and that is surely the most important thing."

"It's amazing that you managed to keep it a secret." Darnley was suitably impressed and a fact that had recently become apparent to me now dawned on him. "My goodness, that's why you kept the discs apart. It wasn't to prevent our countries from using the machine independently, it was because it wouldn't have worked."

"That's right, M'Lord," Rider confirmed. "It isn't meant for decoding at all. In fact, it's the opposite. Some years ago, the Germans invented a coding machine known as Enigma. We based our machine on reports of that one but threw in a few more discs and some extra buttons. It was never meant to function, so we weren't too worried about the way it looked."

"What an audacious plan you pulled off." Darnley no

longer sounded upset to have been left out. "You will surely get a medal for this, Rider. All in secret, of course."

He was so impressed that he took the head of the crypt-analysis department – or whoever Rider really was – for a conversation in private. Briand had turned away for a discussion with his two aides, which just left Bella and me to continue the conversation.

"We're clearly geniuses," I told her. "Rider is a dolt not to sign us up as spies this very minute."

"Very true," she agreed as a troubled expression came over her features. "Although, before you use such an argument, I would recommend checking whether the plural of genius is *geniuses* or *genii*. I can never remember."

I laughed at her, and she gave me a punch on the arm as it had been far too long.

"Come along, Bella, my dear. I'll drive you back to the civil-ising influence of the big city. There are too many spies and trai-tors in the countryside for my liking."

"Not to mention murderers and dead bodies."

"And upstart mystery writers," Primrose walked over to say. We'd apparently been talking rather loudly.

"And spoilt daughters of wealthy lords." Her brother grinned at us, and it was hard to know whether he was referring to Bella, his sister or, more likely, both.

"And whatever it is that you are, Spencer," Bella replied with the same competitive edge to her voice that she'd had for most of their exchanges that weekend. "It's hard to describe you, but there are definitely too many of you around."

He held his hand to his heart, as though he'd been shot, and then mimed a tear rolling down his cheek. "Does this mean you still won't marry me?"

"Alas no. I have eyes for just one man."

For the briefest of moments, I thought she was talking about me, but then I remembered that I'd only been playing the part of her boyfriend and would no longer fulfil that role in real life.

The three of them continued to squabble all the way to dinner that evening. Bella quite forgot about me as she enjoyed re-enacting scenes from her childhood and, even though I spent the day listening to Uncle Arthur's endless rambling, I didn't mind. We'd caught the traitor. What more could anyone want?

THIRTY-ONE

It was hard to go back to normality after that incomparable weekend. A few days after I returned to London, I found myself walking Percy through the park all the way to the GC&CS office on Broadway. I stood across the road for a few minutes and looked up at the floor where I was fairly sure we'd been after our run-in with Inspector Ordinary's doped bottle of champagne. I don't know what I expected to see there. Perhaps I simply wished to prove to myself that I hadn't imagined the whole thing.

"Gilbert?" a voice asked as I stood in a dream. I'd very rarely gone by that name and so it took me a few seconds to respond.

"Hello, Hermione," I replied. "I was hoping I'd bump into you."

"I..." Her voice wavered and it would be some time before she found the courage to speak. I was glad that Percy was there to comfort her, as I wasn't much good at it. "I received a telegram from Ernest last week." She took a sharp breath and forced herself to keep talking. "He told me that he's been dispatched on a mission abroad. It's impossible to say when he'll be back, and he can't reveal any details of his posting."

I didn't know what to say to this. For one thing, Bella and I were the ones who'd written the telegram, which I sent to a soldier pal in Tanganyika, who in turn forwarded it to Hermione. We'd tried to make her missing fiancé sound heroic yet believable, and there was a nervous moment just then when I thought we'd failed.

"I'm sorry. I really—"

"What on earth for?" she replied, her face suddenly brightening. "It's just like him to do something so brave and noble. I don't know what he could be up to, but I have no doubt that he'll be helping those who need it most."

"I'm sure you're right," I said, although, as far as she knew, I'd never met the man and didn't know the first thing about him.

She laughed then. She walked a little closer, put her hand on my arm, and laughed at the simply perfect picture of him that she was able to maintain despite the fact he was locked up in a secret prison somewhere.

"You know, it's the kind of thing that someone would make up to escape from a bad romance, and if it was anyone else, I might just believe that, but not my Ernest."

She seemed so entirely contented that I had to wonder whether the story we'd given her was preferable to the marriage she could have had.

"Thank you," she said, squeezing my arm a little tighter with her eyes fixed on mine.

Yet again, I thought we'd been found out. "Why would you thank me?"

"For doing what you could to locate him. I have to believe that the fact you uncovered the letter he left for me somehow got back to Ernest. That must be why he sent the telegram in the first place. Thank you, Gilbert Baines. You are a terribly kind man."

I would have liked to disagree with her, and Percy would certainly have been happy to remain there, but she turned and walked across the road to her office without a glance back over her shoulder.

I'd already decided to wait a few months and then give poor Ernest a heroic death. I couldn't stand the thought of that trusting woman mourning her traitorous fiancé, but it was better than her wasting her life waiting for the scoundrel to reappear.

Whatever the reason I'd gone to that part of the city, one visit was enough. My meeting with Hermione showed me that it was time to get on with real life once more.

Back in the old routine, I tried my best to get some words down each day for my third book. When the well inevitably ran dry, I would telephone Bella for long conversations in which we relived our adventure. We picked over each detail as though there was some part of the mystery that we still had to solve.

In the weeks that followed, for the most part, I was waiting for something to happen – for the telephone to ring or the doorbell to chime. It was tempting to believe that, in our future cases, were we merely to investigate despicable murders rather than international criminal conspiracies, life would seem rather dreary again. In time, however, I realised that I would happily settle for such simple pleasures, not least because our trip to Buckinghamshire had left me quite paranoid.

Whenever I opened the front door, I wondered whether the postman, baker or butcher's boy were who they claimed to be. On my walks around the city, I was certain that I was being followed, but when I looked, there was no one there. I had the unshakable sensation that the Syndicate had more business with me, and so it was something of a relief when a man with some answers turned up on my doorstep one day.

"I've brought champagne to toast your good health," Rider told me, and I noticed that, just as Inspector Ordinary had, he stood to the side of the door so that he couldn't be seen through the front window.

"Is this a joke, or are you planning to poison me?" I asked as I eyed his gift.

He certainly didn't act as though he were pulling my leg. "It is sealed, Mr Quin. I couldn't possibly have tampered with it."

"So was the last one, and we both know what happened."

He held out the bottle of Louis Roederer Brut, and I discovered that there really was no turning down victory champagne. I took it and he wandered past me into the house, straight into my messy writing room.

"It looks like you've been busy," he guessed incorrectly and, if I hadn't seen first-hand just how capable a spy he was, I might well have doubted it.

"Hardly. I've written a little under a chapter since we came back from Mentmore and, not that this will mean a great deal to you, my hunt for my father is not progressing as I hoped it would."

His face was perfectly blank as he picked up a pile of detective novels and placed them as neatly as possible on the carpet before taking their place. "You're quite right. I don't know anything about Terence Quin, who disappeared in the March of 1918 and has not been heard of since."

Any normal man would have smiled at the trick he'd played on me, but not Rider. He shuffled in his seat to get comfortable, and I went in search of two coupes for the champagne. By the time I'd returned to the room at the front of the flat, Percy had found his usual spot on the feet of whoever happened to be near at the time. He let out a long, weary yawn and fell asleep as Rider and I drank and talked. I'm happy to say that, unlike my dog, I managed to keep my eyes open, even after I'd consumed a whole glass of champagne.

"So how goes it in the world of British intelligence?" I asked my visitor once I was sitting in the armchair opposite his.

"You know full well that I can't answer that question, Mr Quin. You're lucky that I've told you what I have."

"You mean, I'm lucky you haven't locked me up to keep your secrets safe."

A short laugh escaped him, but he didn't smile. "Believe me, if I thought you knew anything important, I wouldn't hesitate to put you somewhere dark and damp." There was a touch of warmth in this horrible threat, and I almost felt like thanking him for being so reasonable.

"Have you managed to work out why the Syndicate wanted the machine in the first place?" I asked instead.

"It's interesting you should ask," he replied with just a hint of animation, "as that is one of the topics which I cannot discuss."

"And Vidocq? Have the French discovered how he came to be recruited?"

"It's interesting you should ask that, as it's another of the topics I cannot discuss."

"Oh, very well, but what about Castleton? Has he blown the gab? Are you any closer to finding his associates?" I asked these final questions, despite the infinitesimally small probability of his answering them.

"It's interesting you should ask, as that is the very topic that I have come here to discuss." He smirked at me. "We've discovered something rather intriguing."

I considered listing several potential (though unlikely) outcomes, but decided it would be best to keep my mouth shut and wait for him to say more.

"I'm not at liberty to tell you anything about the Syndicate as a wider organisation. In fact we've had trouble establishing what their aims really were, but we have been trying to identify the man who recruited you."

"You mean Inspector Ordinary?"

"I'm not going to call him that." He was having none of it and shook his head. "First, we spoke to the children who run messages for the East India Club out in the square here. Only one of them was any help: a little girl by the name of Jamie. She got a good look at the man and gave us a detailed description. She said that there was another chap who'd been hanging around waiting for your return, but we believe he's a petty criminal who has since moved on. We're more interested in this fellow."

He pulled from his briefcase a photograph of a plain-faced man in a beige suit and placed it on the coffee table between us.

"Inspector Ordinary!" I said with some glee, and he still wouldn't take the bait.

"Again, I'm not going to call him that, but I appreciate your confirmation. Your friend Ernest Castleton says he only ever met one figure in the gang. He says that this man recruited him just as he did you. The difference is that he didn't rely on the promise of adventure to win him over. No, he found some compromising material on him and threatened to share it with the police. We imagine he did something similar with the poor sop who Snipe shot dead in St James's Park. It might even be the case that Rochefort and Vidocq were recruited in the same way."

It was almost enough for me to feel sorry for Castleton and the others, but not quite. After all, if Ordinary had discovered something to use against them, that suggested they were far from innocent in the first place.

"You've worked out who he is, haven't you?" I predicted, mainly from the self-satisfied look on his face.

"You could say that." He paused to scratch the three-day stubble on his chin. "And that's where it gets interesting. We've connected this Ordinary fellow—"

"Ah ha!" I couldn't contain my joy. "You said it! You used the name."

He was not amused. "We've connected him to your father."

In a split second, my laughter died in my throat. "No, that can't be. What does Dad have to do with any of this?"

"The man who hired you to find Ernest Castleton was the last client your father represented in court before he disappeared." Rider had to swallow then, as if it was a struggle to get the words out. "His name is Lucien Pike."

A LETTER FROM THE AUTHOR

Many thanks for reading *The Castleton Affair*. I hope you were glued to the book as Marius and Bella raced to solve the mystery. If you'd like to join other readers in accessing free novellas and hearing all about my new releases, you can sign up to my readers' club!

benedictbrown.net/benedict-brown-readers-club

If you enjoyed this book and could spare a few moments to leave a review, that would be hugely appreciated. Even a short comment can make all the difference in encouraging a reader to discover my books for the first time.

Becoming a writer was my dream for two decades as I scribbled away without an audience, so to be able to do this as my job is out of this world. One of my favourite things about my work is hearing from you lovely people who all approach my books in different ways, so feel free to get in touch via my website.

Thanks again for being part of my story – Marius, Bella and I have so many more adventures still to come.

Benedict

benedictbrown.net

 facebook.com/benedictbrownauthor

ABOUT THIS BOOK

I've wanted to write this book for some years, but it didn't really fit with my previous series. If I'm honest, I might even have devised the Marius Quin Mysteries in order to write it. There's something wonderfully old-fashioned about the scenario as a whole. While murder mysteries set in the 1920s are popular these days, they tend to stick to the classic closed-circuit whodunnit format. Of course, if you read a lot of Golden Age detective fiction, you'll know that this was not the only or even the most common form and there were a lot of adventurous, intriguing and conspiracy-driven tales that were hugely popular.

The most obvious ones that are still read are Agatha Christie's *The Secret Adversary*, *The Man in the Brown Suit*, and *The Big Four*, which made up a third of the novels she produced in the twenties. Spy fiction had been popular for some time by then, and the fear of foreign conspiracies against Britain, and even secret military invasions, were only heightened by the First World War. There had long been a trend in fiction to focus on particular countries as the enemy. If you go back to the nineteenth century, France tended to be the classic foe – with Britain and Germany allied against the bothersome Frenchies – but as shown by the publication of the hugely successful *The Riddle of the Sands* in 1903, the public's imagination soon turned to the German threat.

For the next decade, novels, plays and everyday people were obsessed with what might happen as a result of Germany's growing naval and military power. It got to a point at which this "spy fever", and the constant reports of real or imagined espionage, led to newspaper reports detailing the tens of thousands of armed German spies already stationed in Britain. Though this was not true, it placed immense pressure on the government and led to the passing of the 1911 Official Secrets Act – which still exists in a modified form today. It introduced penalties for all sorts of things which might be construed as being supportive of Britain's enemies, including disclosing **any** official information to another country – a law which remained on the books until 1989. It shows how crazy things were that there was no opposition whatsoever to the bill and it made it through Parliament in a single day – which is very rare indeed.

Invasion fiction wasn't quite as popular when Christie was writing in the carefree twenties, so in the books I mentioned before, she focused on the more nebulous threat of all-powerful criminal gangs who secretly manipulated international governments and had a spy in every room in the land. The first draft of this book had a similarly unlikely premise, so thanks must go to my early readers for persuading me to scale things back.

I should probably also mention that this subgenre was often an excuse to include thinly disguised xenophobic, racist and antisemitic plotlines in order to stoke fear in the public. With a lot of the fiction from the first half of the twentieth century, we must look past outdated language and attitudes to enjoy other elements of them, and I hope that all of my readers know that this novel was not designed to vilify anyone (except perhaps snobs, people who talk too much but never listen and, oh yes, murderers).

One example of this kind of literature that my father loved when he was a boy was *Bulldog Drummond*. The first book in the series is a macho tale from 1920 with a gung-ho hero who is only too happy to dive head-first into trouble. It's fun but outdated (for any number of reasons), and in one of those wonderful coincidences that I love, my mum brought it to Spain on a visit just as I was about to write this book. I pinched it off her, and I don't think she's had a chance to read it yet. Sorry, Mum!

What I liked about these stories, and especially the first Tommy and Tuppence novel, *The Secret Adversary*, is the way in which their heroes take on insane challenges without really thinking about the dangers. The first big twist in this book is a spin on that trope, and I hope anyone reading the early stages thinking, *This could never happen*, by the end of the book saw where I was coming from in this affectionate send-up of those old books.

As for the setting, this was another chance for me to spend far too long reading about interesting places in London, and the real highlight was the British Museum itself. I've been there many times since the big refurbishment of the central courtyard was completed, and I had no idea that, inside the rotunda in its centre, the reading room remained.

The rotunda is almost exactly the same size as the Roman Pantheon and opened in 1857 with a delicious breakfast of champagne and ice cream to celebrate. The description of the lavish domed room in this book is as close as I could get to capturing the unique space. As it developed, immense metal stacks (also described) with twenty-five miles of shelving were built around it to fill the courtyard. They were ripped out in the nineties when the British Library was relocated to a new building in St Pancras.

Over its one-hundred-and-forty-year history, any number of famous people read and studied there including Gandhi, Conan Doyle (there's no time for first names), Kipling, Orwell, Wilde, (oh fine, that's Oscar, not Kim) Lenin, Twain, Rimbaud and Woolf. Marx (that's Karl, not Chico, Harpo, Groucho, Gummo or Zeppo) was a regular and, during the hours he spent at one of the long desks, he formulated ideas that would lead to the composition of one of the most influential texts in history. The reading room is a superb space and, though it sadly isn't used a great deal these days, there are occasional special events when you can access it.

All of that is amazing, but my favourite moment of my research surely came when I was writing the first draft of this book and, after a day not getting nearly enough done, I decided to call it a day and watch an old Hitchcock film. I mentioned *Blackmail* in the first book in this series because it is commonly considered the first British talkie. So imagine my joy when I was watching that movie, which I quickly confirmed was filmed in 1928 – the same year as this book is set – and the finale occurs in... wait for it... actually, this is probably really obvious because I was literally just talking about it... that's right, the film ends with the police chasing a murder suspect all the way to (and on top of) the reading room of the British Museum! I watched it on the very day that I'd sent Bella and Marius off in the car to the museum. So when I went to write the key scene the next morning, I had a very good idea of how it should look – though I still had to trawl through photographs and old accounts to work out the layout and colours of the place.

I was also really pleased to discover that the GC&CS – the real code breaking and signal intelligence unit that was the forerunner of the modern GCHQ – had its headquarters just a short walk away from Marius's flat. It really was based at 54 Broadway and the building is still there today. I am certainly not an expert on the early days of the British intelligence services, but I did enjoy working in some elements of truth in my over-the-top scenario. The plaque outside the building didn't advertise a fake lawnmower firm but the "Minimax Fire Extinguisher Company". There really was a Don Carlos high up in the navy who liaised with the code breakers, and the stuff about the stolen code books in the First World War was all true, too. They're not exactly James Bond types, like in MI6, but all those clever people did some amazing things.

Finally, Mentmore Towers was another fortuitous discovery which I came across because of the sorry state in which it now finds itself. It's an incredible house, much as Marius describes it, that was built in the Jacobethan style by Baron Mayer de Rothschild of the Rothschild banking dynasty who assembled a collection of priceless antiques, before the house passed through marriage to the Earls of Rosebery.

A hundred years later, when the sixth earl died, the house and all its contents were put up for sale – there is a brilliant AP News report about it from the seventies on YouTube. Even though the family offered the whole estate to the British government to maintain as a museum for just a few million in reduced taxes, the short-sighted politicians declined the offer. A ten-day auction was held that sold every last thing from the silver tree and dove automaton in Primrose's room (which itself went for hundreds of thousands of pounds and was bought by someone in Iran) to old cutlery and china bed pans. The sale made over ten million pounds, and it makes me so upset to think of all the treasures that were lost when, if things had been different, we could have visited the incredible place today and seen its wonders, just as it is possible with so many other stately homes that are open to the public.

Instead, the building changed hands several times before ending up in the possession of British billionaire (and convicted rapist – though he gave a false name to escape punishment) Simon Halabi. He intended to turn it into a six-star hotel but when the credit crunch hit, he lost a lot of money on his invest-ments and was declared bankrupt – the kind of bankrupt that still allows him to own property all over the world, a fleet of Rolls Royce and a 130ft yacht. So Mentmore Towers sits rotting in the Buckinghamshire countryside, untouched for the twenty-seven years since Halabi bought it.

It is on the Historic England "At Risk" list, and the reason I came across it is because there are loads of videos on YouTube of urban explorers who break into the building to look around at night. The videos are very entertaining, and you can see the gigantic (and frankly rather ugly) Rubens fireplace in the Grand Hall, and several rooms that are covered in glittering decoration. Oh, and the false bookshelf in the library really does give on to a secret antechamber, and the names I've used for all the rooms are the original ones. It is still an amazing building, though in desperate need of repair, which makes it all the sadder that it wasn't preserved for the British public when the chance was there.

One function that Mentmore has fulfilled since its sale, though, is as a filming location. It has featured in *Brazil*, *Johnny English*, **that** scene in *Eyes Wide Shut*, *The Mummy Returns*, *Inspector Morse* and music videos by Roxy Music, Enya, and the Spice Girls. But best of all, it stood in for Wayne Manor in the first Christopher Nolan Batman film, which makes me rather happy as, in the sequel, Wayne Manor is destroyed by the Joker before Bruce Wayne rebuilds it for the third film. The supposedly rebuilt mansion is actually Wollaton Hall in Nottingham, which graced the front cover of my first ever 1920s mystery, *Murder at the Spring Ball*. Thus bringing us full circle. Lovely.

HISTORICAL RESEARCH

A lot of my research this time around focused on the twin topics of the British intelligence services and Mentmore Towers, which I've already mentioned above. So rather than just going deep into their history, I'll tell you a little bit about the parallels between this ridiculous book and real life, along with filling you in on some of the incredible people I learnt about.

I'll start with the original owners of Mentmore Towers, the Rothschilds. Mentmore was Baron Mayer de Rothschild's passion project and was completed in 1854. His inordinately wealthy family built several estates in the Vale of Aylesbury, but Mentmore was considered the most beautiful. Happily, several of the others are preserved and can still be visited. Rothschild was a fan of hunting and horse racing, and Mentmore was known for the champion horses its two stud farms produced.

However, I think the most interesting thing about him was his daughter, Hannah Primrose, who married the Earl of Rosebery. Her husband was a massively popular politician who would go on to be Prime Minister of Great Britain. The Countess of Rosebery was often in his shadow, but she was actually a very important person in her own right. Not only did

she enable her husband to achieve his goals thanks to the finan-
cial heft of her family, she became an important philanthropist
and championed the cause of women, and especially charities
connected with health. Society was extremely antisemitic at the
time, and so for a Jewish woman to hold such a role in society –
to the extent that she and her husband were sometimes said to
be more popular than the royal family – was really groundbreaking. Ironically for a woman who had done so much to look
out for the health of the working classes, she died of typhoid
aged thirty-nine.

Let's move away from the rich and famous to the people
who work in the shadows. As described by Rider and his
colleagues, the intelligence services were in their infancy at the
time of the Great War, and the first peacetime code-breaking
agency was formed in 1919 and given the intentionally
misleading name the Government Code and Cypher School. It
remained part of the navy for several years, before moving,
along with MI6, to Broadway Buildings in 1925. I have no
evidence whatsoever that the building hosted a clandestine
hospital ward, but it suited the story, so I went with my imagination.

GC&CS was run by a rather interesting man called Hugh
"Quex" Sinclair, who became head of the Secret Intelligence
Service. With his own money, he bought the estate of Bletchley
Park, which became the British intelligence hub in the Second
World War. It was there that the code for the German Enigma
machine was broken (and where my dad's secretary Doris
worked, taking down intercepted messages by hand for the
experts to decipher). It is often said that without the work that
was done at Bletchley, the war would have continued for up to
four years longer. I was lucky enough to visit with Doris when
she was still alive, and it is a fascinating place to go if you get the
chance.

The Enigma machine itself was designed in Germany in

1918 and initially sold for commercial uses – so I think it's fair that Marius might have heard of it when he was living there in his lost years after the war. It was eventually adopted by the German military and, by 1932, the Polish Cipher Bureau were working on cracking its code. They made huge inroads and passed not just their findings but reconstructed versions of the machine on to the British, who acknowledged after the war that much of the progress made at Bletchley was only possible thanks to the work that the Poles had done.

In fact, at the outbreak of war in 1939, British Special Operations Executive officers went to rescue the cryptologists in Warsaw, but when they got there, the team had already been evacuated and would spend most of the war assisting the British, while stationed in France. I didn't know much about the SOE until one of my regular readers – the ubiquitous Peggy Craddock – told me that she had been friends with one of their most daring agents, Francis Cammaerts. There's no time to talk about all the incredible things they got up to here, but you should look it up. The SOE was tasked with espionage and sabotage missions, deep within enemy territory, and it's amazing what they achieved.

One person in particular who had an impact on this story was the French Prime Minister and Nobel Prize winner, Aristide Briand. Of course, the only reason he ended up in this book was because he was the French Foreign Minister in the summer of 1928, but it turned out he was a fascinating man. Not only was he an important statesman who held several positions in the French government and served no fewer than eleven terms as Prime Minister, he was a great evangelist for peace.

He won the Nobel Prize for his work on the Locarno Treaties that normalised the relationship between France and Germany after the far more punitive Treaty of Versailles. It was not a perfect solution, but it did help to ease tension in much of Europe, as it guaranteed the geographical borders between the two countries – until Hitler had other ideas a decade later. Briand was also instrumental in establishing the League of Nations, and even proposed a European union in an attempt to avoid another war. His ideas helped shape post-war collaboration and politics even decades after he died.

During one of his terms in office, he was forced to step down because of a game of golf against the British Prime Minister, David Lloyd George. Briand played such a poor game that his enemies in Parliament considered him a disgrace, who was sucking up to a foreign ally. Such was the anger at his performance that the French parliament failed to ratify the security pact he had negotiated, and he had to step down (only briefly, of course) from his role. All that and he once tried to get France and America to renounce war as a government policy, and he was also good friends with Jules Verne. Whether he would have gone along with Mr Rider's plan to flush out the spies in this story is another matter, but he was certainly well-known for trying to get to the heart of the problem rather than addressing its symptoms.

I'll stick with France to tell you about the Sûreté de Paris. Established as the criminal investigative bureau of the Paris Préfecture, it was one of the very first police forces in the world. It inspired the creation of Scotland Yard and was created in 1812 by a man called Eugène François Vidocq. What's particularly interesting about the real Vidocq, and many of the early detectives of the Sûreté, is that he was a reformed criminal. Within eight years of its formation, its thirty officers had reduced crime in Paris by 40 per cent.

The real Vidocq's story is flat-out insane and makes anything that happens in this book seem very tame indeed. He came from a well-off family but had a wild youth and indulged in bare-knuckle fighting and plenty of theft. He spent two weeks in prison after his father had him arrested for taking silver plates from their home, and then it wasn't long before he took a large sum of money from his family bakery and attempted to escape to the Americas. That didn't work out as he was robbed of his ill-gotten gains, but he ended up working in a travelling circus freak show as a fake cannibal (I told you this was a crazy story), and eventually joining the army. He was an expert fencer and killed two people in duels, and, whilst in prison for this, helped another inmate escape. He was in and out of the army for several years – interspersed with more duelling, desertion, womanising, spells in prison and daring escapes.

Perhaps it's enough to tell you that he served as the inspiration for both Jean Valjean in *Les Misérables* and, later in life we can assume, the relentless policeman Javert, as, on trying to escape his life of crime, it would always catch up with him. He faced the death penalty on a number of occasions but escaped each time. At thirty-four, he realised that he didn't want to continue his life on the run, so he handed himself in to the police in order to become an informant in a Paris jail. He worked as an underworld spy for a few years before deciding that the city should have a more established plain-clothes crime-solving unit and setting up the Sûreté using his criminal contacts as undercover detectives.

He is considered the father of criminology and made use of such advanced techniques as ballistics comparisons and plaster casts for footprints, along with patenting different types of inks and papers that were used in investigations. All that and he may have established the first ever private detective agency, and he was good friends with Balzac. There's obviously a lot more to his story, and he has been depicted in countless books, plays and films – including a very early silent one from 1909 right through to a historical epic from 2018 starring the always brilliant Vincent Cassel. It's probably rubbish, but I remember enjoying the 2001 science fiction film in which he is played by Gerard Depardieu.

From the father of criminology, let's look at the father of... checks notes... micropalaeontology! Unlike Bella and Marius, I could just about remember what mycology was, but I certainly know a lot more about it now than I did before choosing it for a passing reference in this book. I picked the topic at random, and then had to spend a few hours reading up on it because... well, I don't know why I did it, but it seemed important at the time.

I wanted to choose a dry topic for the book our detectives have to find in the British Museum, and (ironically as Marius points out) I chose black mould. I then discovered that the first scientific description of *stachybotrys chartarum* was by Christian Gottfried Ehrenberg back in 1818. Ehrenberg wrote the paper as part of his doctorate and did not go on to have a career as a mycologist but branched out into zoology and natural history. He travelled through Africa and Asia collecting thousands of plant and animal specimens, which he would use to write papers on a range of topics. He was one of the most prolific scientists of his day and spent much of his time focused on micro-organisms and would go on to found the discipline of micropaleontology – i.e., looking at tiny fossils through a microscope. But the main reason I wanted to include a paragraph here on this groundbreaking naturalist is because I felt a bit bad for what Marius, Bella and the helpful stranger in the library said about his mould pamphlet.

And then, when I thought I'd finished with all that, I had to include another passing reference that brought me straight back to mycology again. I bet that if you were to ask most people (who had not read the previous paragraph) whether they know the names of any mycologists, they would say, *No, of course not.* But it turns out they would be wrong, as undoubtedly the world's most famous example is the children's writer Beatrix Potter.

Potter was obsessed with the natural world and was interested in fossils, botany, zoology and entomology. She was an incredibly skilful artist and became adept at scientific illustration, which, during the 1890s, led to her interest in fungi. But she didn't just draw them, she studied them and found out things about them and the way they reproduce that no one had known before. She even developed her own theory for the way in which they germinate using spores.

She explained her ideas to the director of Kew Gardens, who was not interested because Potter was just an amateur and (even more scandalous) a woman! Similarly, when she wanted to present her paper on the germination of mushroom spores to a scientific society, she was not allowed to attend, and a male mycologist friend had to speak on her behalf. It was only fairly recently that this academic work was rediscovered, but her phenomenally accurate drawings of mushrooms can be found in collections all over Britain, and they are still consulted to help identify different species. And on top of all that, she created a series of children's books which are still read and adored 120 years after they were first published. I have her full collection and still read them to my children just as my parents did to me.

Let's switch to bullet points for a collection of interesting facts that have no thematic connection whatsoever and can't be stretched to full paragraphs.

- From 1912 to 1948, the Olympic Games didn't just feature sporting events, but artistic ones too. This was the idea of the modern games' founder, and there were prizes for architecture, literature, music, painting, and sculpture that were inspired by sporting endeavours.
- Now, this is weird... Between 1894 and the birth of our current king in 1948, it was one of the roles of the Foreign Secretary to be present at royal births. They were called on to bear witness to the fact that

the child really was of royal issue, which, when you think about it, is totally insane.

- I didn't imagine it being so old, but kiss-proof lipstick really did exist in the 1920s, and the colours I used were real examples taken from adverts in the British Newspaper Archive.
- Meccano, Hornby Model Railways and Dinky Toys, three of the most popular toys in Britain in the twentieth century, were all invented by the same person. Frank Hornby designed the toys for his sons at the turn of the century and would go on to be a multimillionaire off the back of them. All three toys had the distinction of being played with by my dad when he was a child. We still have all his Hornby trains, and my father-in-law in France has a large and still growing collection of Dinky cars.
- I found a quote in the OED from the *Daily Mail* in 1965. It is not connected to this story, but it made me laugh so I'm reproducing it here for you: "Mr. Ranulph Bacon, Scotland Yard Assistant Commissioner for Crime, yesterday gave this advice to the public if they saw gunmen carrying out a raid: 'If you can have a go, have a go.'" Which is quite the worst advice I've ever read. What he should have said was, if you see someone carrying out an armed raid, call the police and then get as far away as you can.
- St Ignatius' College, the university where Ernest Castleton went, is a fictional university that was created by Margery Allingham for her detective, Albert Campion. Readers may also be able to work out that Castleton is my detective Izzy Palmer's great-great-uncle. I like putting these kinds of

connections in my books, though I never know if
anyone notices them.

- I had to check whether the bridge in St James's Park
  was the same in 1928 as it is today. It wasn't and
  that was another fun rabbit hole to dive down. The
  current concrete one replaced a rather pretty green
  suspension bridge in the 1950s. A hundred and
  thirty years before that, there had been an even
  more impressive design which was built to celebrate
  the centenary of the accession of the House of
  Hanover. The bridge was in a Chinese style with a
  seven-storey pagoda. The celebrations included
  naval re-enactments on the Serpentine, a balloonist
  dropping treats to the crowds and, sadly for the
  pagoda, fireworks. The structure soon caught fire,
  though the crowd didn't mind as they thought it was
  part of the entertainment.

Staying in St James's, the Cavendish hotel was a legendary
establishment that sadly only lives on today in name. If you read
any books about the Bright Young Things of the twenties, you're
bound to come across stories of late-night shenanigans there,
and of its landlady Rosa Lewis. It seems that the Cavendish was
the go-to after-party venue once the masked balls and treasure
trails of the in-crowd were done for the night. Lewis was not
only a big character, she was a self-made woman who started
her career in domestic service before becoming a cook and
working for any number of well-known and fashionable people.
She had cooking classes from the King of Chefs, Auguste
Escoffier. She even worked for Winston Churchill's mother,
Lady Randolph – and had to chase the young Winston from her
kitchen – before taking a job with a French count who possibly
helped her to buy the Cavendish.

Whilst there, she caught the eye of the young Prince

Edward and the two were rumoured to have had an affair – though, let's be honest, the list of women that the future king did not sleep with is a short one – and her cooking was so admired by Kaiser Wilhelm II that he gave her a portrait of himself, which she hung upside down in the men's toilets when Britain and Germany went to war. She was in charge of the Cavendish for half a century and hosted all the most fashionable names of the day, whilst maintaining a casual and welcoming atmosphere in an extremely exclusive area of London. She was known for her generosity and down-to-earth nature, and, during the Great War, allowed her rich clients to cover the bills of the humble soldiers she accommodated. However, if a guest was unlucky enough to get on the wrong side of her, she would cart out her classic gag, "You treat my house just like a hotel!" before dealing with them accordingly. Her life not only influenced several characters in contemporary novels by people like Evelyn Waugh, it was also depicted in a British TV show in the seventies called *The Duchess of Duke Street*.

I only have to tell you about cars and songs and then I can have my dinner. There are a couple of French car marques mentioned when Marius arrives at Mentmore, and I hadn't realised before that the American ballerina Isadora Duncan was driving an Amilcar CGSS – a sporty model of the day – when she died. Her love of flowing scarves meant that she donned one for a short journey and it got trapped in the axle and pulled her from the car to her death. Despite her fame and talent, Duncan had a sad life. All three of her children died very young, whereas she met her fate at fifty.

Marius also spots a car made by the French company Delage. The firm was founded in 1905 by a half-blind engineer with the single greatest moustache in history. Louis Delâge was not wealthy and had to borrow money to get his company off the ground. He started off with just three employees, two lathes and any number of ideas. The marque soon developed a reputation for high quality, sales skyrocketed, and the cars won countless motor-racing prizes and grands prix. The larger cars they produced in the 1920s are particularly beautiful. I look at a lot of cars from that era, and these really are special.

Sadly, their success didn't last. The Great Depression took its toll and Delâge himself died penniless having been kicked out of his own firm. So that's two sad demises in a row, however, there is a happy caveat to the story as, in 2020, the first Delage car in almost seventy years was produced and it won the "Most Beautiful Car in the World" prize at the Automobile Awards in Dubai. Supported by the Delage owners' club, Louis Delâge's descendants and some French billionaire, only thirty cars were made, and you can pick one up for a nice round two million euros.

The Welsh song "Sosban Fach" may be familiar to you if you watch rugby, as it is often sung in the crowd – especially by fans of the Scarlets in south-west Wales. I never knew what the words meant, as only a couple of people in my wider family speak Welsh, so I was pretty surprised to find out that it really is about saucepans! In fact, Marius's stab at singing it in English isn't too far off the meaning. It was written as a continuation of a verse from a famous poem and tells the story of an overworked housewife's travails. The verse in the book translates as...

A little saucepan is boiling on the fire,
A big saucepan is boiling on the floor,
And the cat has scratched little Johnny.

It's an insanely catchy nonsense song that encourages the listener to keep working hard even when times are bad. It is sung in the audiobook by my mum's cousin Rhodri, who in his career has not only been a high court judge but was also a club singer and guitarist. It is fitting that he should record it, as he was the inspiration for the character of Bertie, so it's only right that we hear his voice. I recently discovered that the name for a male first cousin of one of your parents is a "Welsh uncle" which is appropriate for me, as all such people in my family are Welsh.

Another silly song is "Frog Went a-Courting" which is the best part of five hundred years old. I didn't know it when I shoved it into this book, but some historians believe that the frog who comes courting Missie Mouse in the nursery rhyme was actually a metaphor for a French prince looking to marry into British royalty. It's uncertain whether that's true, but it would be a nice coincidence to have included it, considering the Anglo-French themes in this book. Hurray for weird coincidences.

Right, I was going to tell you about Louis XV's mistress, Madame du Barry; the origin of the phrase "cut to the chase"; Ebenezer Howard and the Garden City Movement; and finally the silver swan automaton that I saw as a child in Barnard Castle, but I think it's time to— No, wait! I can't resist. I must tell you about that swan.

I have such a strong memory of this incredible mechanical creation that was made of silver and glass. I saw it on a trip to visit friends in Newcastle when I was about eight years old, but I haven't seen it again until searching out a video on YouTube just now. The swan has a very natural movement as it preens itself and then dips its head forward into what looks like running water to capture a small fish. It truly is extraordinary, especially when you consider that it was built way back in 1773 and still functions today.

It was a collaboration between a Belgian inventor, John Joseph Merlin (who is also credited with inventing inline skates), and a British jeweller called James Cox. Both men had their own museums displaying their fantastic creations, and London's wealthiest citizens would pay a high price to enter.

Their creations were totally unique and beyond belief in their intricacy, beauty and originality.

If you happen to be in the north of England, you must call into Bowes Museum at two in the afternoon to see the incredible swan perform its thirty-two-second show. And if you won't take my recommendation, then how about Mark Twain's? In his travel book, *Innocents Abroad*, he says the swan has "a living grace about his movement and a living intelligence in his eyes". But if you can't get to County Durham, then the online video is pretty good too.

Okay, that's it. I mean it this time. I'm hungry, this has taken me all day to write, and I'm off to have dinner.

WORDS AND REFERENCES

Banana-oil – slang for nonsense or inane talk.

Barbary lions – a population of the northern lion which previously existed in the Atlas mountains.

Amaranthine – surely the prettiest word in this book. It means unfading or immortal and comes from a mythical flower that never dies. It can also be a shade of purple.

Foxfire – the luminescent glow on some species of fungi. Another nice word.

Flittermouse, Sweetikin or Cariad – terms of endearment, the last coming from Welsh and meaning darling, but occasionally used in English in the past.

Jumble letters – an old-fashioned term for a wordsearch.

Gabster – a chatterbox.

Corded velveteen – an old-fashioned term for corduroy.

Pied-à-terre – an apartment or home kept as a secondary residence to have a place in the city.

Skeleton at the feast – party pooper!

As ready as a borrower's cap – this is not my simile but taken from Shakespeare's *Henry IV*. It presumably means to be ready as the cap that someone who wants to borrow something will produce to receive the offering.

Set-to – a fight or disagreement, originally a term in pugilism.

Row past our own reach – to do more than you're capable of.

Vickie – this is a joke for my wife alone. We drive an Ioniq, and so our car is known as Nicky. Marius drives an Invicta, and his car is Vickie.

Red-tempered – perhaps slightly confusingly, this does not mean angry but grumpy.

Squash – another word for a cordial to which you add water. Still common with British kids today, the word dates back to 1876.

Call the tune – from the idiom "he who pays the piper, calls the tune". It means to be in control or in charge of something.

Terrazzo – a type of flecked stone flooring that has chips of marble, granite and quartz within it.

Run like the blazes – to run fast (obviously). The blazes refer to the fires of hell.

Jabberwock – nonsense. It comes from Lewis Carrol's poem "Jabberwocky".

Swithered – when someone falters or hesitates.

Cour d'honneur – the courtyard, as originally found at the Palace of Versailles, which is open on one side with two long wings to the left and right.

Red-tapeworm – a bureaucrat. I love this word!

Walkover – something easy. The expression *a piece of cake* wasn't in common use until 1936.

Asleep on her feet – I realised when writing this that Percy is inspired by a guinea pig I once had who would sit on my feet as I wrote. Louise was an excellent pet and she kept me very warm.

Make my toilette – this was a common expression for washing and brushing before bed. It is in my head because the French *faire la toilette* is what is shouted in my house each night when my wife needs me to get our daughter ready for bed.

Susurration – a whisper.

Chariot clock – an elaborate clock set into a large model of a Roman chariot. They were often found in grand palaces like Versailles.

Rankled in – this isn't a typo. It's how they used the verb rankle (to annoy) back then. I'm often torn between matching historical speech patterns and writing what people today will read smoothly, but I left this one in.

Blow the gab – inform upon or reveal information.

CHARACTER LIST

New Characters

The unnamed agent in the first chapter – a mysterious figure who comes to Marius's flat to hire him and Bella to find Ernest Castleton (humorously referred to as Inspector Ordinary later in the book).

Ernest Castleton – a young, hard-working aide to the British Foreign Secretary.

Hermione Ravenscroft – his fiancée who works as a receptionist in Broadway Buildings.

Mr Dillon – a rather theatrical jeweller.

Mr H. Rider – another mysterious figure from British intelligence. Eagle-eyed readers may work out that he featured in one of the Lord Edgington books.

Lieutenants Boyle and Snipe – tough and gloomy heavies who work for Rider.

"Don Carlos" – a shadowy figure. We don't know exactly what he does but he's high up in British intelligence.

Chief Inspector Darrington – a regular in the Edgington books, and a member of the Metropolitan Police based at Scotland Yard. He and Rider go way back.

Lord Darnley – the British Foreign Secretary and owner of Mentmore Towers.

Spencer Darnley – "an exceedingly posh young gentleman" and Lord Darnley's son.

Primrose Darnley – Lord Darnley's rather mischievous and seductive daughter.

Aristide Briand – based on real the French Foreign Minister of the day.

Clément Rochefort – his chief aide.

Monsieur (Serge) Vidocq – Rochefort's aide.

Arthur Darnley – Lord Darnley's middle-aged brother. A big man with a booming voice. He is known to talk a lot!

Monsieur Menier – elderly, grey-haired, stooped-over advisor to Briand. Suspicious of the British and angry in his speech.

Monsieur Lemoine – the young, handsome, dark-featured and more diplomatic advisor.

Already Old Favourites

Marius Quin – soldier in the Great War with a broken heart, turned mystery novelist with a bent for adventure.

Bertrand Price-Lewis – Marius's publisher and friend.

Margery Price-Lewis – his jolly wife.

Lady Isabella Montague – Marius's childhood sweetheart turned friend, the daughter of the Duke of Hurtwood.

Gilbert Baines – Bella's boyfriend, a rather charmless banker.

Uncle Stan – the brother of Marius's missing father, Terence. He has recently bought a bakery in Marius's childhood village.

Auntie Elle (Eleanor) – his brainy wife who lost the use of her legs after a childhood illness.

Marius's mum – self-explanatory, and I still haven't given her a name.

Caxton – Bella's cantankerous chauffeur. He is no fan of Marius's.

ACKNOWLEDGEMENTS

Writing these books with a team of editors is a lot of fun, and my main editor Emily Gowers is brilliant company and support. She propped me up when I was losing all energy and motivation on my last book of 2023 (just weeks before Christmas), and she even came to the theatre to see a musical with my family. Each time we've met, it's felt like we've known each other for years. She's just a very good person, and I'm glad she contacted me to create this series with her. Also, congratulations on the engagement, Emily and Josh!

And the rest of you who deserve thanks know who you are. All my ARC readers who chip away at each book to make it ten times better (especially Joe and Kathleen Martin). My mum for still being a dynamo at eighty and telling everyone she meets to buy my books. My brother Daniel for staying incredibly positive whilst living through something horrid. And my wife Marion, my daughter Amelie and my little golden-haired bundle of cuteness, Osian. What I can't say is whether I will find the time to write another word after he learns to walk. That boy likes to grab stuff!

Thank you to every person who's read this book. I couldn't do it without you.

Printed in Great Britain
by Amazon